ENGEL

BY
NICHOLAS M. KROHN

<u>PRAISE FOR 'SCOEFIELD'</u>

"A 'merry-go-round' of emotions. For me, it's a much needed reminder that Christians need always to maintain and keep our testimonies, and that the world is always watching for us to mess up. I look forward to reading what new things we'll unravel."

– Adam S.

"The best parts of this story and Scoefield himself are owed to the struggles we all face: the want for happiness, the need to provide for those we love, and what that means for the sanctity of the soul. Even at their lowest, the struggles of Henry Engel and Scoefield serve to highlight the truth that lies at the center of it all: That God provides."

– Andre T.

"Very good. I do like your analysis of (the Bible passages). They make it easier for people who don't know God to understand what each passage says. It answers very important questions that I've heard from many people who aren't saved in a clear and concise way."

– Kaylinn T.

Dedicated to my wonderful wife, Marissa. Thank you for always being there to listen, to support, to encourage, and to lift me up in my dark times. You are the greatest joy God has ever given me. I'm excited to start a new chapter in my life with you as parents to our first child.
I will love you until eternity ends.

TABLE OF CONTENTS

<u>CHAPTER ONE</u>

How do you undo something terrible that can't be undone?
I'm an awful writer. Never done it before. It feels girly and I ain't
no girly man.
…But I'm doing it because I should.
This is going to be edited by Sarah so my grammar's good.
But back to my question: how do you undo something horrible
that can't be undone?
You can't. It's that simple.
But don't you wish that you could? With all of your heart, don't
you wish you could undo it? Doesn't it make you stay up all night
in frustration and in tears and you wish you could just sleep? But
you can't. Because what's done is done. And even though it is so
horrible, it can't be undone.
My name is Bradley Scoefield.
And I am a murderer.
But I'm jumping ahead. If I'm gonna' outshow Henry's book, I
need to make this good.
I'm not going to tell you my birthday because I don't like parties.
Like you'd care about my birthday anyway.
I'm not going to tell you dates because I don't have that good of a
memory.
I'm not going to tell you about every little detail of my sorry past
because I know your attention span is already running dry.
I know mine is.
So I'm going to cut to the chase.
Henry Engel was his name. First, he was a stranger. Then, he was
a friend. Then, he was nearly a brother…
Then he was a scoundrel.
I had been caring for my sister, Sarah, for years. She was the most
important thing to me in all the world. Whoever's reading this,
take the person you care about most. Imagine them right now. And
imagine someone else came along and stole them from you. That
person was no longer yours. That person belonged to someone

else.

Engel did something unspeakable to Sarah. It got me fuming just thinking about it. I hated him for it. And instead of owning up to it like a man, he lied about it.

He *lied* to try and cover up what he had done. He was a snake. He was a slithering, slimy critter. And when I had him…when I was shoving him out of my life and Sarah's life…

He took Sarah with him. Sarah was in love with him.

And I wanted to strangle him. I wanted to throw him under a bus. But I couldn't hurt Sarah. And hurting Engel…would've hurt Sarah…

I hurt him anyway, of course. I got some good swings in on his face. I admit, he did get *one* good swing at me. Only one, though. I got in, like, twenty.

But that was it. I couldn't do anything else to him. Sarah was on his side. She betrayed me for him. And no matter how angry I was, I could not hurt Sarah.

So I left.

I went to my old home: a small shack in a Hooverville. Had to chase a family of possums out of it, but I got it back. It actually felt more like home than any other place I had lived at. I had lived there for a number a years with Sarah and even Engel.

That night, I went out. I had been saving up my money for a while, so I had a good chunk of cash in my pockets. I intended to use it that night. And the next night. And the night after that. I was always told that, when you needed to get rid of your troubles, the bottle was the best place to go. Though I hated it because of what it made my pop, I didn't think I had a better option. My attitude was "I've got nothin' else to lose".

"Bradley?" Ronny blinked as I entered my pop's old joint. "Little Bradley? Is that you?"

"Not so little anymore, Ronny." I grunted.

My pop was well-known for his drinking. He went frequently to a bar not too far away from our first house. He brought me with him a couple times, so the regulars and the bartender knew me fairly well.

"What're you doing here, Bradley?" Ronny asked.

"Gettin' a drink, that's what." I snarled as I threw money on the counter. "And the name's Scoefield. 'Bradley' died with my mom. Give me all ya' got."

"Okay then, Mr. Scoefield." Ronny got a mug. "Beer?"

"Whiskey."

"Whiskey?" Ronny raised an eyebrow. "Isn't that a little strong?"

"Exactly." I glared.

"Give it to him, Ronny." One man cheered. "He's a man now. A chip off the old block."

I ignored that. If I thought on it too much, I'd get mad. I hated being compared to my pop, but I was already mad because of what happened with Engel and Sarah only hours before. Ronny got a glass that was about the size of a pebble.

"Hey! You kiddin' me, Ronny?" I growled.

Ronny stopped. I nudged at the glass.

"Bigger."

Ronny sighed. Next, he got a glass the size of my fist.

"Bigger, Ronny." I said again.

"Scoefield…" Ronny began to object.

"Hey, I'm payin' for it, ain't I?!" I shouted. "Bigger!"

Finally, Ronny slid me a beer mug full of whiskey.

And I downed it all as quick as I could.

I really regretted that later. Whiskey is not good. For pete's sake, no giggle water is good. They're like acid. If water could be set on fire and go down someone's gullet, that is what liquor feels like. That's also how harmful it is for you. It's like pouring fire down your throat. But I didn't really realize that until much, *much* later. The moment I downed that mug, I felt like upchucking.

I didn't, by some miracle. But it burned and it didn't even taste good. I should have set down that mug right then and walked out. But drinking was supposed to be for the hard-boiled. It was for tough guys. If you were a weakling, you couldn't drink. And people were watching me. People who knew my pop were watching me.

And I was not going to be upstaged by my father.
"Give me another." I told Ronny. I wanted to sound coarse and rough, like drinking whiskey was nothing. But I was actually coughing and wheezing like a chain smoker.
Some men in the bar laughed at me because of it.
Ronny shook his head. "Bradley, I don't think you should."
I was hot mad. I was not going to accept that.
"Ronny." I hissed. "Give me another."
Ronny was a good fella. Ronny was a big fella, too. He had to be big for all the punks that came in the bar, got drunk, and refused to leave. Ronny had a way of escorting them out. But when I gave him that look…
When he heard the tone in my voice…
Ronny looked scared. And he slid me another mug.
And for the rest of the night, I drank. I drank and drank and drank and drank and drank.

I don't remember much of that night. Or the next night. Or the next. I was in a drunk haze for days. I made a bad decision a habit. Then that habit became a chain.
I went to that bar for weeks. Every penny I had, I spent on whiskey.
Until…
"Scoefield?" A familiar voice said next to me as he sat down. "I didn't think I would find you here."
I slowly turned.
Wesley Butters.
Engel's boss. Engel wrote and sang songs for him and his recording studio. Sometimes Sarah helped sing the songs.
I snarled in response. He reminded me of Sarah. Worse yet, he reminded me of Engel.
I turned away from him and nursed my mug.
"I suppose Henry and Sarah are more of the church type, huh?" Butters continued. "That suits me. To be honest, it's nice to have one of you who isn't so Christian. Christians make me uncomfortable."

I tried to tune him out. But I was drunk and the word "Henry" made my jaw clench. My hand tightened on my mug.

"Have you heard any of the new songs on the radio?" Butters asked me, not catching my less-than-cheerful mood.

I grunted angrily in response.

"Oh, right." Butters chuckled. "I still haven't gotten you three a radio. I'll write that down. I'll get you one tomorrow. How's that?"

"Good evening, Wesley." Another voice spoke as I felt the counter shift. I peered over my shoulder to see Butters' boss had sat down next to him. I didn't know him too well, but I knew he was the owner of the recording studio. Butters usually got nervous around him.

I glanced down.

Yep. Butters' foot was tapping.

"Good evening, sir." Butters said a little too happily. "What brings you here tonight?"

"Beer." Butters' boss said bluntly.

"Oh, of course." Butters laughed nervously.

"Who's this?" Butters' boss pointed to me.

"It's Scoefield, sir." Butters explained. "Henry's brother-in-law."

My free hand immediately curled into a fist. I was breathing hard. The room felt extremely hot.

"Brother-in-law?" I growled.

"Yes, they were married a couple days ago." Butters smiled. "Henry asked off of work for it. Rather rash, but who am I to say?"

"Oh, yes." Butters' boss nodded. "Congratulations to your sister, Mr. Scoefield."

I gritted my teeth. I was going to explode.

"Oh, sir, he doesn't like to be called 'Mr.'." Butters mentioned. "Just Scoefield."

Butters' boss shrugged.

"Now, Scoefield, would you be able to give Henry a message for me, if convenient?" Butters asked. "As you know, he and Sarah are on their honeymoon and I won't see him until-"

I broke.

I curled my right fist, swung around to Butters, and plowed my knuckles right into his kisser.

The fat man toppled off of his seat and landed hard on the floor. But I wasn't done.

I pulled him up by his collar and gave him another punch to the face. All eyes were gawking at me in pure shock and confusion.

I kept landing blows on Butters' chubby face. But I didn't see Butters anymore.

I saw Engel.

Butters' boss tackled into me from behind.

"What're you doing, son?!" He shouted at me, trying to get me away from Butters. He was tall and intimidating, but not very strong.

I threw back my elbow and nailed him in the nose. He backed off, but now he was my target too. I spun on my feet and fired my fists at him.

Soon, the entire bar was trying to stop me.

Ronny, my Pop's drinking buddies, everyone.

I was a raging bull. I rumbled the whole place like an earthquake.

I fought like a spitting-mad gorilla. Before long, though, the police arrived. They came charging through the door as I was whacking someone with a chair. They stepped into the bar and blew their whistles loud and clear. As soon as I turned to thrash them, I was clocked in the nose by one of their nightsticks.

I was knocked to the ground and pummeled until I was black, blue, and nearly dead to the world.

As I was being dragged outside, I heard several people chit-chatting about how I just flew off the handle for no good reason. Just like my pop.

CHAPTER TWO

I woke up in a jail cell. I was lying in a pile of puke. My head
ached like it had blown up. That was either from the alcohol, the
beating, or both. I rolled over, wiping the gunk off my face.
"Finally up, eh?" A voice boomed outside of my cell. I placed my
hands over my ears. Everything was so loud.
I moved my blood-shot eyes to the iron bars where the voice had
come from.
A middle-aged policeman was staring at me through the bars. He
looked at me like I had slapped his wife.
"Quit starin' at me." I barked at him. "Don't ya' have somethin'
better to do, like savin' a cat in a tree?"
The policeman scoffed. "Just like ol' Amos."
I immediately flew at the bars. "Say that again, Buttons, and I'll
give you a one-way ticket to see him! I ain't nothin' like Amos
Scoefield!"
The policeman didn't even flinch. He curled his lip at me. It may
have been from my smell, but I figured it was more from disgust
towards me. For a long while, he just looked at me like that.
Maybe he was considering giving me another good beating.
But he turned away from me. He began to walk away from my
cell.
"Keep telling yourself that." He called as he continued walking.
I growled in anger. It was true that I was a spitting image of my
father, both in looks and character. But I denied it. I wouldn't let
anyone say it. I refused to allow anyone compare Bradley
Scoefield with Amos Scoefield.
But that policeman was right.

For the next week and a half, I sat alone in my jail cell,
awaiting my trial. I was being charged with aggravated assault and
destruction of property.
Felonies. Not misdemeanors. I was in trouble.
As I waited there, I found that I had actually been thrown in the

same jail cell that my father had once sat in. On the back wall, I found words etched into the cement.

SARAH SUNFLOWER – MAY 31 1916

Amos was in jail at the time Sarah was born. My mama sent him letters about it all. She loved him dearly, as much of a monster as he was.

And here I was, sitting in his cell for the same crimes.

"That was quite some fight you started." A calm voice echoed from outside my cell.

I flicked my eyes toward the bars. Wearing a dark-green uniform proudly, a polished-looking army goon stood there, smoking a gasper. I snarled at him. I hated cigarettes.

"They let you have butts in here?" I glared.

"That offend you?" The soldier grinned. "Fine."

He put his cigarette out.

"Oh, no. Don't mind me." I said sarcastically. "Feel free to poison yourself and me all you like."

"Says the guy who downed mugs of whiskey before he took on an entire bar."

"Get lost, ya' chowder-headed cad." I spat.

"That's exactly what I would expect someone like you to say." The soldier couldn't stop smiling.

"What do you want?" I asked.

"I want you to join the army, Scoefield." The soldier told me. "Use that fiery, fighting spirit for the protection of this great country."

"Ha!" I laughed. "That's a good one. Now what do you really want?"

"Listen, Scoefield. I'm Sergeant Doug Davis. I'm an army recruiter. My job is to look for qualified personnel to enter the army."

I took a deep breath. "And how do you know my name, Doug? You been askin' the coppers about me?"

"They do know you well." Doug shrugged.

"They know Amos Scoefield." I fumed. "Not me!"

"All-right, all-right." Doug said calmly. "But hear me out. You're facing some bad charges."

"Yeah, don't remind me." I sneered.

"What if I told you I could make them go away?" Doug asked.

"Do I get two other wishes, miss fairy?" I chuckled.

"I'm serious." Doug was getting impatient. "I can talk to the judge for you. Without me, you'll be in a prison cell for many years. You think this jail is bad? Wait till you get there."

I considered what Doug was saying. I didn't want prison.

"You got a lawyer?" He asked.

"No."

"You think the people you thrashed are going to let you off easy?" Doug questioned.

"...No."

"Then will you listen to me?" Doug folded his arms.

I sighed. I didn't really have any other option.

"Okay." I muttered. "I'll listen."

"You may be seated." Judge Miller said to all of us as he sat down on his big throne. I'm told it wasn't a throne, but it sure did look like one. Judge Miller gazed at the papers with his beady brown eyes.

"We are here for the case of Scoefield vs. Butters."

Several people in the courtroom made snorting noises, trying to hold in laughter.

I smirked. It was Butters' curse.

I was sitting in the very front of the courtroom. My pathetic excuse of a lawyer was next to me and Doug sat behind us. I glanced across from where I was seated. Wesley Butters was not present. In his place was his boss, whose nose was covered with some sort of cast. His eyes also had bruises under them. Must have been what I looked like after Engel got his lucky punch on me. Other than his bad nose job, he was in a very crisp and dashing suit. His eyes were filled with utter determination that I was going to be fried.

"You are Wesley Butters, then?" Judge Miller questioned Butters' boss.

"No, your Honor, my name is Vincent Doeler. Wesley Butters is my employee and my friend."

"So, that's what his name is." I muttered to myself.

"Where is Mr. Butters?" Judge Miller asked.

"He is currently in the hospital for treatment. He has recently had difficulty breathing."

"Problems with his lungs, Mr. Doeler?" The judge asked.

"No, your Honor. With his nose and jaw."

"He was hurt that badly?" The judge marveled.

"We have many eye-witnesses." Doeler nodded. "This boy is a menace."

At that moment, both the judge and Doeler gave me a vicious look.

I was dead.

"I believe it." Judge Miller said.

So dead.

"And the state of the-" The judge was about to continue.

"Your Honor, if I may…" Doug stood up. "Before we continue, I believe I have a wonderful solution to all of this."

Judge Miller gave Doug a frustrated stare.

"Sergeant. Here you are in my courtroom again." Judge Miller sighed. "What? You want to take this young man and throw him in the army? The army cannot solve every case, Sergeant."

"No, your Honor. However, I do believe it will with this case." Doug persisted.

The judge stuck his nose out at Doug. "This is the third criminal you've wanted to recruit since April, Sergeant. You better have good reason for this one. He put a man in the hospital, and I am told that Mr. Butters did nothing to deserve it."

"He didn't." Doeler confirmed. "We were attempting a friendly chat with Mr. Scoefield."

"Yes, but-" Doug stuttered.

"And, as it says here in the police report, that he destroyed several

tables and chairs of a bar owned by a Mr. Ronald Faraway." Judge
Miller read. "He even attacked the police and resisted arrest.
These are not trivial, Sergeant. This young man sounds qualified
for the asylum."
I lowered my head.
"Your Honor." Doug spoke. "Allow me a few minutes to plea my
case for Mr. Scoefield."
Judge Miller puckered his lips in thought. "Hmm. I will allow it.
Do convince us, Sergeant."
"Thank you, your Honor." Doug said as he stepped up beneath the
judge's throne.
"Adolf Hitler. Benito Mussolini." Doug spoke out in a clear voice.
I was confused. Was he speaking a different language?
"Some know these names, but I still believe far too many do not.
They are leaders in Europe. Dangerous ones. Hungry for more
than what they already have. Tension has been on the rise in
Europe for quite some time."
Doug turned, slowly eyeing everyone in the courtroom.
"Gentlemen. Ladies. War is coming."
The courtroom became deathly quiet.
"Naturally, you may wonder what that has to do with Bradley
Scoefield tearing up a bar here in New York. Dear people, this
man took on nearly an entire bar full of strong, capable men by
himself. He even gave the police a handful. He is dangerous. Why
not use that frightening power and spirit for something useful:
protection."
Mutters came here and there.
"War is in Europe, and it may not be long until war could
potentially come to our very shores. We need to be ready. We need
a military that will defend this wonderful nation. And the army
can take men like Bradley Scoefield. Men that are violent,
terrifying, and brutal. The army can take them and transform them
from a monster into a machine. A machine that will maintain
peace and security in the United States of America."
He went on like that for some time. I rather didn't like that he kept
referring me as someone who was scary and destructive.

But I was.

And though I didn't think it would happen, the judge **was** convinced after some time. But it came down to the money.

"Mr. Scoefield is charged with the expenses for new furniture for the bar and Mr. Butters' medical bills. What of those, Sergeant?"

Doug thought a moment before giving a hesitant answer.

"I'll pay for them."

"Will you now?" Judge Miller was surprised.

"...Yes."

"Does that suit you, Mr. Doeler." Judge Miller asked.

Doeler gave me an accusing glare, but nodded his head.

"Very well, Mr. Scoefield is sentenced to a minimum of six years in the service of the army. Mr. Butters and Mr. Faraway are to receive their expenses by Sergeant Davis. Court is adjourned."

Judge Miller slammed down his hammer.

"You did it." I gawked at Doug as we exited the courthouse. "You got me off scott-free."

"Scott-free?" Doug raised an eyebrow at me. "You're joining the army."

"Eh, not a big deal." I grinned. "Besides, I need a new job anyway. Oh, thanks for payin' for all that too. I don't have any money."

"Yeah, don't remind me." Doug groaned as he lit a cigarette. "But you'll make it up to me, I can promise you that."

"What's next?" I asked him.

"Basic training. You'll love that."

"Will it be in the city?" I questioned.

"City?" Doug laughed. "The closest one is Camp Jackson in South Carolina."

"South Carolina?" I breathed.

I'd never been out of the state, let alone in the south. Then a thought immediately popped in my noggin.

Sarah.

What about Sarah? I'd be so far away. What if Engel hurt her? What if she needed me?

But I had no choice now. I was going to the army whether I

wanted to or not. No going back.

"I need to do something before we go."

"What's that?" Doug turned to me.

I knocked on the door. I was already trying to keep my anger down. The house itself just made me mad.

Worse yet…

Engel answered the door.

It took me a lot to not immediately punch his lights out.

"Scoefield! You came back!" He cheered happily.

"Did he forget what happened between us?" I thought. *"Why is he so happy?"*

"Not for long, Engel." I hissed at him. "Now, if ya' would be so kind, I'd like to talk to my sister."

That wiped Engel's smile clean off of his face. That was rather pleasing.

"But Scoefield, I-"

"Oh, sorry. I gotta' ask permission, don't I? After all, she's **yours** now, ain't she?"

Engel started to look really sad. His face went from pleasing to bothering. I didn't want another cry-fest on my hands.

"No, Scoefield, it's not like that-"

I couldn't take anymore of his blubbering.

"Get me Sarah, Engel." I clenched my fist. "And get outta' my face. And then, I promise you, you will never see me again. Got it?"

For a moment, Engel just stared at me with his pathetic, miserable expression.

But he left without saying anything else.

"Thank goodness." I took a breath. *"I hate that stupid look of his."*

After a couple minutes, my baby sister was at the door. My anger faded. I felt guilt and regret rise up in my throat like a poison. She didn't say anything to me. She waited for me to speak first. I didn't want to say it, but I had to tell her.

"I'm leavin'." I said, looking down at the floor.

"You already did." Sarah said, unflinching and arms folded. "Why

come back just to say that?”
She sounded like she didn’t understand, but I could see in her eyes
that she was really upset. Maybe mad. Maybe sad. Maybe both.
“I mean I’m leavin’ New York.” I told her. “I’m joinin’ the army.”
At that point, Sarah’s hard look dropped. Worry was in her eyes,
her expression, even her body language.
It felt nice to be worried about.
“The army? Bradley, please!” Sarah pleaded. “Don’t do that!
Please forgive us! Come back and live with us!”
She wanted me to come back. I didn’t want to come back. Be
around *Engel* again? No sir. And even if I wanted to come back, I
couldn’t.
“Don’t ya’ tell me what to do.” I got angry. “Ya’ chose him, ya’
got him. Ya’ don’t need me. So, I’m gone.”
“You’re going to get yourself killed, Bradley.” Sarah told me.
I swallowed. I never actually thought about dying. Doug said a
war was coming. A war that I might be a part of because I
smashed up a bar. I lowered my head again.
“Well, maybe I deserve that.” I mumbled.
“Bradley.” Sarah started tearing up. “Please don’t do this.”
The crying only fueled my anger again.
“Don’t you cry in front of me!” I yelled at her. “It ain’t gonna’
work! I’m headin’ out tomorrow and I’m not coming back. So this
is goodbye, Sarah.”
“I don’t want to say goodbye!” Sarah’s eyes were shooting out
tears.
“Well, too bad.” I growled. “And tell that grifter if he ever hurts
ya’ or if he ever leaves ya’ for a floozy, I’ll kill him. And I don’t
mean I’ll beat him up. I mean I will end his life. Ya’ got me?”
I really did mean it, too. I had fantasies of how I would kill him.
“Bradley…” Sarah sniveled.
That was it. I said what I had to. Doug wanted me back with him
in an hour’s time anyway. I had to go.
“Goodbye, Sarah.”
And I left.

For the next day, I was traveling on a bus to a basic training camp somewhere in the south. I kept thinking about Sarah the whole way down.

Would Engel really take care of my baby sister? Out of everyone that I knew, he was the last person I wanted taking care of her. But I had no choice now. So, I just kept staring out of the window until the guy in front of me turned around in his seat. He held out his hand to me.

"Hi. I'm Kenneth."

He was smaller. Of course, most people are smaller than me. He had chestnut brown, wavy hair. He wore glasses that made him look like a goof. I wanted to simply ignore him and keep gazing out of the window. A "buzz off" would've done nicely with it as well. But I was in the army now. I had no family and no friends. It would be a good idea to make some.

I shook his hand. "Scoefield."

"Oh, right." Kenneth chuckled. "Since we're going to be in the army, I guess we should only use last names, huh? Mine's Taggart."

"Kenneth Taggart?" I asked.

"Yeah."

"There's probably going to be a problem with me then." A fellow in the seat on my left spoke up. "My last name is Smith. Do you know how many Smiths there are? None of us will know who anyone is talking to."

He was even shorter than Taggart. He had rough, black hair and creamy brown skin.

"Well, then what's your first name?" I asked him.

"Johnny."

"John Smith?" Taggart laughed. "You have the most generic name in all of America."

"Yeah, my parents were real jokers." Johnny looked annoyed.

"Where are you from?" I asked him.

"I bet you're thinking it's Mexico." He eyed me.

"Nah, I was thinking Russia." I said sarcastically.

"How did you know?" Johnny gasped mockingly.

I laughed. "It's that rough, cold accent of yours."

Johnny laughed back. "I like you. I don't meet many guys as sarcastic as I am."

"We're a special group of chumps, we are." I smirked.

"Well, I suddenly feel ostracized." Taggart muttered.

I turned back to him. "Oh, you're too kind."

"Kind?"

"You think I'm smart enough to know what that means." I acted touched.

"Don't read much, do you?" Taggart responded.

"If we were big smarty-pants, we probably wouldn't be joining the army." Johnny commented. "I'm here because I got fired from the only job that'd have me. How about you boys?"

Taggart sighed deeply. "Parents. My dad tells me I need to learn what it's like to be a man. Not some twerp that accidentally blows up houses. He said the army will whip me into shape."

"'Accidentally *blows up* houses'?" I coughed.

"I was messing with some ammonium nitrate." Taggart said sheepishly. "Just out of curiosity. Turns out I mistakenly made a very efficient…uh, bomb."

"The army'll love you for that." Johnny grinned. "So, big guy, why are you here?"

They both looked at me.

Awkward.

I folded my arms uncomfortably. "I...smashed up a bar pretty bad."

"Smashed up a bar?" Taggart blinked.

"Yup." I nodded. "Put some fuddy-duddy in the hospital. Beat up a few drunks. Fought some coppers. I could'a chosen prison or the army. I chose army."

Johnny and Taggart grew very quiet. All they knew about me was that I was twice their size and I was thrown in jail for ripping up a bar.

Taggart immediately shrunk away from me. Johnny seemed intimidated, but curious.

"Why?" Johnny asked.

An anger began to burn up in my chest. "'Cause a German took my sister from me."

"Well, that's good news for you." Taggart chuckled nervously. "Because they say we might be fighting Germans soon."

"Good." I growled.

Of course, I went to boot camp in 1934. I wasn't going to be fighting any Nazis anytime soon like everybody thought.

CHAPTER THREE

Monday, November 24th, 1941

Dear Bradley,

You know how I've been so glad you've decided to write back to me, even though it's not your style (to say nothing of your terrible grammar and spelling). But, big brother, I would really love to see you again. Face to face. Writing, calling, it's all good...but when's the last time we've been in the same room together? And I know...I know it's because of Henry. It's definitely not because you "still have time to serve in the army". I don't believe that baloney for a second, Bradley. We spoke to your judge after we found out what happened at Pop's bar. He told us you only had _six_ years to serve as your punishment. Not ten, like you say. And even still, doesn't the army give leave, or something? Can't you take a weekend

and come see me? Henry doesn't have to
be there. But, you know, there's not a day
that goes by where he isn't sorry. He is
willing to do <u>anything</u> to make it up to
you. In fact, he's willing to do anything
just so you'll come and see me. Not him.
Just me. I'll leave the decision up to you.
Even though our old diner is under new
management now, it's still pretty good.
Maybe we could both get a bite to eat
there?

Anyway, I'll stop beating that horse for
the moment. As for answering your
questions about what's new with me...
well, nothing's really new. Henry, the
kids, and I have all worked into a
routine. Speaking of the kids, though,
Lucas and Gary are growing more and
more everyday. In different ways, I guess
you could say. Even though they're twins,
they are so different. They don't even look

alike. It's like Jacob and Esau. Lucas is already so huge. In a couple of years, he'll be taller than Henry. Lucas reminds me of you. He's tough for a six-year-old. Him and Henry wrestle from time to time and Lucas gives Henry bruises! He's got an incredible arm in baseball, too. At least, for his age. He says he wants to be a "copper" when he grows up. It's so cute. He loves watching police officers do anything. Even just when they patrol down the street. Gary is more...well, like Henry. He's a bit of a crier, but boy is he smart! He's already reading books of the Bible that I have trouble understanding. Honest to goodness! I was reading 1 Corinthians 7 and having a hard time comprehending what Paul was saying. He uses phrases like "render unto the wife due benevolence". Gary found me whispering that phrase to myself and muttering "what on earth does that mean?". Gary just looked at me and said, "Mama, 'render unto the wife due benevolence' means that Papa should treat you right". Then he just walked away. He blows my mind sometimes. Honestly, I think Henry gives him Bible lessons behind my back or something. As for baby Michaela, she's doing well, too. I should probably stop calling her 'baby Michaela'. She hates being called that now. She's only five, but she acts like she's all mature sometimes. She already "knows" who she's going to marry. Guess who it is? Bing Crosby. I mean, she could definitely do worse. Henry jokingly told her that he's a way better singer than Bing Crosby, so she should just stay with him for the rest of her life. You know what Michaela said? "Papa, Bing Crosby is a beautiful angel. His singing voice is like cake to my ears. But your singing voice is like carrots". It was so cute! I had to walk out of the room to keep from laughing in front of both of them. Needless to say, all of the children are doing wonderful and we are proud of all three of them.

As for Henry, I want to tell you how he's been. I know you're still angry at him, but he's my husband and a part of my life. If you're going to hear about me, I can't leave him out of it. Mr. Butters is calling him golden because of how his songs are doing on the radio. Most of the time, neither of us are the ones who are singing them anymore. Mr. Butters' boss was the one who started that. He says that Henry and I are good at singing, but not _that_ good (Evidently, Michaela wasn't wrong about the "carrot" voice). So, Henry pretty much only writes songs now. His latest song is called "Looking Up, Looking Down". It's a bit on the poetic side, but I think you might like it. Mr. Butters' boss say he'll put it on the radio soon to see how it does. Listen for it, okay?

Now, about you. You're a sergeant now, huh? Congratulations! I don't know much about the military and what a sergeant does compared to a corporal (or was it private? I forget what order they go in), but moving up the ranks must be good! And, I mean, it just sounds nice. Sergeant Scoefield. That has a very nice ring to it. Do you have anyone you order around? Do you get any perks for being a sergeant? Tell me all about it in your next letter, okay? And tell me what you want for Christmas! It's only a month away! Your present will probably be late. I'm sorry about that, but it's your own fault since you won't tell me what you want. By golly, you're getting a present, even if I just have to send you money!

Anyway, I've probably gabbed on for a lot longer than you have time for. I'll let you go now. Answer all of my questions in your next letter. And please come see me sometime. Merry Christmas!

Your sister,
Sarah Engel.

I shook my head with a click of my tongue.
"She adds in 'Engel' just to poke at me." I said aloud with a growl. I was in my bunk alone. The other boys were out, doing whatever. It was Sunday. Time for church and everything, if you wanted to go. For me, it was the only time I could be alone. That was when I would read Sarah's letters and write back to her. I didn't want the other boys thinking me girly.
Sarah's letter made me mad, to be honest. I still hated hearing about Engel. I didn't like how she scolded me through her letters, either. Who was the older sibling, anyway? I kinda felt like Engel was turning her into another person. That was part of the reason I actually **didn't** want to see her. The first reason is that I was still bitter against her and Engel after everything that had happened. Sarah herself had said to me "Leave us alone, Bradley! Stay out of our lives!". Now, she was thinking that she could just guilt-trip me into coming back? I don't think so. Secondly, she had kids. I had no idea what to think of that. It was all too weird. My baby sister? A mom? But, lastly, I was just plain scared. Scared that if I did meet her in person…that I wouldn't meet the Sarah I used to know. I was scared that I would meet a different Sarah. A Sarah who was not as much my sister as she was Engel's wife.
And I just couldn't do it.
So, as I sat down at my desk and took out a piece of paper, I tried

to think of an excuse to tell Sarah why I couldn't come see her. It was getting harder. She found out I was lying about my sentence. She was right about the army giving times of leave. I decided to start writing and wait for whatever lie or excuse I would use next to dawn on me.

Sunday, December 7th, 1941

Dear Sarah <u>Engel</u>,

Thanks for the congrats. Sargint Scoefield does sound pretty nice, huh? I do getta boss some peepull around, but Im no captan. I can't come see you yet thoh. See, its becuz-

I paused. I didn't have a clue as to why I **couldn't** go see her. I had plenty of reasons why I **didn't** want to go see her. But none of them were **couldn'ts**.

"What am I gonna' say?" I asked the air around me.

I shrugged when nothing came to me. I put the pencil in my mouth and started to chew on it a bit.

Then, the door swung open.

"Hey, Scoefield." Johnny said as he walked in. "Or should I say 'Sarge'?"

I snatched up my letter and stuffed it in my desk drawer. Then I glanced back at Johnny, trying to look like normal.

Johnny looked at me.

Then he looked at the desk drawer.

Then he rolled his eyes.

"This is the part where I act like I didn't see that, right?"

"See what?" I coughed.

"See you writing to your sis." Johnny chuckled. "Come on, Scoefield, we all write to our families. And we all know you do, too."

"Hey! I ain't no girl, Johnny." I snarled at him. "I don't write."

"Sure you don't." Johnny nodded sarcastically. "Well, does the

not-girl want to stop not-writing and play some cards?"
"That's Sergeant to you, Corporal." I pointed at him as I stood up.
"And I would. Who's all playing?"
"The usual." Johnny told me as we headed out of the room.
"Davis, Taggart, Larkin, Sheldon, Calvin, and Bratt."
"Bratt doesn't know how to play poker." I smiled.
"He says he does." Johnny shrugged. "I decided to let him in.
We're just waiting on you."

Some stuff had happened in the seven years I was in the army.
No war, like Doug had said (at least, not for America), but stuff.
Doug had actually come to boot camp with me, Taggart, and
Johnny. He decided to put away his recruiter hat and get his
combat boots back on. Being a sergeant, he was in charge of us
new recruits.
And let me tell you, boot camp was hard. Anyone tell you
differently, they're lying.
But I won't bore you with the really short hair-cut, the push-ups,
the running, the early mornings, the drill-sergeants that want to
make your life miserable, the throwing up, the aching muscles, all
that jazz.
It's about as fun as playing barefoot hacky-sack with a hedgehog.
But hey, they're not training puppies for the army. They're
training boys to be killers. That's not exactly a walk in the park,
you know.
I kept in touch with Sarah after a while. She started writing to me
soon after I left. I didn't start writing back until a year later. I have
to hand it to my little sister: she's got some stubborn bones. She
kept writing to me until I finally gave in and wrote her back. I
only wrote to her occasionally. She would tell me about her life. I
would tell her about mine. Though many of her letters talked
about Engel and God, the two people I didn't want to hear
anything about, I read every single word.

Johnny and I popped into the rec hall. The usual boys were
lounging around a small table with a dim light overhead.

"About time you got here, Scoefield." Doug grinned, sucking on a cigarette.

"I won't stay here long if you don't put that butt out." I pointed.

"There's nothing wrong with smoking." He rolled his eyes, annoyed that I still hated his smoking. "How many times do I have to tell you that?"

"Ever been in a fire before, Doug?" I asked as I pulled out a seat.

"No."

"Well, I have." I grunted as I sat down. "And let me tell ya', breathing in fire-smoke doesn't feel good. It sure ain't good for you. Makes you hack like you're chokin' and you just can't breathe right. Cigarette-smoke ain't any different. Those things will kill ya', mark my words."

Doug shrugged. "Whatever you say."

He put out the cigarette.

Doug had gone far since I first met him. He used to be a sergeant. Two years back, he had been promoted to Captain Doug Davis. Out of our little gang, Doug was the highest ranking officer. Most of the time, he called the shots.

Unless I said otherwise.

I was the second-in-command, so to speak. I was the only sergeant.

The rest of the fellows in our little outfit made up pals that Doug and I had made along the seven years I'd been in the army. Taggart and Johnny were the first, even though I scared both of them at the beginning. Taggart was a bookworm. He lived up to the glasses he wore. Always said words that were too big for me to understand. He also knew a couple languages, architecture, strategy, and whatnot. Johnny was more interested in fun times. Loved to play cards, which was why we were there instead of doing something else. He got all of us addicted to poker. Except Bratt, but I'll get to that later.

Johnny knew how to take care of himself. Being from San Salvador, he wasn't treated the best. He didn't like to fight much. Lived by his wits instead of his fists. I respected that.

Through boot camp, we met a few others who stuck it out and didn't quit like wimps.

Mel Larkin. He was from Kansas. A cooky carrot-top, but grew up on the streets, like me. Knew how to hold his own and was a great shot. His only problem was his belly. He loved to eat and it definitely showed. He wasn't the fittest of all of us, but he sure was a soldier.

Jack Sheldon. A dreamer, for sure, but we all have some girly habits. Had an average build and weird habit of smiling. He grew up in Florida and knew a lot of boy scout stuff like knots and camping and whatever.

Roger Calvin. A Texan that was a tad bigger than I was. Wasn't much on the smart side, but knew everything important. He was the best shot out of all of us. Grew up hunting. He was rougher than sand paper. Grammar was horrible. Had a nasty temper. Had a severe problem with authority. Thought war was more like a game.
Let me tell you, Texans are something else.

Lastly, there was Allan Pratt from Indiana. He was the youngest. Just a kid. Didn't know what he was doing or what he was getting into. Slimmer than a pole and awkward as a bald man in a barber shop. He didn't even know what a gun was, let alone how to hold and shoot one. Because of all that, the drill-sergeants really picked on him in basic training. Called him "Bratt" instead of "Pratt". He could run, but all the other exercises nearly killed the boy. Many of us bet that he would be the first to quit.
But he wasn't.
He wasn't the second to go, either.
He wasn't the third, or fourth, or fifth.
He kept at it. Sooner or later, we saw grit in that boy and we accepted him as one of us. As for the nickname "Bratt", the boy kinda wore it like a badge of honor. And it stuck. Soon enough, we

all called him "Bratt", and he liked it.

What a booger.

"Deal me in, pallies." I said as I took a sip of whiskey and slapped down some money.

"Okay, so a full house is what again?" Bratt asked Taggart as he fumbled through his cards.

"Bratt, you shouldn't even be playing." Calvin laughed gruffly. "You should just hand over your money right now."

"I made it through basic training, I can make it through poker." Bratt said confidently.

"Well, Private Pratt, I admire that you're willing to try, even though you're going to go broke again." Doug chuckled with a cough.

"Laugh now." Bratt smirked. "But by the end of this game, I'll be able to buy enough sodas to last a month."

"Sodas?" Johnny scoffed. "Oh, you're such a kid."

Bratt lost all of his money in that game. I did, too, but I didn't care as much as he did. Johnny whooped us all, like he did most times. The guy was good with cards. Calvin swore that Johnny was cheating, but we all knew Calvin was just blowing his top.

"Why don't we pop into town, maybe see some girls?" Johnny asked as he counted his money. "Buy 'em a couple of drinks, you know? Ladies love men in uniforms."

"I'll pass." I sighed as I leaned back in my chair and closed my eyes.

"Oh come on, Sarge." Taggart nudged me. "You need some social stimulation of the female sort. Interaction with them could provide far more satisfaction than us men. Who knows? It might even open doors of opportunity to a deeper companionship. It'll do you good."

I opened one eye at Taggart. "Speak English, Taggart."

"Girls smell nice." Doug translated, smoking at the other end of the rec hall. "And if you ever want to get married, you better learn how to talk to girls."

I took a deep breath as I glanced over at Bratt and Calvin. They were playing a game of billiards.

"What do you think, Bratt?" I asked him.

"I get too nervous around girls." Bratt admitted. "Don't know how to talk to them."

"We'll teach you, boy." Calvin punched him in the shoulder. "And if you listen to us, you might get *lucky*."

Calvin winked. Bratt blushed a bit.

"Hey." I growled. "Stow that kind of talk."

"What?" Calvin shrugged, holding down a grin.

"Women are not circus animals." I glared at Calvin "You don't just throw 'em treats to get them to do what you want. Women aren't prizes, or trophies, or slabs of meat. They're people. Wonderful people that you'd better respect, Private."

"You're telling me you've never just tried to have a good time with one?" Calvin sauntered over to me. "You're being too preachy. What's wrong with a little lovin'?"

My mouth twitched slightly. "Tell me, Calvin, just how did you get that 'little lovin'? Did you promise her anything? A ring? A courtship? Marriage?"

Calvin shrugged, still looking smug. "Sure. Just some little white lies is all."

"And let me guess." I stood up from my chair, fists clenched. "You dropped her like a sack of potatoes after that, didn't you?"

"Oh, come on, Bradley." Calvin frowned a bit. "You're not telling me that's so bad, are y-"

I socked Calvin right in the face, launching him into a table and over it.

Before Calvin could he even realize what just happened to him, I bounded over to him and grabbed him by the collar. Everyone in the rec hall was dead silent, staring right at me.

"You listen here, chum." I growled at Calvin. "First, you better learn to quit promisin' girls things you don't intend to deliver on."

"Why do you care?!" Calvin's temper started to show.

I punched him again. "Why?! 'Cause I got a sister! And don't you interrupt me again! Second, don't you ever tell me I'm bein' preachy! I hate preachers! Third, if you ever call me 'Bradley' again, I'll break your arms. You got me, **_Private_**?"

"Yes." Calvin said, barely holding back his anger.

"Yes, what?!"

"Yes, Sergeant Scoefield!"

"That's more like it." I let go of Calvin's collar. "And instead of you headin' out into town, you'll be cleanin' the barracks. Understood, Private?"

Calvin stood up slowly. "…Yes, sir."

"Go on, then." I ordered.

Calvin headed out, his head simmering. The rec hall started to get back to normal. I sat back down in my chair and Doug walked over to me.

"You know, you're a natural leader when you get angry." Doug laughed.

"Meh." I muttered. Then I glanced at Taggart and Johnny. "Still thinkin' of going into town, boys?"

The two boys looked a little spooked by how I had just thrown the biggest guy in our outfit over a table. Johnny was the first to speak.

"If that's all-right with you, sir." He said respectfully.

"Well, mind your manners and make sure Bratt doesn't embarrass himself too much."

"Yes, sir." Taggart and Johnny said at the same time. Then, they promptly stood up, got Bratt and Larkin, and left the hall.

"You're not going, Sheldon?" Doug asked Sheldon, who was over by the radio.

"No, sir." Sheldon answered as he was switching through channels. "I'm feeling a little lazy today. Thought I'd just listen to some tunes."

Then he stopped it on a certain channel.

"Oo, this sounds good!"

At first, I didn't recognized it. But after a bit of listening, I picked up on the fact that it was one of Engel's songs. I knew what his words sounded like.

I LOOK UP TO SEE YOU
BUT YOU AREN'T THERE
YOU'VE BEEN GONE SO LONG, I CAN'T REMEMBER YOUR
FACE
AND THE PAIN IS MORE THAN I CAN BEAR
BUT I LOOK UP
YES, I LOOK UP

LOOKING UP, I KNOW THAT YOU ARE WITH HIM NOW
LOOKING UP, I KNOW YOUR PAIN HAS CEASED
LOOKING UP, I AM GRATEFUL FOR THE TIME THAT I HAD
LOOKING UP, I KNOW THAT YOU ARE AT PEACE
I HOPE YOU LOOK DOWN WITH A SMILE
I'M TRYING TO BE WHAT YOU TAUGHT
I CAN ONLY DREAM OF WHAT YOU ARE THINKING
OF THIS MAN WHOM JESUS HAS BOUGHT
YOU MAY LOOK DOWN
PLEASE LOOK DOWN

LOOKING DOWN, I PRAY YOU CHEER OF WHO I'VE BECOME
LOOKING DOWN, I HOPE I BRING YOU GLEE
LOOKING DOWN, I WISH THAT MY LIFE BRINGS HIM PRAISE
LOOKING DOWN, I WANT YOU TO SEE CHRIST IN ME

WE MAY NOT HAVE BEEN BLESSED TO HAVE YOU IN ALL
OF OUR LIFE
WE MAY NOT HAVE ALL THAT WE DESIRE
BUT WE CAN GO ON, KNOWING WHERE YOU ARE

"Yeesh, that was sad." Doug said to Sheldon.
"You're telling me." Sheldon scratched his head. "Good tune, though."
"What does it even mean?" Doug asked.
"It's talkin' about his parents." I spoke up, looking at the ceiling.
"What?" Doug looked at me.
"The one who wrote the song…" I answered. "His parents died when he was a kid. He's talkin' about how he knows they're in heaven now. He's lookin' up to them. They're lookin' down to him. Get the picture?"
"How do you know that?" Doug eyed me.
I didn't answer him.
"Never took you for an artsy type, Sarge." Sheldon told me. "Thought you said it was girly."
"It *is*, Sheldon." I sneered. "And you better shut your pie-hole before I send you to clean the barracks with Calvin."
"Yes, sir." Sheldon replied.

The rest of the day was…well, boring. Ugh, I'm not good at this writing thing. So much details…it makes my head smart. Look, I don't remember it much, okay? I'll probably have other parts of this book where I do that.
Deal with it.
Anyway, the night was what was important. I couldn't sleep. I was…troubled. I had read Sarah's letter *and* heard Engel's song. Usually, Sarah's letter by itself got me into a sour mood. Each

39

letter I read would often smack me with the facts that I always tried to forget.

Sarah was gone. She was Engel's now. She wasn't a Scoefield anymore. She had been my best friend and my only living family. And she was gone now.

That **alone** would leave my stomach churning. But then, right after I read her letter, Engel's new song was shoved into my face. The worst part…was that I actually liked the song. The music was catchy and I could relate to the words.

My parents were dead, too. Just like Engel's. But I didn't believe in heaven. I didn't believe in God. I didn't believe in anything. And it was **Engel's** song. So, I was left angry as ever. And that meant no sleeping.

All I could think of was my mama. Sarah looked a lot like her. Acted a lot like her, too, except for Sarah's fiery attitude. Mama didn't have that at all. She was complete sweetness. She didn't have a mean bone in her body. She had a way to make anyone smile, even Amos Scoefield. She made the best grits. Made a mean quiche, too. She would always make me feel better after Amos came home and beat us.

With her…there was always at least one ray of light.

Then Amos killed her.

And, as I sat in my bunk, thinking about my dead mother…I wondered if she was looking down on me right in that moment. I wondered if Engel **was** right. If he was…well, I knew that my mama believed in all that God stuff.

Then anger boiled up in me. My mama did believe in God, but she also believed that Amos Scoefield was a good man. For all the good that she was, my mama was stupid. Plain stupid to marry a dirtbag like Amos Scoefield.

I eventually fell asleep, somewhere between sad and angry.

"Scoefield, get up." An arm shook me.

I shot my eyes open. In the army, no one woke you up gently. If they did, it was weird.

I jolted up. It was Doug.

I glanced out the window. Still dark out. Not yet time for the revely.

"What's wrong?" I whispered to him.

"Hawaii was attacked."

"What?!" I gaped. "By the Germans?"

"The Japanese." Doug told me. "The President is talking about it on the radio now."

I immediately got up, threw some clothes on, and ran with him to where we kept the radio. The entire barracks was up, listening closely.

"Why was I the last one to have been woken up?" I growled inwardly.

But I threw that thought away, because I could hear President Roosevelt on the radio:

"Mr. Vice President, Mr. Speaker, members of the Senate, and of the House of Representatives: Yesterday, December 7th, 1941 – a date which will live in infamy – the United States of America was suddenly and deliberately attacked by naval and air forces of the Empire of Japan. The United States was at peace with that nation and, at the solicitation of Japan, was still in conversation with its government and its emperor looking toward the maintenance of peace in the Pacific. Indeed, one hour after Japanese air squadrons had commenced bombing in the American island of Oahu, the Japanese ambassador to the United States and his colleagues delivered to our Secretary of State a formal reply to a recent American message. While this reply stated that it seemed useless to

continue the existing diplomatic
negotiations, it contained no threat or
hint of war or of armed attack. It will
be recorded that the distance of Hawaii
from Japan makes it obvious that the
attack was deliberately planned many
days or even weeks ago. During the
intervening time, the Japanese
government has deliberately sought to
deceive the United States by false
statements and expressions of hope for
continued peace. The attack yesterday
on the Hawaiian islands has caused
severe damage to American naval and
military forces. I regret to tell you
that very many American lives have been
lost. In addition, American ships have
been reported torpedoed on the high
seas between San Francisco and
Honolulu."

Doug swore under his breath. Taggart took of his glasses and
rubbed his forehead, clearly upset. The rest of the boys simply
stood still, looking rather shocked. I was clenching my fists.
People. Innocent people were killed without warning. Why would
anyone do that? President Roosevelt continued:

"Yesterday, the Japanese government
also launched an attack against Malaya.
Last night, Japanese forces attacked
Hong Kong. Last night, Japanese forces
attacked Guam. Last night, Japanese
forces attacked the Philippine Islands.
Last night, the Japanese attacked Wake
Island. This morning, the Japanese
attacked Midway Island."

I didn't know where any of those places were. My eyes, along with the eyes of a few others, instinctively turned to Taggart. Taggart, catching on to our glances, cleared his throat. "Hong Kong is the capital of China. The rest are all islands in the Pacific Ocean."

We nodded as we started listening in again:

> "Japan has, therefore, undertaken a surprise offensive extending throughout the Pacific area."

Taggart pointed to the radio, nodding. "There you go."

> "The facts of yesterday and today speak for themselves. The people of the United States have already formed their opinions and well understand the implications to the very life and safety of our nation. As commander in chief of the Army and Navy, I have directed that all measures be taken for our defense. But always will our whole nation remember the character of the onslaught against us. No matter how long it may take us to overcome this premeditated invasion, the American people in their righteous might will win through to absolute victory. I believe that I interpret the will of the Congress and of the people when I assert that we will not only defend ourselves to the uttermost, but will make it very certain that this form of treachery shall never again endanger us. Hostilities exist. There is no blinking at the fact that our people,

Silence rang through the whole room. President Roosevelt was done speaking.

"I hate to say it…" Doug nervously took a cigarette out of his pocket. "But I saw this coming."

I sat back down at my desk. After seven years, Doug had finally been right.
America was going to join the war.
I took a deep breath as I noticed my letter to Sarah still sticking out of the desk drawer.
I looked around before pulling it out.
I looked at the last sentence that I had been writing.

I can't come see you yet. See, its becuz

I took my pencil. I finished the sentence.

Im goin to war.

I put the letter back in the drawer.

CHAPTER FOUR

Tuesday, April 25th, 1944

Dear Bradley,

Hey. Look...I know I say this every single time I write to you now, but...I hope you're still alive. I pray urgently every single morning and night that you're still alive. You're a real jerk, you know that? I haven't seen you in ten years. Ten years, Bradley! You left to go and fight in North Africa in the biggest war of our lifetime and you did it without even coming to see me first?! You could die! You're not invincible like you think you are! And I can't bare to think that one of these days, I'm going to get a letter or be told by some military men that my big brother was killed hundreds of miles away!

Look, I'm not mad at you for what you are doing. It's incredibly honorable.

You're fighting for some very good things. You're combating against some very evil people. And I'm so delighted to tell everyone that. My big brother is Sergeant Bradley Leonard Scoefield. I'm so proud of you. Know that, Bradley. I just miss you. And I love your letters. I really do. But it's nothing compared to actually getting to see you. Don't misunderstand me now, you <u>better</u> keep writing me. It's the only way I know you're alive. And I do enjoy your letters. Your grammar is getting so much better! You'll be a proper author in no-time, just like Henry!...That was a joke, don't get mad.

Speaking of which, did I tell you that Henry wrote a book about you? He even titled it "Scoefield". I edited it and drew the cover. It was wonderful to read it. Henry really captured your attitude and character. Seriously, it's like you wrote part of it. Well, _I_ helped Henry a bit with it, so maybe that's why it sounds like you. The children love the book. Gary has read it three times. It's the only thing they know of their uncle. Lucas really wants to meet you after reading it. He says you're the "coolest" uncle ever. Have you ever heard people use that word like that before? I haven't. Lucas says it all the time. Henry told me that it's a slang word that's being used in a lot of jazz circles. A "cool" person is supposed to be admirable in some way. I have no idea how cold and admirable go together, but kids say the darnedest things nowadays, don't they? I was thinking of sending the book to you, but I thought instead that I'll keep it so you have a reason to not die and come see me after you're done over there.

Nothing's really new with us. I've been put on rest recently because of a slightly serious influenza infection. But don't worry, I'll be fine. The doctor says that I'm doing phenomenal compared to my last check up. Henry's been worrying his head off, but trust me, I'm doing great. How are you? Meet anyone new? Any ladies? Any _special_ ladies? Be careful of those foreign girls. They may seem innocent, but you never know who could be a spy. That's what Henry tells me, anyway. He's been reading spy novels lately. It may be getting to his head. He doesn't like to use the phone very much because of it. Says the government is listening or whatever. Anyway, that's all with me. Tell me everything that's going on and _DON'T GET SHOT_. If you do, Bradley Leonard Scoefield, so help me, I will come over there and beat you like I spank my seven year old daughter.

I love you,
Sarah.

I downed the rest of my whiskey. "Beat me like she spanks her seven year old daughter? I'd love to see her try. At least she stopped puttin' 'Engel' at the end of her letters."
"Sarge!" Larkin called. "We're moving out! You coming?"
"Yeah, yeah." I muttered back as I stuffed Sarah's letter in my jacket. I grabbed my pack, slung it over my shoulder and jogged out of the bar.
It would be the last time I saw one of those in a while. Me and the boys were getting on a ship and we would be on that ship for a while. We had been in scorching-hot North Africa for some time, giving the Nazis all we could. It was the first time I ever saw warfare. And it was awful.
And really, I don't want to talk about it much.
They shot at us. We shot at them. No need to get into the bloody details. Too many nickelodeons and books go too far when it comes to that stuff. Look, people, you don't need to fill your minds with gore and guts and stuff. I went through the horror of war so you didn't have to know what that's like.
So, expect to only get the brass tacks from me when it comes to that kind of stuff. But we were moving out of North Africa. On ships. We weren't told much at all except for that. We weren't told where we were going or why. The tittle-tattle going around was that we were going to invade Nazi-occupied France.
Some operation called "Overlord", or "Sledgehammer".
Most were calling it "D-day", though.
And for much of the trip, that's what me and the boys talked about.

"What do you think the 'D' in 'D-day' stands for?" was the question that popped up.
"Delivery-day." Taggart offered confidently.
We all looked at him. Our faces basically said "that's stupid".
"What?" Taggart asked. "We're being delivered to France. Delivery-day."
"Delivery-day?" I scoffed. "What? Are we having a baby?"
"Okay, how about…" Taggart thought. "Due-day?"

"Even worse." Doug rolled his eyes.

"What?" Taggart said again. "It's when the German's will face what is due them."

"Still sounds like a baby thing, Taggart." Johnny told him. "I reckon it's 'Doomsday'."

"Doomsday?" Bratt gulped. "For the Germans, right?"

Johnny shrugged. "Us. Them. Maybe it's for both."

"Nah, the 'D' stands for 'Dark'." Sheldon stated. "It'll be a dark day when we march onto those shores."

"Not bad." I nodded to Sheldon.

"How about 'D-'." Calvin was about to say.

"Calvin, we all know what you're already thinking." Doug interrupted him. "So save the cursing for when the fighting starts. We don't need your foul language around here."

Calvin grumbled testily, but shut his yapper.

"I'm thinking 'Decision-day'." Larkin put out his two cents.

"That doesn't make much sense to me." I chewed on that. "The decision's already been made. What decision will we be makin'?"

"The decision to fight?" Larkin said with more uncertainty.

"I'm thinkin' it stands for 'Defend-day'." I suggested. "We're defending innocent people from the Germans."

"But, Sarge, we're not defending." Taggart corrected me. "It's actually the opposite of that. We'll be on the offense here. We're attacking the Nazis."

I hated it when he was right. Made me feel like a numbskull.

"If that's what you think." I huffed.

"Designated-day." Bratt finally said. "It's the day that's designated for this mission."

The lot of us thought on that one.

"That's pretty good, Bratt." Sheldon clapped his hands.

"That might be it." Doug added in. "You never know."

"Nice one, boyo." I winked at him.

"...I still think it *could* be 'Due-day'." Taggart mumbled.

Eventually, we all glanced at Doug.

"What do you think, Captain?" Larkin asked.

Doug raised an eyebrow. "Honestly, I don't think it stands for

anything. From what I've heard, the big boys in Washington have tried to keep this all quiet. No one's supposed to know much about this 'D-day'. I've even heard that they're trying to make the Nazis think this operation is happening somewhere else so we can have an upper-hand. So, I think they added a 'D' to it just to confuse everybody. Make it sound mysterious. Make everyone wonder what the 'D' means."
Calvin made "phhht!" noise. "Yeah, right, Cap. That can't be it. Frankly, that's the dumbest one I've heard yet."

We may have sounded hard-boiled talking about D-day like it was a walk down the street…but we were scared. That's why we were talking about it. Most fellas on that boat didn't talk much. They were thinking. Praying. Hoping they'd see their families again.
We didn't know exactly what we were in for. Until we could see the shores of Normandy with our own eyes.
I took a deep breath. It was dark and cloudy out. Not yet morning. Everyone's eyes were locked onto the shores of France.
"You look scared, Scoefield." Doug whispered next to me. He was fumbling through his pockets as he spoke. "Didn't think I'd ever see the day."
"Zip it, Doug." I muttered. "You're scared, too."
"I am. So what?" Doug said unashamedly. He snatched a cigarette from his breast pocket and popped it in his mouth.
I gave him a sour look.
"Oh, I'm sorry, your highness." Doug scowled back. "Do I have her majesty's permission to poison my lungs one last time before I die?"
"You're not gonna' die, Doug." I sighed, looking away from him.
"I wouldn't be too sure." Doug shivered, lighting the cigarette.
"You see what we're up against? We're sitting ducks. The Krauts have shelter in bunkers with machine guns aimed right at us. What do we have? I'm thinking…we all might die."
A dangerous hush fell on everyone around Doug when he said that.

We all knew he was right. Dead on.

Bratt looked up at me, fear blazing in his eyes.

I flicked my eyes back at Doug. "You thinkin' of runnin'?"

Doug gave a stupid grin as he blew out some smoke. "You think I'm all talk when I go on about America being so great, don't you?"

"If the shoe fits, wear it." I shrugged.

Doug's grin disappeared as he looked at me. His eyes were wide and serious.

"I love America, Scoefield." He almost growled. "And if any no-good, low-down, rotten piece of garbage ever dares to threaten her, I'd sell my soul to the devil before thinking of running."

Mutters of agreement came from the men around us.

"What about you, Scoefield?" Doug asked me, gravely. "Are you thinking of saving your own skin at the expense of our great country?"

My mouth formed a sort of sneer. "I'll be honest, I don't care for the politics of the United States. I don't like how some dirtbags get all the good stuff while decent folks have it hard. But I know plenty of wonderful people in New York."

My sneer changed into a smile. "And they're worth much more than anythin' anyone could offer me. And I'll fight for 'em. And I'll die before any worthless Germans get anywhere near them."

Doug nodded proudly as I heard some fellas around me grunt in approval. Doug reached into his pocket and offered me a cigarette.

"Hey!" I said in disgust. "Get that away from me!"

"It'll calm your nerves." Doug told me.

"I don't need to be hackin' and wheezin' right before the fight of our lives!" I told him.

"Yeesh, I try to be friendly." Doug grumbled as he put it back in his pocket. "For a drunk, you sure don't like gaspers."

"There's a reason they're called **gaspers**, Doug." I rolled my eyes. "And don't you call me a drunk."

"You **are** a drunk." Doug laughed. "Remember why you're here?"

Suddenly, we both noticed movement next to us. A colonel was making his way towards me and Doug.

"Are you a bloody blunderbuss?!" He whispered violently at Doug. The man was clearly British. The colonel slapped the cigarette out of Doug's mouth and stomped on it.

"How blind do you think Jerry is?! Lighting a bine in the dark?! You could have made this entire operation a ball of chalk, Captain!" He hissed at Doug. "Why don't you wave a sign?! 'Hello, Jerry! Shoot right over here, would you? There's a good chap'!"

Doug swallowed roughly. "I'm so sorry, sir. Forgive me, sir. I didn't-I didn't-"

"Just button it before I have you thrown off of this Higgins." The colonel snapped before turning his back on Doug. He slowly made his way back to where he came from.

Doug muttered under his breath. "Why is he even here? I thought the British were supposed to be going to the Gold, Juno, and Sword beaches. This is Omaha."

"Young guy, too." I shrugged. "Must'a gotten lost. By the way…

I nudged Doug with a grin as I pointed at his cigarettes. "Told you those things are deadly."

Then I used my best British accent. "Get off the bines, why don't you? There's a good chap."

Doug gave a grin back at me and used his best British accent. "Just button it before I have you thrown off of this Higgins, **Sergeant**."

We snickered at that. And that was incredibly precious. I mean it. Most men were either shaking, throwing up, or praying.

There was no laughing on that Higgins except for that short moment. And it didn't stay for long, either. We looked back at those dark shores. They were getting closer.

"Doug…" I breathed deeply. "If I don't make it, will you go yourself to tell my sis? I want someone to go who'll have known me."

Doug nodded. "Yeah, Scoefield. I'll go for you. And…And if I don't make it, will you-"

He never finished. Because, ahead of us, the firing was starting. The shouting. The panic. The fever of combat.

It all raced at us like a runaway train.
D-day had begun.

CHAPTER FIVE

For some reason, my first thought was keeping Bratt safe. He was just a kid. He had been through North Africa with us, yeah. He had done just as much fighting as the rest of us. So why was I momming him? Call it some weird older brother-ness I had for him, or whatever. I felt like I needed to protect him.
Also, because he was kind of…drowning.
"Keep movin' boyo!" I shouted behind him, pushing him forward with a free arm. "One foot after another! Go! Go! Go! Go! Go! Don't ya' dare stop! Keep runnin'!"
See, when we ran off those boats, we were running into ocean. Not land. We hadn't gotten close enough for that. For most of us, the water was up to our shoulders. For Bratt, the water was slapping above his head.
So I kept pushing him. Literally. And whenever he would slip too far under the water to breathe, I'd yank him back up. Sometimes, I just plain carried him. But that was just *one* of many things that were happening.

The Nazis were mowing us down like a bowling ball does to pins. Machine guns, rifle fire, some explosives even.
If you stopped even for a second, you were dead. Even if you kept moving, you could be dead at any time. It just depended on where the Nazis were shooting at. The water was more red than blue already. People were screaming. Bombs were exploding. If you stopped to look around you, you'd go into shock. I had just one thing on my mind: keep running. And let me tell you, running is *hard* when you're in shoulder-deep ocean while carrying a truckload of weight on you and keeping your gun above water.
Just because of that, many guys didn't make that desperate plunge towards shore. We were easy targets.
But everyone in my little group did. We were out of the water and onto Omaha beach.
And that was a whole other ball-field.

Again, I will not go into the details. Omaha beach was the most horrific nightmare I've ever been through and you shouldn't want to know all that happened on that strip of land. But I will give something. Just not everything. Omaha beach had a bunch of cliff-like terrain. Bunkers and trenches were up there with who-knows how many Nazis stationed in them. They had an enormous higher-ground advantage. They could just pick us off as we ran off of our Higgins. Air support was supposed to have taken a lot of them out, but something had gone wrong, I guess. We were also supposed to have a wave of nearly thirty Sherman tanks come on to shore with us.

I only found two.

There was hardly any cover for any of us. The Nazis just kept firing and firing and none of us had many places to hide. About the only things that helped cover us from German sight was smoke and Czech Hedgehogs.

There were…a bunch of American bodies that littered the ground. Hundreds bobbed in the water, too. The first wave that had come to shore was all but gone.

It was a miracle that I didn't die that day.

I dragged Bratt behind the shelter of a Czech Hedgehog. They were these "x" shaped pieces of metal that kept our landing vehicles from coming ashore. Thankfully, they also provided cover for some of us Americans.

Doug met us under that Czech Hedgehog.

He started off that conversation by shouting out many swear words. I will not repeat them.

"Got any idea what we do now, Cap?!" I shouted back at him. "We move out of this, we're dead!"

"We stay here, we're dead!" Doug screamed back. Then he pointed to a piece of land that was right below the cliff bunkers. The sand sloped up just enough for some of our men to be able to lay down and not get shot. Right after that slope were fences of barbed wire.

"See that?!" Doug shouted. "Meet me there! Then I'll tell you

what to do!"
"Yes, sir!" I said.
I turned to Bratt. "You got that?!"
Bratt nodded, his eyes filled with panic.
"Let's go!"
The three of us stood up and bolted for that slope. Between us and that slope was hell on earth.
And that's all I really need to say about that.
I pulled Bratt behind me. I acted as a bit of a shield for him. Partly out of care for him, partly because he just wasn't running as fast as I was. He had short legs compared to mine. I was dragging him for part of that run.
Doug was ahead of us, keeping his head low and running like a bull.
He was actually gaining speed away from Bratt and I.
"He's gonna' make it!" I thought with some hope. *"Doug's gonna' make it!"*
Doug was nearly to the slope. Other American soldiers were already there, keeping their heads down and looking for the officer in charge.
I took half a second to glance up at the German bunker. The machine gunner had his sights on a group of soldiers behind us. He wasn't aiming anywhere near Bratt or me.
*"**We're** gonna' make it!"* I said with a little bit more hope. *"**We're** gonna' make it!"*
Doug was about to dive to the slope, when he turned his head to glance at Bratt and I.
"Hurry up, Scoefield!" He said.
And that was the last thing he ever said.
Captain Doug Davis stepped on a land mine. He was gone.

Bratt and I dove to the base of the slope, right before the fences. Bratt was upchucking. I was shivering at what I had just seen. I could feel myself going into shock.
But I was slapped out of it before long.
"Answer me, Sergeant!" A familiar voice on my left broke through

my haze.

"What?" I choked.

It was the British colonel. He was lying down next to me, shouting in my face.

"Where is your captain?!" The colonel snapped. "The fellow with the cigarettes!"

I was breathing really fast at that. "He-he-he…He's gone, sir!"

"Blast!" The colonel growled. He looked around for a moment before turning back to me. "Fine, then. You'll take his place, Captain. Now, can you lead that half of the men-"

He pointed to all of the men on my right.

"While I lead this half?!"

He pointed to all of the men on his left.

"Yes, sir!"

"Brilliant!" He shouted angrily. Then he shouted to some men running around the beach. "Where are my bloody bangalores?!"

The men started bringing several bangalore mines and began prepping them.

I put two and two together. We were going to blow our way in through the fences.

"Once we blow the barbed wire, you take your half to take out that bunker!" The colonel ordered me. "Understand that, Captain?!"

I glanced back at my right. Amazingly, Johnny, Taggart, Calvin, Larkin, and Sheldon had all made it to the slope next to Bratt and I.

"Yes, sir!" I said back to the colonel.

The bangalores were ready.

"Fire in the hole!"

We covered our ears and sheltered ourselves as best we could before the explosion.

We heard the "boom".

And we ran for the bunker.

We lived that day. Me, Bratt, Taggart, Johnny, Sheldon, Larkin, Calvin. Even the British colonel.

Doug didn't.

Thousands others didn't.

Omaha beach was the worst part of D-day. We were told later that some other beaches were taken pretty easy and with fewer casualties. We just got the short end of the stick. And Doug gave his life for the country he loved so much. Thousands of American men did. That was a truly hard thing to accept. See, when you go through something like that, you can feel guilty just for living when others don't. People always say that you shouldn't feel guilty. They say "it wasn't your fault" or "you couldn't control what happened".

But it doesn't really help. In your mind, the voice still echoes: "It should have been me, not him."

As for my new promotion, it stuck. I wasn't sure how, but I was made a Captain. It worked, I guess. It felt nice to be an officer, now, but…

I didn't want it. It made me feel like I was taking Doug's place.

"To Captain Davis." Sheldon raised his glass.

After the fighting was over and after we got some time to lay down our guns for a second, the boys and I went to a bar. Each of us got the biggest glass of alcohol we could. It varied. I, of course, got whiskey. Others got beer, scotch, brandy. All except Bratt. He got a glass of water.

"To the Cap." Calvin raised his mug of beer.

"To Captain Davis." The rest began to say, each raising their glass. Then it came to me.

"To Doug." I said quietly, raising my glass of whiskey. Then, each of us downed our drink.

It helped us forget. It helped us lose our minds a bit, which is what we wanted at the time.

But I got to say it again: the drinking never *really* helped. In fact, it only made things worse in the long run. Alcohol isn't a life-line. It's a noose.

We played poker after several rounds of drinking. We were at the point where we were acting like a bunch of idiots. Well, some of us, anyway. Calvin and me were, definitely. Taggart kept talking

about how he was going to prove his pop wrong. Johnny could hold his liquor pretty good, so he wasn't so bad. Larkin was laughing like a hyena at *everything*. Sheldon was passed out on the table.
And Bratt? He was quietly playing poker, completely sober. Seriously, the guy was a real champ to choose not to drink around us.

When my head started to clear, I noticed that the British colonel who was with us on Omaha beach was sitting at a table by himself in the corner of the bar. I sauntered over to him as the boys were starting up another game.
"Let me buy you a drink, Colonel." I offered as I pulled up a stool next to the British colonel.
"Whatever for, Captain?" He asked without looking at me. I could tell by the look on his face that he was feeling the weight of dead comrades just like I was.
"For slappin' a big oaf like me back into action when I needed it." I told him honestly. I held out my hand. "Name's Scoefield."
The colonel glanced my way. He shook my hand. "Charles Eckelstein."
The name sounded really familiar to me. I had heard some higher-ups talking about that name.
"I've heard that name before." I told the colonel bluntly. "The first name was…Alfred? No. Allen, I think. Allen Eckelstein. Ya' know him? He your cousin or somethin'?"
Colonel Eckelstein gave me an "are you kidding me?" look.
"Are you referring to *Albert Einstein*?" He enunciated slowly.
"Yeah!" I pointed, not yet noticing my slip-up. "That's him! He-oh wait…"
"I apologize for him!" Taggart called from our table.
"Hey! Is he talkin' to you, Taggart?!" I shouted, pretty embarrassed. I looked back to the colonel.
"Sorry, sir…" I blushed. "How 'bout that drink?"
I waved at the bartender. Just as I did, though, Eckelstein shook his head at him.

"Save your money, Captain Scoefield." Eckelstein told me. "I don't approve of liquor outside of the medical field."

"Even after what we saw today, sir?" I asked him.

Eckelstein nodded. "For two reasons: firstly, as a devoted Christian, I believe the drink does nothing but pollute the soul and drive the Holy Spirit from the body. Thus, inviting other, darker spirits to inhabit the heart. Secondly, as an officer, I know for a fact that the drink clouds and disturbs the mind. Since we have not yet won this war, I would very much enjoy a quick mind whilst in battle."

Inwardly, I groaned.

"Christian, eh?" I said not so politely. "With all due respect, sir, I don't see how anyone could have run on that beach and still think there's a God out there who's all about love and stuff."

"I don't see how anyone could have run on that beach without calling out to a God who is 'all about love and stuff' as you say." Eckelstein replied. "As for your comment, war is not the Lord's design. Mankind invented that. It's a miracle that you and I are still here."

I scoffed under my breath.

"But enough about religion." Col. Eckelstein stood up from his stool. "I am glad that you're here. I would like to assign to you and your men some reconnaissance missions."

I blinked twice. "I-uh, think I should report to my commanding officer, sir."

Col. Eckelstein blinked back. "I *am* your commanding officer."

"You're British."

"Ah, yes." Eckelstein chuckled. "A common mistake. I was born and raised in England for most of my childhood. However, Captain Scoefield, my family and I came to New York before the Great Depression. I am an American citizen and an American officer. Why did you think I was on Omaha beach?"

That stumped me.

"And did you think I would have the authority to promote you if I wasn't an American colonel?"

Again, stumped. But I felt like I had to say something.

"But you talked like…a British person." I stuttered.

"I was recently in England." Eckelstein told me. "Revived the Queen's English in me. But no worries, I'm learning to embrace my Yank again."

"Oh…" I said stupidly. "Okay then…What kinda missions do ya' have in mind?"

<u>CHAPTER SIX</u>

Saturday, July 22nd, 1944

Dear Bradley,

I have some news you'll never believe, big brother! My husband can now defend himself! Remember, when we were kids, how Henry took a thrashing from the Tanner boys? Well, Henry was out on church visitation and he led a boxer to the Lord! This guy isn't too famous or anything, but he agreed to teach Henry how to fight so he could protect me and the kids. You know, in case a dangerous situation ever comes up. Maybe when you get back from war, you can test Henry. See what he's learned. I know you, being a military <u>CAPTAIN</u> now (so proud of you! Congratulations!), would definitely be able to show him a thing or two.

Which makes me wonder, Bradley...

will you come back to New York? It's been so long. And I know, I know, you're fighting in a war right now. I'm not talking about that. I'm talking about after. I say that I want to see you in almost every letter, but you haven't once said that you'll come by sometime. You haven't once said that you want to come see me. Or my children. You never talk about Henry, either. You don't say anything good or bad. You act as if he doesn't exist. And, I'll be frank, I'm getting a little sick of it. It's been a decade, Bradley! Are you still so bitter? We messed up, I acknowledge that! We've asked for forgiveness from you! Will you never accept our pleas? You won't, will you? You won't ever come see me. You won't ever see your nephews and niece. You won't ever talk about Henry again. So why do you even write to me? If you think I'll be satisfied with that...If you think that you can still be my big brother, but at a distance, <u>YOU'RE WRONG</u>.

I'm sorry...I got a little hot-headed there. A little bit of Pop is in both of us, huh? My point is this: I need you. I need you back in my life. It's so hard being this way. Henry was not the only one who sinned against you. I did it, too, Bradley. Willingly. He did not force me. He did not persuade me. I did what I did because I wanted it. And I am sorry. So sorry, big brother. I want us to let that evil time go. I want us to meet up again. I want us to move on. Promise me, after the war, that you'll come by? Promise me that we can try to get past what happened? We all want you back. And I know you were hurt. I know you're still hurting. But you have no idea how it feels to have done wrong and not be forgiven for it. Let's

That was not how I wanted to start out my day. I'm guessing that Sarah thought that letter would make me tear up like a sap, or make me want to go home to see her, or something like that.
It didn't. It made me boil up like a tea pot.
I had gotten that letter before heading out on another reconnaissance mission. I was reading it later because it was the first time I was really able to. Colonel Eckelstein had been using me and my small group to scout out areas and report back. It was now October.
And we had come a long way from Normandy. The Allies were at the borders between France and Germany.
But me and my men?
We were in enemy territory. We had slipped past the front and began scoping out areas in Germany. It was scary stuff, but we had gone through several missions without any hiccups.
Eckelstein made sure that we had some German uniforms snagged for us to keep us from getting into any trouble. If anyone saw us (which we usually tried to avoid), sometimes they would just nod at us and leave us alone. If they ever did talk to us, Taggart took over. He was, after all, fluent in German. And smart. He knew how to talk his way out of trouble when it came to that.

The boys were still sleeping. We were hiding out in an abandoned barn. I was the one keeping watch, but let's face it, nobody was around. So, I finally had time to read Sarah's letter. And like I said, it made me spitting mad.
"Who does she think she is?!" I grumbled in my thoughts. *"Ever since we met Engel, Sarah's turned into some holy guilt-tripper! I*

hate that stupid German! Oh, I'll come by, Sarah! I'll come by to snap that punk squirt's neck! Then you'll be sorry ya' ever wrote to me like this!"
I took a couple breaths to try and calm myself down. And as I did, I began to replace my anger with sadness.
Sarah had changed. She had changed so much. She wasn't my sister anymore. She was Engel's wife. The mother of his kids.
I lowered my head, rubbing my eyes.
That's why I couldn't go back to see her. It would be too…much, I think is the right word.
Too much anger.
Too much sadness.
Too much for me to hold back. I'd probably kill Engel and then start crying. That'd be weird.

I tucked the letter into my pocket. The sun was starting to rise. We needed to get back and tell Eckelstein what we had seen. And report Private Roger Calvin to Eckelstein. Since we had started being spies, Calvin had become more of a problem. Every time we saw Germans, Calvin would grab his rifle and try to shoot them. He was being a bigger idiot than I gave him credit for.
At one point, I had to sock him to the ground. The guy wasn't thinking that, if he fired, he would let everyone know where we were and that we were not really Germans.
For that, his rifle was taken from him and given to Larkin. This was the last mission I was going to have him on. Most of the time, he would tell us that he just wanted to shoot something. He hadn't fired a shot since D-day. It may have been true, but I wasn't about to endanger my men and myself to a stupid brute that was getting trigger-happy.

Several hours later, while we were walking back through some dense woods, it began to snow. It's cold in Germany and it snows a lot sooner in the year than New York. We were soon trudging through snow and, let me tell you, snow is noisy.
And when you're trying to be quiet, that's annoying.

"Where we at, Johnny?" I called back as I was looking around at the trees. Johnny was the map-guy.

"I don't think we're far, Cappy." Johnny told me. "We'll be back at camp before sunrise, I think."

I groaned. We had been walking since sunrise. It was now night. I was tired, cold, sour, and hungry.

"Cappy, house ahead." Bratt told us. He was several yards ahead of us, looking out for anything that might pose a threat.

"All-right, boys, ya' heard him." I said to the rest. "Let's move southward so we ca-"

Something silenced me. A horrible scream. The kind that isn't fake. The kind that means "help me!". The kind that makes your bones shake and your hair stand up.

It came from a woman.

Without a word, each of us took cover. Me, Larkin, and Johnny all dove behind a large tree that had fallen over. Calvin, Bratt, and Taggart all hid behind trees.

"Bratt!" I called quietly. "What's goin' on?"

Bratt looked out from behind his tree. "It came…from inside the house."

I glanced at the house. It wasn't as fancy as the president's, but didn't belong to a poor guy, either. It was a good two-hundred yards away from us. The lights were on in the upstairs.

"Larkin!" Calvin hissed from behind us. "Give me my gun!"

Larkin turned to look at Calvin. Larkin seemed like he wasn't sure whether or not he should give Calvin the rifle.

So I just made it clear.

"Do **not** give him that rifle." I growled at Larkin. Then I whipped towards Calvin. "You'll be holdin' no firearm until we make it back to Eckelstein!"

"What if it's Germans?!" Calvin fumed.

"Hey! We look like Germans!" I spat. "You're goin' to get all of us killed, ya' dunderhead!"

Calvin sneered at me, but said nothing. I turned back to look at the house. A second scream erupted from it. It was just as chilling as the last one.

"There's a lady in there that needs help." I said out loud.
"I don't think that's a good idea, Cappy." Johnny advised me.
"Remember, we're in enemy territory."
I thought on that for a second. Johnny was my right-hand man.
When I was promoted to Captain, I made him Sergeant. He had a
good head on his shoulders. He wasn't a brainiac like Taggart, but
he thought through problems a lot and I liked that. So, when he
gave me advice, I usually listened.
Johnny kept going. "It's probably just Germans. A German guy
and a German girl. May not even be soldiers. We don't have any
business with them. We should just keep going."
A third scream.
"Ya' hear that, Sergeant?" I asked him. "We can't ignore that. She
may be dyin'."
"Who cares?" Johnny asked me.
I sighed. "I do. You all stay here. And keep a close eye on
Bazooka Bob for me, eh?"
I was referring to Calvin. I leapt over the tree and quietly ran
towards the house. It was stupid, I knew.
But I went anyway.

The locked front door wasn't hard to kick in. As soon as I
walked in, I could hear banging coming from upstairs. I moved up
the stairs carefully, trying not to make any sound. I didn't want
anyone hear me coming, especially if someone was aiming to hurt
people.
Once I was at the top of the stairs, I heard noise coming from the
bedroom.
I put my ear to the door. Inside, there was definitely something
going on. A fight or a struggle. I could hear things slamming into
the wall. I could hear furniture being shoved.
And then I heard another terrible scream of a woman.
With a hot breath, I stepped back and charged at the door. Like a
bull, I thrusted my shoulder into the door and split the wood off of
its hinges.
I glanced around madly for whatever I had heard on the outside.

Then, I spotted them. There was a man in the corner of the room.
He was trying to pin down a woman against the floor.
The scene before me was unmistakeable. This man was trying to
rape the woman underneath him. Thankfully, he had not gotten far
at all. The woman was still fully clothed. She was bruised a bit,
but not too harmed.
When I had come raging through the doorway, they had both
stopped and gaped at me.
But the terrorizing part was…It was Engel.
It was stinking Engel. And his filthy arms were around…Sarah.
My little sister, Sarah.
She was being pinned down by the grifter, Engel.
Engel was trying to rape my sister.

Without any hesitation, I unleashed an animal-like roar. I
threw my gun to the ground and bounded at Engel before he could
even blink. I took him by the throat with my left hand and grabbed
the back of his shirt with my right. I ripped Engel off of Sarah and
threw him as hard as I could. Engel went flying into the wall on
the opposite side of the room. He landed, gasping horribly.
But I wasn't done. I rampaged at him and dropped my knee on his
chest. Engel wheezed as he clawed around for anything to save
him. I reeled back a clenched fist and pounded it right into Engel's
nose.
Then I fired another fist.
Then another.
Another.
Another.
Another.
Another!
Blood was covering my fists. But I didn't care. He was trying to
rape my sister! My sister!
He would never get the chance again.
After I had slugged in Engel's face to the point where my fists
were aching, I stood up off of him. I lifted my left leg and stomped
on him about six times. Pressing down all of my strength and

weight through my leg, I would crunch my boot against Engel.
Some on his chest. Some on his ribs.
Several loud cracks were splitting the air as I did this. The sounds
of bones snapping.
Once I was done with that, I glanced around the room.
Instinctively, I grabbed the closest thing and slammed it on top of
Engel.
It was an eight-drawer, wooden dresser.
The dresser cracked and split when I crushed Engel with it.

It was only then that my rage had calmed. My madness had
cleared.
I was done.
But…I had actually realized what I had done.
I had just killed a man.
And, to my surprise, it actually **wasn't** Engel.
How could it have been? Engel was with Sarah in New York.
They were married.
They were…happy.
The man I had just pummeled to death was a German I had never
met before.
I shook my head, looking closer at his face.
I didn't know him at all.
"The girl!" I thought. *"Sarah!"*
I turned around to see her. She was quivering on the other side of
the room.
She was just a teenager. Probably not even eighteen.
She was tiny. Almost as tiny as Engel himself. She had very large
ears. They seemed like they didn't belong to her head. Besides
that, she was pretty. Very pretty. She was plump, but not fat. I
guess the right word would be "well-fed".
…Hmm, maybe not. That doesn't sound right.
How about…"healthy"? "Healthy" sounds better. Basically, her
cheeks pooched out a bit, she wasn't slim, but she still could turn
plenty of guys' heads.
There. That's about right.

Her hair was thick, and had a very rich brown color to it. Her nose reminded me of a button. Which, I guess that's why, in fairy-tale stories, they call them "button noses". It was cute.

Her eyes were light brown and big. Huge. Like a puppy's.

And her mouth was thin and delicate. It looked like a great mouth to kiss.

But the most important thing that I realized was that she was not Sarah. She was not my sister.

She was just a very pretty German girl.

And I had just killed a man in front of her.

I glanced back at her rapist. Confusion and guilt began welling up in me.

I stepped away from the dead German, breathing hard with shock. *"I just killed that man…"* I thought. *"I just killed him…I didn't…I didn't mean to…"*

But I took some slow breaths as I examined him further. He was a soldier. A German soldier. His uniform was unbuttoned, but it was still easy to tell he wasn't a civilian. That made it easier to accept the fact that I had just killed him. I had killed other German soldiers. Plus, this man had tried to rape a teenage girl.

He wasn't exactly an innocent victim.

With that, I did my best to make myself feel a little better. Then I turned back to the girl. She looked absolutely terrified.

I lowered my head in shame. I hated it when people looked at me like I was a monster.

But in reality, I was a monster.

True, I had probably just done her a favor, but I probably didn't have to kill him. I could've knocked him out easily.

Then, it clicked in my head that the girl didn't know why I had just killed her rapist. I was an American soldier. For all she knew, I could've been there to kill her, too.

I swallowed nervously. I looked back at her to see she was still panicking.

"I'm not gonna' hurt ya'." I tried to reassure her. "It's okay. My name's Scoefield. It's okay."

Then, I remembered that she was German. She didn't know

English.

I shrugged, not knowing what else to say.

"Uh…" I mumbled. "I…I heard your screams. I came to help."

"Help?" She questioned me in perfect English. "How can I believe you? How do I know you will not finish what he started?"

I raised my eyebrows. Her accent was thickly German, but the English was spot on.

"What?" I blabbered. "Finish what he-? No. No! I'm not goin' to-. I'm not like that."

The girl sneered. "*All* men are like that."

"Not me." I shook my head.

"How do I know that?" She interrogated.

I lowered my head. "I…have a sister. Somethin' like this happened to her."

The girl instantly softened. "Your sister was raped?"

In absolute truth, Sarah was in no shape or form raped by Engel. But I was bitter, so I lied.

"Yeah."

The girl sat up some, relaxing just a bit, but still breathing hard. "Well, then…thank you, Mr. Scoefield."

Then, she frowned, looking uncomfortable.

"Forgive me." She apologized. "'Mr. Scoefield' does not suit you. I understand you are no civilian. I would address you by your position, but, to be frank, I do not know it. That uniform you are wearing is that of a lowly *Wehrmacht soldat*. Essentially, what you would call a 'private'. From what I can tell, though, you have the constitution of an officer."

I narrowed my eyes at her. Something was off about this German girl. She could speak perfect English (she probably had better grammar than me), and she could tell just by my 'constitution' (whatever that is) that I was an officer.

But, I shrugged away those thoughts. She was a teenager. Not a soldier or a spy. Just a German girl.

"Captain." I told her.

"Captain Scoefield." The girl nodded her head. "*That* suits you. Thank you, Captain Scoefield."

"You're welcome." I said to her, looking back at the dead man in her room. "Um, sorry about all this."

"Do not be." The girl told me as she eyed the dead man in disgust. "He was a pig. I am glad to be rid of him."

I chuckled a bit. "Well, uh, I wasn't talkin' about him. I was talkin' 'bout the dresser…Oh, and the door."

"Oh, it is nothing." The girl waved her hand dismissively, finally calming her breathing back to normal. "I can buy more. Surely you have seen my house."

"***Your*** *house, huh?*" I noted inwardly as I looked around. "*Not bad.*"

But I knew I had already spent too much time there. I was an American in German territory. I had helped the girl. It was time to go.

I tipped my helmet to her. "Ma'am."

She bowed her head back. "Captain."

Then, I began to head out what remained of her door.

As soon as I did, I heard something to my left. I turned to look.

It was the butt of a rifle. It hit me right in the face.

And I was out.

<u>CHAPTER SEVEN</u>

I awoke much like I had when I was thrown in jail after smashing up Ronny's bar in 1934: My head ached like it had blown up.

Luckily, there was no puke this time. That was nice.

My vision was coming back to me and I saw a soldier with a rifle standing over me. I was moving around, for some reason. I was feeling bumps.

I was in a vehicle of some sort. A transport.

But I didn't have much time to piece it together, because the soldier noticed I was awake.

And he hit me in the face with the butt of the rifle. I was out again.

When I awoke again, there was no soldier standing over me.

But there was something far more worse.

I awoke in a barracks. It looked like an army barracks.

But after waking up, letting my head clear, and glancing around, I knew...

I was in a prisoner of war barracks.

"Cappy!" Taggart ran over to me after I had woken up. I was on the lower bed of a bunk bed. I rolled off as Taggart came to check on me. Following him was Johnny and Bratt.

I rubbed my head as they all stood in front of me.

"Don't tell me we're where I think we are..." I groaned.

"Yup." Johnny sighed. "Welcome to Stalag III-D, Cappy."

I swore at that. I didn't usually use foul language, but I felt like it was a pretty good time for it.

"Watch your mouth." An irritating voice piped up from the other side of the room.

I gave a look towards where the voice had come from. In the corner of the barracks, a black-haired soldier was lying on his bunk, reading a book. He glared at me with a kind of look that a parent would give to a naughty five-year-old. I'm pretty sure the fella was two-feet-tall. He was an American, all-right, but he was just **so small**.

I shrugged and turned back to my guys. "What happened?"

"I think you better tell us." Johnny told me. "It wasn't two minutes before you went into that house that it got surrounded by a bunch of krauts."

"What?" I gasped.

"They raced in like angry hornets." Taggart nodded. "They dragged you out of the house. You were out like a light and a teenage girl was following after the soldiers, screaiming something like…."

Taggart thought for a moment. "'Let him go! He is innocent!'."

"So why are *you* boys here?" I asked them. "They spotted you, too? You should have stayed out of sight."

"Oh, we were." Johnny said quietly. "But Calvin wasn't okay with that."

A bad feeling was filling my stomach. "What did he do?"

Johnny rubbed his forehead. It was then that I noticed that he had a bruise on his head.

"He started telling us that we needed to kill the Germans that had you." Johnny explained. "That we couldn't let you be captured. I told him no and tried to think of what we should do next, but he hit me. He took my gun and fired on the Germans."

"Idiot!" I yelled.

Johnny nodded. "That's what I yelled at him, but before I finished the word, Calvin was…"

It was like a brick was thrown into my lungs. "They shot him?"

Johnny, Taggart, and Bratt all nodded.

I looked at them. They were only three of my guys.

"…Where's Larkin? Sheldon?" I asked slowly.

"Both dead." Bratt said hoarsely.

"No…" I breathed sharply.

"The Germans open-fired on us." Johnny explained sadly. "I was shouting at everyone to just throw down their weapons and surrender, but Larkin and Sheldon didn't listen. We were out-numbered, out-gunned, out-everything. Sheldon was still alive when they captured us. We begged them for medical supplies to save him. But they laughed at us. And, after they threw you into

the back of the truck, they left Sheldon behind in the snow."
"Then he could still be alive!" I tried to grasp at some hope.
Taggart shook his head as he wiped his glasses. "They shot him in
the neck. He had already lost so much blood. Johnny was doing
his best to keep Sheldon from bleeding to death, but the Germans
beat Johnny off of him. Sheldon couldn't have survived that. He
was barely alive when we left."
I hung my head.
But I didn't have time to mourn. The door suddenly swung open.
Two German soldiers walked in, scanning the barracks.
"Captain Scoefield!" They called.
The rest, they yelled in German.
In my anger, I stood up and glared at them. "Ya' better learn how
to speak English, boys, 'cause I got no idea what you're sayin'!"
They didn't take that well.

   I was dragged outside into the cold night after being beaten by
the two soldiers. I was a little dazed, so I didn't remember much
of the trip.
But when everything stopped spinning, I realized I had been
dragged to some very nice quarters. I was thrown into a chair as
everything began to clear. The two soldiers stood on either side of
me.
And a very official German officer was standing in front of me.
He, like most people compared to me, was small. Not as small as
Midget-Potty-Words in my barracks. But small. Very thin, too. He
stood with excellent posture, his arms folded behind his back. His
shoulders were sharp and his hair was cut rather short. In some
places, he was actually beginning to bald.
But his face looked…familiar. Like I had seen him before.
His eyes were like a falcon's. They stared at me, unblinking. Big
and fierce. His nose was wide, but not pointed. He had very large
ears. Almost like they didn't belong to his head.
"Do I know you?" I asked groggily.
The German officer looked at the soldier to my right. The soldier
slugged me in the face.

"You will not speak unless I command you to, Captain Scoefield."
The German officer told me calmly as I recovered from the punch.
"I am *kommandant* of this Stalag. My name is *Oberst* Blume.
'*Oberst*' is a rank that could be compared to your 'colonel', so I
will permit you to address me as 'Colonel Blume'. This Stalag and
everything in it is under my authority, which now includes you."
"Joy." I groaned.
Kommandant Blume looked to the soldier to my left. Another fist
in my face.
"I have some questions for you, Captain Scoefield." Blume
continued as he sat down at his desk. "You **will** answer them."
Blume paused as he stared at me with his unflinching gaze. I
looked at the two soldiers next to me, then back to him.
"Am I supposed to answer now or will your thugs punch me
again?"
I got another slugging for that. The soldier on my right again, but
this time he did it himself. It wasn't Blume's order.
Blume stood up and shouted in German at the soldier who hit me.
Blume pointed to the door and the soldier hesitantly left.
"You may speak freely now, yes." Blume told me calmly as he
poured some alcoholic drink into two tiny glasses. He set one in
front of me.
I looked at it suspiciously.
Blume rolled his eyes. "If I wanted to kill you, Captain, I would
simply shoot you. Drink it or give it to Johann, there."
Blume nodded to the soldier who was still standing on my left.
I took the glass and downed it. Blume slid back into his seat
behind his desk. "Firstly, there is the matter of the two men you
and your Americans killed."
"I've no pity for 'em." I coughed to Blume. "After all, you killed
three of my men. Though, the one who started shootin' isn't
makin' me cry too much. His name was Roger Calvin. He was a
blockhead from Texas. Didn't like to think much."
"Hmm." Blume pursed his lips. "And what of my other man?"
"What'cha talkin' 'bout?" I shook my head.
"The one **you** killed." Blume pointed at me. "We found you and

him in the same room together. He was *Obersoldat* Norbert
Schleim. His face was barely recognizable, however. And he had
been crushed by a rather expensive, hand-carved dresser."
I gave a sneering smile. "So, he was one of yours, eh? Well, I'm
glad to report to you that the piece of trash suffered plenty before
he kicked the bucket."
Blume scowled. "Do not push me, Captain."
"You should be thankin' me." I folded my arms. "The fella wasn't
worth the breath in his lungs. He was tryin' to put his hands on a
girl without her permission. You get me?"
Blume's mouth twitched angrily, but he nodded slowly. "I do. And
speaking of which, what were **you** doing at that house in the first
place?"
I scratched my neck. "I just told ya'. I helped the girl who lived
there. She was in trouble."
"Oh?" Blume asked sarcastically. "You just happened to know she
was being attacked by a German soldier?"
"As a matter of fact, yeah." I taunted back. "I have these strange
ways of knowin' when someone's in trouble. I hear this terrible
sound. It's called 'screaming'."
"Watch your tone with me, Captain." The *kommandant* boiled
slightly. "I have been patient with you, but my patience is thin."
Even though I was about as angry as this guy was, I decided to
listen to him. I knew he could kill me. I knew he could kill my
men.
"Sorry, sir." I apologized.
"That's better." Blume simmered down. "Fortunately for you, your
story matches up with Irmgard's. And you have my thanks."
"Come again?" I asked him.
Blume stood up and walked to his window, gazing out of it.
"Irmgard. She was the girl you saved from Schleim. Irmgard is my
daughter."

A lot of thoughts ran through me at that moment. It explained
some things. The girl knew perfect English and understood
military ranks. And it explained why Blume looked familiar. He

had the same ears as his daughter. But I wasn't sure if it was good or bad that I had saved a *kommandant's* daughter. That is, I wasn't sure if he would treat me good or bad for it.

I didn't say anything to his "thank you". So, eventually, Blume began talking again.

"I had set them up as a couple." Blume confessed. "I thought they would be a good match. Schleim was respectable and good-mannered. Followed orders well. He had a drinking issue at times, but don't we all? My daughter is almost eighteen years old and has no prospects, so I decided to set them up on a date. All is quiet for most of the night, until I get a phone call. I hear her voice. She was crying for help. Most of it was incomprehensible and the line was quickly cut off. I phoned the closest military unit I could think of and sent them straight to her house. Lo and behold, I am told there was an American Captain in my daughter's bedroom. And, I am told that his men, who were waiting outside, fired upon the German soldiers who were sent. Naturally, you can understand why some of your men are no longer with us."

Suddenly, Blume turned back to me. "And you should consider yourself lucky that you are still alive, Captain Scoefield. The soldiers reported to me that two of my daughter's doors were knocked down, and a soldier of mine was beaten to death. Needless to say, it didn't look good for you. Those men there were about to end your life when my daughter explained that *you* saved her from one of *my* men. It was indeed a very peculiar situation. An enemy of the Germans, saving one?"

Then he sat down at his desk and pierced his eyes deeply into mine.

"And what I want to know is this: why?"

A thick silence hung in the air for some time while I thought on Blume's question.

He wanted to know why I, an American, would save a German from another German.

Instead of just blurting out my answer, I actually wanted to ponder on it before I told him.

"Why did I save her?" I asked myself as I lowered my eyes from Blume's fierce gaze.

Then, once I knew what I was going to say, I looked Blume straight in the eye.

"She was a girl who needed help." I started. "Think whatever you want about us Americans. We think the same thing about you Germans. But she's not involved in this war. She's a human, like everybody is. And she needed help. What kind of guy would I be if I did nothin'?"

Blume continued to stare at me. "Are you some moral man of God, Captain Scoefield?"

I spat. "There is no God, Colonel. Anybody who thinks there is one is a fool. But I would think myself decent, if that's what you're askin'."

Blume finally softened his gaze as he poured another two glasses full of alcohol. "Then, as I said before, you have my thanks."

He slid one of the glasses to me and we both drank.

"That being said…" Blume folded his hands together. "Your life has been spared and I have personally thanked you. From this moment on, you will be treated no better than the other prisoners in this Stalag. Follow my orders and the orders from my men, and you will be treated as you deserve, Captain. Though we are enemies, we can co-exist here. Am I understood?"

I had heard about prison camps. If anything of what I had heard was true, death and torture were common visitors to prisoners. This man sounded reasonable. But he was the leader of a death patrol. No prisoner's life really mattered to him. In fact, he probably smiled every time a prisoner was found dead in his bunk. And now, I was at his mercy.

"Yes, sir." I said anyway.

CHAPTER EIGHT

All-right, look, I'm about to start talking about how life was in a P.O.W. camp. Being a smooth-talker is not my strength, if you haven't seen that already. I say things how they are. At least, that's what people say about me.
Now, I'll say it again about my experiences in war: ***I don't want to go into everything***. And you shouldn't want me to. P.O.W. camps were not places where Axis and Allies held hands around a fire, singing Christmas tunes.
We were enemies. We hated them. They hated us. Both us and them wanted the other person to choke on their breakfast.
If you know a man who lived through a P.O.W. camp, you ought to **thank** him for his sacrifice and his service. We went through unspeakable things. Things that people don't think ever happened in those days.
In the eyes of the Nazis, we weren't men. We were dirt that needed to be swept off the porch. The only thing that kept them from mowing down all of us with machine guns was the Geneva Convention.
But that didn't mean they didn't shoot some of us. That didn't mean they didn't want us to die. That didn't mean we were given warm meals and cozy beds.
We were given barely enough to survive. We were treated a little worse than garbage. We were forced to work for the Germans. We had to do any labor they "asked" us to do, as long as it wasn't dangerous or supported the German war effort. Most of this was stuff like coal mining, stone quarrying, saw-milling, railroading, foresting, or factory…ing.
As an officer, I was told I didn't have to do work alongside my guys. I could sit back and supervise, if I wanted to.
But I didn't. I worked with my men. Call me old-fashioned, but a man isn't good for much if he lets others do his work for him.

We met a bunch of guys who had already been at the P.O.W.

camp. French, American, British, people from all sorts of places.
The one who sticks out the most, though, was a Russian. His name
was Tikhomir Izmennik. He was funny at times and had a warm
spirit. Easy to get along with. Liked to be around me and my men,
too, so we basically made him a part of our little group. The only
problem was that none of us could pronounce his name. After
many failed tries, we just decided to nickname him "Tim".
Before I had met any, I assumed that Russian men were always
big. And some are, but Tim wasn't. He had a good build and was
average height, which was just a little shorter than me. The two
eye-catchers about him were his eyes and his mustache. His eyes
were whitish-blue. Ghostly blue. You could almost see them in the
dark. It was downright creepy if you didn't know the guy. He
could stare down anyone. Those eyes looked like they could burn
right through you.
He even made some Germans nervous when he just stopped and
looked at them for a few minutes. I loved it when he did that.
His mustache, on the other hand, was the envy of every man that
wanted good facial hair. It was a perfect mustache and Tim tended
to remind everybody now and again. Even I got a little sore about
it. I could grow a beard, but it didn't look good on me.

We were given only one day a week to rest while in that camp.
One. The other six, we were out working like honeybees, and not
because we wanted to. That day off just happened to be Sunday.
And even though we got to relax on that day, I hated Sunday most
of all.
One reason: Isaac Trevor.
He was the most annoying pain in the neck I have ever known.
Even more so than Engel. Engel, at least, was polite. Trevor was a
loud-mouth. And he was just plain weird. See, because of all of
the stuff we had to go through in that camp, most of us were just
plain miserable.
Not Trevor.
He didn't let any of that get to him. He smiled. **Smiled**, for Pete's
sake.

It was the short guy who told me to "watch my mouth" when I first got there. No matter what happened, he always tried to encourage us.
Let me show you what I'm talking about…

"Take courage, boys." The pipsqueak approached us. "We've got plenty to be thankful for."
Stares went towards him from all over the barracks. Angry stares. Confused stares. Stares of all sorts.
"You're bonkers." Johnny sneered at him.
"Ever heard of the story of Joseph?" The runt asked Johnny.
"There are a lot of Josephs." Johnny folded his arms. "Which one are you talking about?"
"The Joseph in the book of Genesis." The squirt clarified.
My ears twitched at the sound "Genesis".
I groaned. *Not another Engel…*
"Ever heard of that story?" The small-fry asked again.
"Don't read the Bible, Shorty." Johnny told him. "My parents were hypocrites when it came to church stuff."
"Trevor." The little guy said. "My name is Trevor. Chaplain Isaac Trevor. How about you, Ace?"
"Johnny."
Trevor turned to Taggart. "And you, Glasses?"
Taggart frowned. "That's not polite. Name's Taggart, Reverend."
Trevor laughed. "Reverend? Nah, I'm Baptist."
"What's the difference?" Taggart shrugged.
"Oh, if only I had the time." Trevor snickered. "See, Reverend is a-"
"Let me tell you the rules, boyo." I slunked off of my bed. I had already had enough of this guy. I stood over him and folded my arms. The guy was sure a midget. Especially to me.
I jabbed a thumb at myself. "I am the highest rankin' officer here, so I am in charge of these barracks."
"No one's arguing that, Captain Brad." Trevor smiled a goofy grin.
"Wipe that smirk off your face, Half-Pint." I snarled. "And don't

ever call me 'Brad' or 'Bradley'. To you, I am Captain Scoefield. You can call me 'Cappy' on one of my good days."

"I doubt you'll have a good day here, sir." Trevor kept smiling.

I was…surprised by his attitude. What was with this guy? Was he actually happy?

"Zip it and let me finish." I barked at him. "You'll also not ever be spoutin' off about anythin' in that book of yours."

I nodded towards his Bible.

"It's all fairy-tales anyway." I growled.

Finally, Trevor's smile vanished. "Well, I can't do that, sir."

I let out a grunt. "And why not?"

Then, his goofy grin was back. "Well, if I don't, I might get depressed."

I grabbed him by the collar and lifted him up to my face. "Hey! You makin' fun of me, Pipsqueak?!" I roared.

Trevor wasn't bothered by this one iota. He just smirked back and said: "No, sir."

I had no idea what to say back to that. I couldn't really beat him up. I had no reason to. Except for that stupid smile, but I didn't think of that at the time.

So, I kinda just…threw him back down and returned to my bed.

This happened for a long time. Trevor would try to start talking about the Bible and I would threaten to beat him up. It went on for a couple of weeks, until one night…

"I will personally smash you to smithereens, Half-Pint, if you bring up that stinkin' Bible one more time!" I shouted at him from my bed.

Trevor turned to me.

No smile, this time.

"Do it." He challenged.

"What did you just say?" I questioned, rising up from my bunk.

"Do it." Trevor said again. "Beat me up. Teach me a lesson. If you can."

I stomped over towards him. "I could destroy you, boy."

Trevor gave a tiny smirk. "Sure. How about we make a little

wager?"

"Like what?"

"You and I have a little match." Trevor offered. "If you win, I'll put my Bible away and never speak of it again in this barracks. But if I win, you and your men have to attend my devotions every single Sunday night."

I laughed heartily. "Done! I'll mop the floor with ya'!"

Trevor took a step back and lowered himself in a wrestling-like stance. "Then do it, *Brad*."

That instantly got to me.

I moved at Trevor, swinging a right hook. It was sloppy, but I figured this fight would be just like any other fight I had ever fought: A guy would mess with me, I would pound the snot out of him, and he would go crying to his mama.

But Trevor rolled underneath me. He seriously rolled under my punch and between my legs.

The guy was quick and small. I didn't really consider that. Most guys I had fought before weren't that small to me, except Engel. But, to be fair, Engel didn't have one fighting bone in his body. Okay, maybe he had *one* fighting bone in his body, but Trevor? Trevor had 206 fighting bones.

I spun around, trying to find where the little guy had gone. Before I knew it, though, I felt my leg slip and I toppled right onto my face. Trevor had grabbed my right foot as I was turning around and had thrown me forward. Before I could even roll onto my back, Trevor had body-slammed me.

He was heavy for a short guy.

I had the breath knocked out of me just for a minute, but then I swatted him off me. I pulled myself up to my knees and tried to get back up. But as soon as I got up on my feet and turned around, I saw Trevor running full-sprint at me. He looked like a puny bull. If I wasn't so mad at him right then, I probably would've laughed. He looked so dweebish.

He tackled right into me, pushing at me with all of his might. I stopped him easily. It made me step back awkwardly, but I stopped him in his tracks.

"There's no way ya' can tackle me to the ground, ya' nitwit!" I growled at him.

But then I noticed something. Trevor suddenly ducked down and placed one of his hands behind my right knee. The other, he slapped over my left knee. And in one big shove from his shoulder, Trevor launched my off of my legs and I fell hard on my side.

I let out a couple swear words right then as I jumped back up. I began swinging wildly at Trevor, trying to plow his face in any way I could. But he was too fast for me. He just kept dodging punch after punch as I yelled out at him. Then, finally, he got behind me. He pushed into me from behind and wrapped his arms around my gut. For a moment, I thought he was trying to knock me down or tackle me.

He wasn't.

I was caught off-guard when I saw that Trevor had locked his hands over my stomach. Then, with one big thrust, Trevor started lifting me up into the air.

Me.

The biggest guy in the room was being lifted up by the smallest guy in the room.

I started kicking my legs furiously, not knowing what to do. I was going higher and higher. The ceiling came into view as I was being flipped upside down.

I crashed hard on the cold, wooden floor. My shoulders and neck were throbbing instantly.

Trevor suplexed me. I had always heard of people doing that in wrestling.

And before I could blink, Trevor was on me again.

"Yield!" Trevor shouted at me as he pulled my arm back further. Boy, it was painful. He had me in some hold where he was bending my arm back as his legs pushed against my side.

"Never! Ya' scrawny, hi-ho-in' midget!"

He pulled back further and tightened his legs. I could feel my arm

straining. The dwarf could break my arm, I knew. And living in a
P.O.W. camp with two good arms was hard enough.
"…Fine." I grunted.
"What was that?" Trevor grinned goofily. "I can't hear you over
the screaming of your injured pride."
"Let me go, ya' buck-toothed hamster!"
He let me go.
I shoved him back as I stood back up. I was still red-hot mad, and
my face told everyone that.
I had just gotten beaten by a Bible-thumping twerp.
Thankfully, Trevor didn't rub that in my face. He simply stood to
his feet, wiped the dust and dirt off of his shirt, and said "I'll see
you boys for devotions in a little over an hour."
We all grumbled at that. I turned to my men feeling absolutely
humiliated. I had never before lost a fight to anyone.
"Sorry, fellas…" I coughed quietly.
Most of them were nice about it.
"You did your best, Cappy." Taggart told me. "It was a good
effort."
"He just got lucky." Bratt nodded along. "That's all it was.
Beginner's luck."
"He is too small and squirrel-like to pin down easily, Captain."
Tim added.
Then, Johnny. His arms were crossed and he wore a heavy,
disappointed frown on his mug.
"I'll tell all of you what just happened." He scoffed. "You got your
tail whipped by a bug, Cappy. And now we have to go to church
every Sunday until it kills us."

CHAPTER NINE

"Genesis 37:2." Trevor began as we were gathered in a small circle in my   quarters.

Being the highest ranking officer, I got a room to myself. It wasn't really fancy, but it was nice to get a place where I could be alone sometimes. And, since I had the greatest authority in the barracks, I got to choose where we had our little devotions. I wanted to sit on my bed and that's exactly what I did.

At least I got a small win in that.

"'These are the generations of Jacob'." Trevor continued.

"'Joseph, being seventeen years old, was feeding the flock with his brethren; and the lad was with the sons of Bilhah, and with the sons of Zilpah, his father's wives: and Joseph brought unto his father their evil report'."

"Wow." Bratt snorted. "You're going to need to explain all that fancy talk. The only one here who speaks fancy-sphmancy is Taggart."

Taggart rolled his eyes. "Why am I always the one who is the center of all the antics?"

"That's why." Johnny chortled. "Only you would say 'antics'."

"Fair enough." Trevor said, addressing Bratt. "I'll give some explanation."

Then he paused. "How many of you have heard this story before?"

Taggart raised his hand. Then he glanced around with an unbelieving look. "Oh. Just me?"

Then, embarrassed, he slowly put his hand down.

"Very well, then." Trevor clapped his hands together. "Then I'll give background information as well."

Trevor lifted up his Bible. "Joseph, who I'm going to talk to you boys about, was one of the sons of Jacob. Jacob, otherwise known as Israel, was the son of Isaac."

He let his goofy grin shine at that moment. "Whose name means 'laughter'."

"Yeah, you're hilarious, Half-Pint." I groaned.

"And Isaac was the son of Abraham." Trevor continued, ignoring my remark. "Abraham was chosen by God to be the father of the Hebrew people. He obeyed and believed God and thus, Judaism began with him."

"You speak of the Jews." Tim told him. "Be careful, little man. The Germans seek to eliminate them. I do not think they would want you to say that they are God's people."

"I will speak truth, Tikhomir." Trevor declared without apology, still holding up his Bible. "And truth lies within this book. If they want to kill me for that, well, they're only threatening me with heaven."

Trevor flipped back open to Genesis 37. "Now, Jacob (Abraham's grandson) had twelve sons. Joseph was-"

"Twelve sons?" Johnny blurted. "Holy cow! *Twelve* kids? That can't be right."

"I said twelve sons." Trevor corrected him. "They had a daughter, too. So, thirteen altogether."

"Can people even have that many children?" Bratt asked with an amazed look on his face.

Instinctively, we all looked at Taggart. Once Taggart noticed, he cleared his throat. "It is very possible. Just not very common. At least, it's not common between one man and one woman, though there have been instances where that took place. So, yes."

"Wow." Johnny muttered. "Whoever Jacob's wife was, she was a poor woman."

"Jacob had four wives." Trevor suddenly told him.

"Four?" Bratt's mouth dropped. "I can't even get one!"

Tim was laughing heartily. "Ah, some men simply are too much for one woman to handle. My father is such a man."

Trevor gave him a worried look. "Uh-huh. You know, having four wives is not a good thing. God intended one man and one woman together for one lifetime. Anything against His plan will only be problematic and-"

Suddenly, Trevor shook his head. "We're getting off track. I'll talk about God's plan for marriage later. Yes, Jacob had four wives and

thirteen kids. But out of all of them, Jacob loved Joseph the most."
He began reading out of the Bible. "'Now Israel loved Joseph
more than all his children, because he was the son of his old age'."
"Sounds like my brother." Bratt grumbled.
"Exactly." Trevor pointed at him. "That's exactly what we're
about to get to. Joseph's brothers had the same kind of animosity
towards him because of the way their father treated him: 'And
when his brethren saw that their father loved him more than all his
brethren, they hated him, and could not speak peaceably unto
him'."
"And how does this have **anythin'** to do with us, Half-Pint?" I
questioned impatiently.
"I'm getting to that, Brad." Trevor gave off his goofy grin again.
"Patience. It's a story. Give it time."
Trevor then turned to the rest of the boys. "So now, his brothers
hate him because Dad loves him more than the rest. Being the son
of Jacob's old age, and the firstborn of his favorite wife, it **does**
make sense. I'm not saying it's right, but it does make sense. But
now, it gets even better. Joseph dreams a dream."
"What difference does that make?" Tim pointed out. "He probably
had some late night borscht. That always gives me bizarre
dreams."
"This dream was sent by the Lord." Trevor explained. "In those
days, Bibles weren't around. God spoke to mankind in a different
fashion. In that day, God used dreams, visions, and even His
audible voice."
"That would make things easier." I grunted. "Why doesn't God do
that nowadays? Prove that He's out there?"
"Because He's already spoken." Trevor patted his Bible gently.
"'For we have not followed cunningly devised fables, when we
made known unto you the power and coming of our Lord Jesus
Christ, but were eyewitnesses of His majesty. For He received
from God the Father honour and glory, when there came such a
voice to Him from the excellent glory, This is my beloved Son, in
whom I am well pleased. And this voice which came from heaven
we heard, when we were with Him in the holy mount. We have

also a ***more sure word of prophecy***; whereunto ye do well that ye take heed, as unto a light that shineth in a dark place, until the day dawn, and the day star arise in your hearts'. 2 Peter 1:16 – 19."

"What does that mean?" Bratt asked what we were all thinking.

"I'll not get too much into it, but it points out that God's written Word is much better than His spoken." Trevor explained.

"How do ya' figure?" I grumbled.

"Let me give you an example." Trevor thought for a moment.

"Say, you're buying a car. The car dealer says 'I'm going to give you this Chrysler Imperial 80% off."

Johnny whistled. "Oo, I could use that kind of deal. I ***love*** Chryslers."

"Right." Trevor nodded. "But what's your first thought after that?"

"Get that in writing." Taggart told him.

"Bingo." Trevor pointed to Taggart with his goofy grin on. "Get it in writing. Why? Because there can be problems with what people hear: Human memory can be faulty, people can twist what was said, and plenty of other things. But if it is written…"

Trevor again held up his Bible for all of us to see.

"If it is cemented down where people cannot wish it away, forget it, excuse it as some bad borscht, or twist it to mean what they want, it is indeed a more sure word of prophecy."

Suddenly, Trevor began muttering to himself. "Though some still try to twist it to mean what they want…"

Then, he was back talking to us. "But it's also for our benefit in this way: God made plenty of promises to us and He's written them all down to assure us that He ***will*** do them."

"Then why hasn't He?" I snapped.

"Why hasn't He what, Brad?" Trevor shot back. "Do you even know any of God's promises?"

Oh, I hated him calling me "Brad". And to be honest, I didn't know any promises from God.

But I lied because I wanted to sound smart.

"Yeah." I squinted at him. "He promised He'd give us happy lives."

"Wrong, Brad." Trevor said flatly. "God has not once stated that

He would make our lives comfortable and pleasant. In fact, He promised the opposite. God is not primarily concerned about your happiness or mine. This life is not about you. It's about Him."

"That's selfish of Him, then." I accused.

"If He was like us, yes." Trevor noted. "But He's not. He's perfect and holy. Without evil. 100% good. Glorious beyond imagining. If you saw Him, you'd fall flat on your face and acknowledge that God deserves everything we can give Him and more."

"I beg to differ, Half-Pint." I folded my arms. "How do ya' know He's good?"

"Are you asking 'cause you want to know or are you asking 'cause you want to just try and trip me up?" Trevor asked bluntly. I didn't say anything back. Everyone, including Trevor, knew why I was really asking that question.

"Well, I'll tell you anyway." Trevor breathed. "God is good because He gave me life. Because He sent His Son to come down to this sin-sick world and live a perfect life and die as a sacrifice for my wretched sin so I don't have to spend eternity in a fiery lake of fire after I die. Because He's answered my multiplicity of prayers. Because He put me into a good family. Because He gave me His Word to read and nourish my soul. Because He made this wonderful world for me to live in. Because He gave me free will. Because He called me to preach the Gospel."

Trevor paused. "I can go on if you wish. It's a *very* long list."

"What about the bad stuff, eh?" I hissed. "If God's so good, why is there so much bad stuff in the world? Like this war?"

Trevor leaned closer to me and whispered. "Who started this war, Brad?"

"…Hitler." I grumbled.

"So why are you blaming God?"

"Because God allowed Hitler to do it." I shot back.

"God allows free will, like I said before." Trevor put up his hands. "He's patient for men to come to repentance. He gives people multiple chances to turn to Him. It's another example of how God is good."

We kept at it like that for a good while. It was really just me trying to find something wrong with Christianity. But Trevor was smart and quick. Whenever I threw something at him, he was ready with a baseball glove to catch it.
I tried to make him and God look like a fool.
Instead, it backfired on me and I was the fool.
I hated that guy so much.
"Well, that's all the time we have for tonight." Trevor glanced at his watch. "The guards will be checking on us soon."
"But we just started the story." Taggart reasoned. "We haven't even gotten anywhere."
Trevor shrugged. "Looks like we needed to hammer some things down tonight before we got too far into it. Don't worry, boys, the story will still be there next Sunday."

CHAPTER TEN

"Evening, gentlemen." Trevor began a week later. We were in the same spot as last time: in my room, around my bunk.
"Now that we've had some things settled down last Sunday, I think we'll be able to actually dive in to the meat of the story today."
No one really said anything in response to that.
Trevor's goofy grin appeared on his face. "So, let's begin, shall we? Joseph dreamed a dream. Remember, this was a dream sent by God Himself. 'And Joseph dreamed a dream, and he told it his brethren: and they hated him yet the more. And he said unto them, Hear, I pray you, this dream which I have dreamed: For, behold, we were binding sheaves in the field, and, lo, my sheaf arose, and also stood upright; and, behold, your sheaves stood round about, and made obeisance to my sheaf. And his brethren said to him, Shalt thou indeed reign over us? or shalt thou indeed have dominion over us? And they hated him yet the more for his dreams, and for his words'."
"This Joseph is not the brightest star in the sky, is he?" Tim shook his head.
"Wait, what?" Johnny looked back and forth between Trevor and Tim. "You understood all of that?"
"Mostly." Tim answered. "The boy had a dream that his sheaf was being bowed to by the sheaves of his brothers. That is to say that he was superior to them. If he is the second youngest son, that would be a mockery to his elder brothers. Younger brothers are not supposed to be superior to the older. And, he told them his dream. They already hated him for their father's greater love for him. Now, they hate him even more because he is telling them that he is better than them."
"That's pretty much it." Trevor nodded approvingly. "Well done, Tikhomir."
Tim nodded back. "It would seem that this boy either did not know of his brothers' malice, which is unlikely, or he simply

95

enjoyed boasting to them. Either way, I do not think it was wise of him to tell them the dream."

"I don't think Joseph was being a punk here." Trevor offered. "He may have just have been excited about the dream. I mean, you know when you have a weird dream, you just want to tell people about it? Anyway, you are right, Tikhomir, it wasn't the best idea for Joseph to tell them. At least, *I* don't think it was the best idea. Anyway, moving on."

He glanced down back at his Bible. "For sake of time, we'll skip the second dream. Joseph had a second dream that basically said the same thing as the last dream. So now, we find Joseph being sent out on an errand for Jacob. 'And his brethren went to feed their father's flock in Shechem. And Israel said unto Joseph, Do not thy brethren feed the flock in Shechem? Come, and I will send thee unto them. And he said to him, Here am I. And he said to him, Go, I pray thee, see whether it be well with thy brethren, and well with the flocks; and bring me word again. So he sent him out of the vale of Hebron, and he came to Shechem. And a certain man found him, and, behold, he was wandering in the field: and the man asked him, saying, What seekest thou? And he said, I seek my brethren: tell me, I pray thee, where they feed their flocks. And the man said, They are departed hence; for I heard them say, Let us go to Dothan. And Joseph went after his brethren, and found them in Dothan'."

Trevor looked up at us. "Any interpretation needed?"

"We're not idiots, Half-Pint." I scoffed.

"Very well." Trevor went on. "'And when they saw him afar off, even before he came near unto them, and they said one to another, Behold, this dreamer cometh'."

"It's just like my little brother." Bratt shook his head annoyingly. "Always sent after me to make sure I'm doing what I'm supposed to. And he's a pathetic dreamer, too. I relate with these brothers."

"Whoops!" Trevor laughed. "I accidentally skipped a part. Let me read it again. 'And when they saw him afar off, even before he came near unto them, *they conspired against him to slay him.*

And they said one to another, Behold, this dreamer cometh'."
"Hold the phone." Bratt's eyes widened. "What did you say? *Slay* him?"
Trevor nodded, finishing the verse. "'Come now therefore, and let us slay him, and cast him into some pit, and we will say, Some evil beast hath devoured him: and we shall see what will become of his dreams'."
"I take it back! I take it back!" Bratt waved his hands frantically in front of his face. "I *don't* relate with these brothers! I love my little brother, Nigel!"
"Why did they want to kill him?" Johnny asked. "Isn't that a bit extreme?"
Trevor sighed. "It was a divided house. Remember, none of these brothers were full-blooded brothers to Joseph. They were all his half-brothers. Most of them were the sons of Leah, while Joseph was the son of Rachel. Rachel was the beloved wife while Leah was neglected. Leah was bitter against Rachel for that and that bitterness bled into the children. The fact that Joseph was Jacob's beloved son only compounded that bitterness. They did not love their half-brother, Joseph. They truly hated him."
"That's real nifty, squirt." I name-called Trevor. "But what does that have to do with us in a prisoner of war camp in Germany?"
"I'm getting to that, Brad." Trevor teased right back. "Hold your horses. You've got to hear the story before you hear the application."
"Oh, ya' know I just *adore* fairy-tale time." I groaned sarcastically.

"Did the brothers kill the boy?" Tim asked Trevor to get the story moving again.
"No." Trevor replied. "Reuben, the oldest brother, convinced them not to. Instead, he told them to throw Joseph in a pit. But Judah got an idea. Here, let's read it. 'And they took him, and cast him into a pit: and the pit was empty, there was no water in it. And they sat down to eat bread: and they lifted up their eyes and looked, and, behold, a company of Ishmeelites came from Gilead

with their camels bearing spicery and balm and myrrh, going to
carry it down to Egypt. And Judah said unto his brethren, What
profit is it if we slay our brother, and conceal his blood? Come,
and let us sell him to the Ishmeelites, and let not our hand be upon
him; for he is our brother and our flesh. And his brethren were
content. Then there passed by Midianites merchantmen; and they
drew and lifted up Joseph out of the pit, and sold Joseph to the
Ishmeelites for twenty pieces of silver: and they brought Joseph
into Egypt'."

"They sold their own brother?" Bratt marveled.

"Better than death." Tim offered. "Brothers selling brothers into
slavery is not unheard of in Europe and Asia. No…let me correct
myself. It is common."

"Really?" Taggart fiddled with his glasses.

"Oh, yes." Tim assured us all. "Even in Russia, family will turn on
family if they need to. But better to be a slave than a dead man."

"I don't think you understand, Tikhomir." Trevor said somberly.
"When Joseph's brothers were selling him into slavery, it was a
death sentence."

A chilling quiet came over all of us.

Trevor continued. "In those days, slaves were worked without
mercy or concern for their lives. Slaves didn't live too long."

"So he did die." Johnny's shoulders sank.

"No." Trevor smiled a hopeful smile. "But it's only because God
was with him. But we'll talk about that tomorrow night. It's
getting late."

"You're darn right it is." I sighed gratefully, lying back on my bed.
"It's 'bout time."

…The next Sunday night…

"'And the Midianites sold him into Egypt unto Potiphar, an officer
of Pharaoh's, and captain of the guard'."

"That's good, right?" Bratt asked. "I mean, the captain of the
guard? It could be worse right? He could've been put to work on
the pyramids."

"No, Allan, the pyramids weren't built then, they…" Suddenly

Trevor stopped and started thinking. Trevor then looked at Bratt with a blank face. "Hmm…To be honest, I don't really know when the pyramids were built. I mean, I assume they were built in the time of Moses, when the Hebrews were all enslaved in Egypt, but I can't be dogmatic-"

"What?" Bratt gasped. "The Egyptians got the rest of Joseph's brothers, too?"

"Who is Moses?" Tim scratched his head.

Trevor blinked, looking between Bratt and Tim. "To answer your question, Allan…not exactly. The Hebrews become enslaved by Egypt generations later. Pharaoh made slaves of the descendants of Joseph and his brothers."

"Wow, Reverend, way to give away the ending." Taggart chuckled.

"Oh, come on." Trevor huffed. "The King James Bible has been available since 1611. That's over three-hundred years! I'm not spoiling any big surprise here. You boys just need to read more."

"*I've* read it." Taggart said smugly.

"All of it?" Trevor challenged. "All sixty-six books of the Bible?"

Taggart's smug grin disappeared. "Well, not-"

"Then zip the lip, Glasses, and don't get so proud about your reading abilities." Trevor told Taggart.

Taggart grumbled, involuntarily touching the rims of his glasses.

"As for your question, Tikhomir." Trevor finally addressed Tim. "I'm sorry, but that's a whole other story. We'll get to that later."

"Very well." Tim said, satisfied.

"Now, back to it." Trevor turned back to his Bible. "Sure, I suppose getting sold to Potiphar had its perks. But that's not important, because I believe that no matter who had bought Joseph, Joseph would've been okay. You know why?"

Taggart raised his hand.

"Not you. You know the story." Trevor shushed him.

Taggart put down his hand with an angry look.

"Because God was with him." Trevor announced for the rest of us. "It says it here in chapter 39:2 – 6. 'And the LORD was with Joseph, and he was a prosperous man; and he was in the house of his master the Egyptian. And his master saw that the LORD was with him, and that the LORD made all that he did to prosper in his hand. And Joseph found grace in his sight, and he served him: and he made him overseer over his house, and all that he had he put into his hand. And it came to pass from the time that he had made him overseer in his house, and over all that he had, that the LORD blessed the Egyptian's house for Joseph's sake; and the blessing of the LORD was upon all that he had in the house, and in the field. And he left all that he had in Joseph's hand; and he knew not ought he had, save the bread which he did eat. And Joseph was a goodly person, and well favoured'. See, but that begs the question: why was God with Joseph? Why did God bless Joseph?"

No one said anything. Then, Taggart slowly raised his hand again. "All-right, Ken." Trevor chuckled. "I've given you a hard enough time. Tell us why."

"The most appropriate and reasonable answer would be that Joseph was faithful to his God." Taggart answered. "As James states: 'God resisteth the proud, but giveth grace unto the humble'. Or, as another verse in James says: 'Draw nigh to God, and He will draw nigh to you'."

"That's right." Then Trevor grinned. "Do you feel good now? Being able to expound some of your deep knowledge to the rest of us?"

Taggart smiled happily back. "I know you're making fun of me again, but yes."

"Well, good." Trevor commented. "God blessed Joseph because, even though Joseph was sold into slavery, he honored God. I believe Joseph put God first and God honored him for it."

Trevor then glanced at me. "Brad, you'll be happy, because we're about to get to application."

"We're almost done?" I asked, getting excited.

"Oh, I didn't say that." Trevor shook his head. "I just said we're getting to the 'what does this have to do with **us**, Half-Pint?'."

"You're gonna' make fun of me?" I growled.

"I make fun of **everybody**." Trevor grinned his goofy grin. "And

yes, I will make fun of you, Brad. It builds character.”
“I could wallop you.” I threatened.
“You tried that already.” Trevor shot back. “I didn't feel so
‘walloped’ then.”
“You wanna go again?!” I shouted.
“Sure, but not now.” Trevor was unfazed. “First, I got to tell
everyone the application before everyone forgets the story.”
Trevor then leaned forward, looking to each one of us. “Joseph
was taken to a foreign land against his will. He was sold as a piece
of property to a man who probably cared little for his life. Sounds
a bit familiar, eh?”
Nods came from all around.
“We're here because Hitler decided to try and conquer the world
with his hate, god-complex, and the German people.” Trevor
explained to us, though we didn't really need the explanation.
“Fighting for our countries, each of us were captured. Taken here,
against our will, to work and survive until someone wins this war.
God willing, America.”
Then he glanced at Tim. “No offense, Tikhomir.”
Tim shrugged. “You are an American. It is only natural for you to
wish for your own nation's victory. I, however, would not put
Russia out of the race, yet. We are a strong people.”
“That you are.” Trevor agreed, then returning to the application.
“So, we're in a situation not unlike Joseph's. What should we do,
then? Escape? Or should we take this situation to glorify God?”
Everyone glanced at each other, confused.
“We should escape, right?” Bratt said, unsure. “Because we need
to beat these guys. We can't do that from in here.”
“Can't we?” Trevor asked back.
“You mean sabotage?” I asked, liking the idea. “I suppose the
Germans'd never expect prisoners bombin' their own stuff. We're
near Berlin, too. We could strike hard against ‘em!”
I smiled wide, really getting excited about the idea. Everyone was
praising my plan, too. We all really liked it. Except for Trevor.
“No.” He said sternly. “That's not what I meant.”
“What did ya' mean, then?” I raised an eyebrow.

"Do you think Potiphar was a slave-loving guy?" Trevor asked all of us.

"What does that have to do with anythi-?"

"Do you think Potiphar cared about Joseph when he first got there?" Trevor interrupted me.

"No." Johnny answered.

"No, he likely didn't even consider him as a person." Trevor nodded to Johnny. "And we don't matter at all to the Germans around here. But Potiphar came to respect Joseph because of his work-ethic and his spirit. Potiphar's perspective was changed when it came to Joseph. And that is what we, as prisoners, can do to these German soldiers."

Trevor let all of that settle in us for a moment.

I folded my arms and sat back, a deep frown on my face. "So, Half-Pint, you're tellin' us that we need to make the Germans our friends? We need to gain their respect? What'll that do?"

"What did it do in Joseph's life?" Trevor asked. "He came to become a ruler in Egypt."

"He did?" Bratt barked. "Potiphar made him a ruler?"

"He didn't become a ruler until he was thrown in prison." Taggart told Trevor. "Potiphar had nothing to do with Joseph's ascension to the second-in-command of Egypt. Joseph being kind to Potiphar did nothing but allow him to be promoted within Potiphar's household. Still as a *slave*. Being kind to the Germans will do us no better. In fact, it may not even do *any* good. Your application is faulty, Reverend."

"Second-in-command?" Johnny looked at Bratt, surprised.

"Look, I'm just saying that maybe God has us here in this place for a reason." Trevor offered. "The Germans may have meant it for evil, but maybe God means it for good."

No one looked like they agreed with Trevor.

"Fine." Trevor huffed out, frustrated. "Let's just move on. 'And it came to pass after these things, that his master's wife cast her eyes upon Joseph; and she said, Lie with me'."

"Hot snot!" Johnny shouted excitedly. "The boy's got it made!

Now Potiphar's wife wants him? What a turnout!"

"Johnny, it doesn't exactly-" Taggart tried to say.

"Though I do not know this Joseph very well, I must say that I am proud of him." Tim folded his arms with a broad smile on his face. "He is truly a man now."

Bratt looked to Tim. "Is that what it means to be a man?"

"No, Bratt." I told the Private. "You're already a man. You made it through boot camp and fought for your country. Any guy who does that sacrifice *is* a man. Bein' with a lady doesn't make you a man."

"You only say that because you haven't been with one." Johnny smirked.

"Johnny, shut your yap before I shut it permanently." I threatened. "And for your information, I respect women. It'd be better for ya' to do that, too, instead of aimin' for a good time on a Friday night."

"Well, I'm glad to see there's some sense in that thick head of yours, Brad." Trevor spoke up. His eyes were calm, but angry. His mouth was creased in a mad frown. "Shall we read on instead of you people talking about sexual sin like it's nothing more than gastronomic indulgence?"

"What?" I asked.

"Come again?" Bratt asked.

"Is that even English?" Tim asked.

"He's speaking 'Taggart'." Johnny marveled.

With that, we all looked at Taggart.

Taggart groaned. "He said, basically, that you were talking about sex like it's nothing more than eating a meal."

"Oh." We all said together, turning back to Trevor.

"Indeed." Trevor still looked mad. "Let's see what Joseph had to say about all this. 'And it came to pass after these things, that his master's wife cast her eyes upon Joseph; and she said, Lie with me. But he *refused*, and said unto his master's wife, Behold, my master wotteth not what is with me in the house, and he hath committed all that he hath to my hand; There is none greater in this house than I; neither hath he kept back any thing from me but thee, because thou art his wife: how then can I do this great wickedness, and sin against God?'."

A pause arose from all of us.

"He was just nervous." Johnny excused. "It's understandable."

"He was *not* nervous. He knew it was wrong!" Trevor pointed accusingly at Johnny. "Did you hear his words?! 'How then can I do this great *wickedness*, and *sin* against God?'! Does that sound like he thinks it's okay?!"

"Whoa, calm down, Half-Pint." I told him. "I'm all for standin' up for the ladies, but she wanted it too, right? What's so wrong about that?"

"What's so wrong about that?" Trevor repeated, shaking his head. "Why don't you tell us, Brad?"

Everyone looked at me.

"What'cha talkin' 'bout?" I asked Trevor, not sure what he was asking. "Hey, it's like Johnny said. I've never done that."

"No, but you've been hurt by it, haven't you?" Trevor asked.

I was still confused. I went over his question in my mind a couple times before it hit me.

Engel and Sarah. Trevor was talking about them.

I lowered my head, anger and embarrassment boiling up inside of me. Anger because, well, Engel. Embarrassment because Trevor was throwing Engel's back-stabbing actions in my face right in front of my men.

"Trevor, we are *done* talkin' about that." I said slowly through gritted teeth.

"I'm just trying to make a point." Trevor sat back. "You all think sex is just a free-for-all. How dare you. Sex was invented for intimacy between a husband and a wife and you all talk about it like it's just a good steak."

"We're not here to listen to your judgmental accusations, Reverend." Taggart said tensely. Johnny and Tim looked just like he did: arms folded, stern faces, and eyes that held back resentment.

"'Doth this offend you?'" Trevor quoted John 6:61. "And they're not my words. The Bible is God's words. Listen to this: 'Marriage *is* honourable in all, and the bed undefiled: but whoremongers and adulterers God will judge'."

Trevor took a few moments to look at each one of us. "The Greek word for 'whoremongers' is 'pornos'. It's where we get the word for pornography. All sexual acts and even lustful thoughts that are outside of marriage are wicked. Only in marriage is sex honorable and undefiled. And you boys better learn that quick because God will judge those who use sex just as a 'good time on Friday night'."

Trevor turned back to his Bible. "And Joseph knew that. He loved God more than his own desires. See here: 'And it came to pass, as she spake to Joseph day by day, that he hearkened not unto her, to lie by her, or to be with her. And it came to pass about this time, that Joseph went into the house-'."

"Trevor, I think we're done for the night." Johnny cut him off.

"I couldn't agree more." Taggart nodded.

"*Da*." Tim grunted.

"What they said." I growled.

The only one who didn't agree with the rest of us was Bratt. He simply looked at all of us, then back to Trevor.

Trevor sighed but closed the Bible. "Very well. We'll continue this later."

"Good. Bedtime." I said with mock enthusiasm. "All of you get out of my room. But Taggart and Johnny? You two stay. I want a word with ya'."

Taggart and Johnny exchanged worried looks.

And they were right to.

Once everybody else was out of my room, I closed the door. Then I grabbed both of them by the collars and dragged them up to my face.

"Which one of you bozos told Trevor about Engel and my sister?" I fumed at them.

"It wasn't me!" Taggart yelped.

I glared at Johnny. He was shaking his head frantically. "I didn't say a word, Cappy! You think I would try and get into long conversations with that twerp?”

“One of you is lyin’.” I growled. “Now, I like both of ya’, but if you push me, I *will* pummel it outta’ you!”

“It was me, Cappy.” Bratt’s voice suddenly came from the doorway. He creaked it open, looking guilty.

I set down Taggart and Johnny. “Bratt? Why would you tell that punk about my sister and lousy Engel?”

Bratt hung his head. “I’m sorry. I like talking with Isaac. We talk a lot. And he asked me why you always seem like there’s a thorn in your foot. I told him it might be about Engel. Of course, he didn’t know about Engel, so I explained it to him.”

Bratt glanced up for a moment and then hung his head again. “I’m sorry, Cappy. If you want to wallop me, I’m okay with that.”

I took a deep breath. I turned to Taggart and Johnny. “I’m sorry for thinkin’ it was you two. To make up for it, I’ll give you both a share of my rations. You can go to bed.”

They hurried off and shut the door behind them.

I sat down at my desk. “Bratt, I’m not gonna’ wallop ya’. But did you have to tell Trevor about *that*? You couldn’t have told him somethin’ else?”

Bratt shrugged, still looking at the floor. “I tend to be honest, Cappy. It’s the best policy, you know.”

I nodded at that. “And I admire your honesty. Thank you. Just next time, take a couple moments to think about what’cha tell people. Ya’ got me?”

“Yes, sir.”

“Go to bed, pally.”

“Yes, sir.”

And he was gone. I turned out my lamp and laid on my rusty bed. *“Now Trevor knows.”* I thought to myself as the comforting darkness surrounded me. *“Great. That’s just what I need. Another Engel knowin’ about my past Engel. That’ll be fun.”*

<u>CHAPTER ELEVEN</u>

"Since we ended a little abruptly last time…" Trevor began as he flipped through the pages of his Bible. The sound had become quite familiar with us. "I'm going to start with verse 10 of chapter 39: 'And it came to pass, as she spake to Joseph day by day, that he hearkened not unto her, to lie by her, or to be with her. And it came to pass about this time, that Joseph went into the house to do his business; and there was none of the men of the house there within. And she caught him by his garment, saying, Lie with me: and he left his garment in her hand, and fled, and got him out'."
Tim leaned over and began whispering to me. "This is the part where he makes us all feel like savage animals."
"Seems to be a thing with preachers." I whispered back.
"So." Trevor started. "As you can see-"
"Can we skip this part?" Taggart asked. "We talked about it last time. We know how you feel about it and you know how we feel about it. There. No need to go over it twice."
"Feeling conviction already?" Trevor raised an eyebrow.
Taggart shifted uncomfortably.
"To answer your question, Ken, I don't think that would be a good idea." Trevor told him with a gentle tone. "I get it. We've all done things that we're not proud of. We've all done things we don't want to talk about. But we need all of the Word's counsel."
A groan came from the men. If I hadn't lost the bet, I knew that none of them would be here for this part of the Bible story. Except Bratt. He seemed eager to hear more.
"*Poor kid.*" I thought. "*He's buyin' all of this.*"
"However…" Trevor said quietly. "This isn't quite the right place for it. I might touch on it a bit, but this passage isn't the best for addressing sexual sin."
"It's not?" I raised an eyebrow.
"Not exactly." Trevor nodded. "Joseph's life does not necessarily make for a case as to why people should abstain from sexual sin. There are plenty of other places throughout the Bible that make

that case far better than this one. And I don't think hopping to those places would be beneficial. I wanted to take you boys through the life of Joseph. Jumping all over the Bible for every issue would just get complicated."

"So, what does Joseph's life make a case for?" Bratt quizzed Trevor.

"Joseph's life makes a case for why we should trust God and do good. No matter how bleak our circumstances seem."

I scoffed. Johnny did something similar. Trevor noticed, too, but didn't say anything about it.

"So, picking up where we left off." Trevor started again. "Joseph refused Potiphar's wife. Even to the point where she grabbed a hold of him. It would be wise of us to imitate Joseph's reaction to this."

"And that is?" Johnny asked him.

"Get you out." Trevor said with a chuckle. "Basically, run from the temptation. Flee from it. Get it out of your life. If the temptation is coming from a girl, avoid her. If-"

"Surely I cannot avoid every woman I come in contact with." Tim interrupted.

Trevor looked at him skeptically. "***Every*** woman that you meet throws herself at you?"

Tim smiled and stroked his mustache. "A gift or a curse. You be the judge."

"Tim, I think you have a major problem with vanity." Taggart told him.

"It is not vanity if it is truth." Tim stroked his mustache again.

Trevor rolled his eyes. "We definitely don't have time to address that issue tonight. Getting back on track, verse 13 – 20: 'And it came to pass, when she saw that he had left his garment in her hand, and was fled forth, That she called unto the men of her house, and spake unto them, saying, See, he hath brought in an Hebrew unto us to mock us; he came in unto me to lie with me, and I cried with a loud voice: And it came to pass, when he heard that I lifted up my voice and cried, that he left his garment with me, and fled, and got him out. And she laid up his garment by her, until his lord came home. And she spake unto him according to these words, saying, The Hebrew servant, which thou hast brought unto us, came in unto me to mock me: And it came to pass, as I lifted up my voice and cried, that he left his garment with me, and fled out. And it came to pass, when his master heard the words of his wife, which she spake unto him, saying, After this manner did thy servant to me; that his wrath was kindled. And Joseph's master took him, and put him into the prison, a place where the king's prisoners were bound: and he was there in the prison'."

"What was that?!" I pointed at Trevor. "He got thrown in jail for doin' right!"
Trevor nodded. "Considering where we are right now, I would think you would understand that happens sometimes, Brad."
"Why didn't God do somethin'?!" I shouted.
"God *was* working." Trevor replied softly. "It just isn't how we often want or plan. As for being falsely accused by Potiphar's wife, that was her doing. Not God's. Each of us have a free will to do right or wrong. But, being thrown in prison was of God. After all, he could have been executed."
"It makes sense." Bratt said. "If I was a captain of the guard and my wife told me that somebody tried to rape her, that guy would be dead."
"Exactly." Trevor smiled at Bratt. Then, looking at me. "Don't worry, Brad. It'll get better. You'll see."
Then he turned back to his Bible. "'But the LORD was with Joseph, and shewed him mercy, and gave him favour in the sight of the keeper of the prison. And the keeper of the prison committed to Joseph's hand all the prisoners that were in the prison; and whatsoever they did there, he was the doer of it. The keeper of the prison looked not to any thing that was under his hand; because the LORD was with him, and that which he did, the LORD made it to prosper'."
"The same thing happened in the prison that happened with Potiphar." Taggart marveled. "I had forgotten about that."
"I thought you said you read this story." Tim looked over at him.

Taggart held his palms up. "I can't remember *everything*."
"Though he's not too far from it." I grinned. "Watch this. Taggart, what's the capital of Arizona?"
"Easy." Taggart smiled smugly while wiping his glasses. "Phoenix."
"What's the tallest mountain in the world?" I asked further.
"Are you kidding me? Mount Everest."
"What was the thirteenth president's middle name?"
"Come on. Give me a hard one." Taggart folded his arms confidently. "Millard Fillmore didn't have a middle name. Although, he was the last president to not have been affiliated with either the Republic or Democratic party."
I gestured out my hand to him as I looked at everyone else. "I rest my case, gentlemen."
"We're getting off track." Trevor cleared his throat. "And if I'm going to get through this passage tonight, you all better listen up." We did so.

"This is the part that I wanted to get to from the very beginning." Trevor said solenmly as he continued looking at his Bible. "The fact that Joseph did right, yet he was met with imprisonment."
Trevor glanced up at me. "Application time."
"I'm singin' 'hallelujah' already, Half-Pint." I muttered.
"We're men that have sacrificed for the good of our nations. We are on the side of right. Hitler and the rest of the Nazis are clearly on the side of evil. Messed up in cults and demonic power, they have done terrible things to Europe. To the world even. We each got involved and, by one way or another, have been taken prisoner by the enemy."
Trevor spoke slowly and firmly, looking at each one of us. "Joseph was not a prisoner of war, but he was in a similar situation. He was doing nothing but right, yet he eventually found himself in an Egyptian dungeon. But he trusted that God was there with him, and God was. God caused his life to prosper because Joseph lived for God."

"So, if we live for God, God will make the Germans put us in charge?" I asked, laughing.

Trevor gave me a glare. "Some of us are in more prisons than one."

I knew what he meant. It just made me angrier.

"Don't push it, Half-Pint."

"No, Brad." Trevor shot back. "*You* don't push it."

Trevor suddenly turned his attention back to the rest of the guys. "Have any of you taken into account that you're actually lucky to be here?"

"Oh! You know what, you're right!" Johnny gasped sarcastically. "How fortunate of us! How come I didn't think of it before? I've always wanted to live in a prison! It's the perfect place to-"

"You could be dead instead." Trevor interrupted him. "If I remember correctly, you boys had some friends that were with you before you got captured. You think they would choose to be here instead of where they are now?"

Johnny shut his mouth, his look completely changing.

"Each of us were captured alive." Trevor stated. "But we didn't have to be. God was gracious enough to allow us to live in this prison. We may be in a prison, but we are alive."

"What would God save us for?" Tim asked. "I do not believe we will change the hearts of these Germans like Joseph changed the heart of the prison-keeper."

"You never know." Trevor offered. "I would like to think that God put me here to influence the Nazis to stop following a demoniac."

At that word 'demoniac', all of us (except Taggart) gave Trevor a look of confusion.

"What's a demoniac?" Bratt asked.

"Is that like Frankenstein?" Johnny guessed.

Taggart glanced at Johnny with a laugh. "The movie?"

"I hated that feature." Bratt whispered to me.

I shrugged back. "I never saw it. Heard about it, though."

"What is a Frankenstein?" Tim asked, looking at the rest of us. "Is that German?"

"Actually…" Taggart thought. "Frankenstein *is* a German

scientist."

"Enough about Frankenstein." Trevor spoke with strained patience. "I was talking about Hitler."

"Oh"s came from all of us…except Taggart.

"I was just trying to say that I think he's demon-possessed." Trevor said, rubbing his eyes. "And I think that maybe God put me here to help these German soldiers recognize that. But the more I'm here, the more I think that God actually placed me here for you boys."

Silence broke out for a minute as Trevor looked at all of us.

"Us?" Taggart asked.

Trevor nodded. "See, because I'm able to give all of you the gospel. As I said with Brad, some people are in more prisons than one. Each of you are in two prisons. One physical. The other, spiritual."

"Stop trying to convert us." Johnny grunted.

"I'm trying to save you." Trevor corrected. "Or rather, lead you to salvation. As I said before, each of you could have died. It's of God's grace that you didn't. But death is still coming for all of us. For all we know, we may never leave this stalag."

A grave weight started to hang in the air over all of us. None of us had any guarantee that we would ever go home. None of us knew if we would ever see our families again.

That made me think of Sarah.

"The reason I say this, fellas…" Trevor said as he was getting his words together. "Look, I know you guys don't believe in what I believe in. But you need to realize that there is a God. And you need to realize that there is a literal place called hell. God is holy and we are all sinners. God cannot abide in the same place as sin. That's why He sent His Son, Jesus, to-"

"Jesus." I scoffed. "You mean the long-haired weirdo that loves everybody? Fairy-tales, I tell ya'."

Trevor shot me a nasty look.

"Whatever you may think of Jesus Christ, know that He is very real." Trevor emphasized. "Even if you don't recognize Him as

God, He was recorded in history. He, at the very least, did exist as a man. That's a fact acknowledged by Christians and atheists alike."

Then, Trevor smiled wilely. "And, thanks to your exceptional fighting skills, Brad, you've agreed to have your men and yourself endure this sound doctrine."

"I hate you." I growled at him.

"God sent His Son, Jesus, to become a sacrifice for our sin." Trevor continued. "To redeem us. To save us. To cleanse us from our sin. To bring us the gift of salvation. But gifts can be rejected. And if you reject the gift that Jesus offers you, you will one day experience death and go to a literal place of fire and darkness and torment. And when death comes, there will be no more time for any of you. You have this life only to call upon Jesus. After this life is over, you won't have an opportunity then."

"Why do you say that?" Tim swallowed, looking uneasy. "Are you trying to frighten us?"

"Honestly, if that would get you boys to face the reality, yes." Trevor said in a serious tone. "Because it ought to terrify you. Hell is not something to laugh at."

Trevor rubbed his hands together as he kept intense eye-contact with all of us. "Truly, without the Lord Jesus Christ, no person would ever be transformed. And that's the only transformation that will really last within a person. To regenerate. To make a new person. Because the very best that you can do and the very best that you can be by yourself is not sufficient to earn God's favor. There are no good works that can get you to earn God's favor."

"But I was baptized as a child." Johnny offered.

"That's a work." Trevor replied. "And baptism is not something that regenerates a man. Infant baptism isn't even Scriptural. It won't save you. Good deeds won't save you. Being kind to others won't save you. They will not be enough to earn forgiveness of your sins. With men, this is *impossible*. But with God, salvation is possible. 'But God commendeth his love toward us, in that, while we were yet sinners, Christ died for us', Romans 5:8. 'For whosoever shall call upon the name of the Lord shall be saved', Romans 10:13. And that word 'whosoever' means exactly that: **whosoever**. That means anybody. That means you boys. You all can be saved tonight if you would just call upon Jesus. There are no qualifications. No stipulations that say 'unless you've done this', or 'unless your of this ethnicity', or 'unless you've been a sinner this long'. Jesus can free you from that spiritual prison that you're all in. He can free you from the power every vice, every sin, every snare of Satan."

Johnny scoffed. "You're telling us that if we give our lives to some ancient, religious guy, we'll never sin again?"

"No." Trevor shook his head. "We're still sinners until eternity, but Jesus can keep you from being overcome by sin, if you submit to Him."

"Then why hasn't He?" I snapped. "I submitted to Him once and nothin' was made better. In fact, it was made worse!"

"Brad, you're still defeated by sin because you don't belong to Jesus." Trevor said flatly. "You're not saved. None of you boys are. Jesus can't work with someone who isn't His child. You need to be saved first."

I was about to say something else at Trevor, but I was drowned out by Tim. The big Russian jumped to his feet with a pleading look in his eyes.

"Then tell me, friend, how do we get saved?" He nearly shouted. "I want to be saved. I know you speak the truth and I know I need your Jesus. Tell me, please!"

"Me too!" Bratt spoke up.

Taggart didn't say anything, but he was nodding frantically. So much so that his glasses were almost falling off of his head.

I was completely dumbfounded. I didn't even know what to say. They were buying this? They seriously thought this was the answer to their problems?

Johnny voiced my thoughts. "You can't be serious. Have you all gone bonkers? This is stupid, religious baloney!"

"Forgive me for saying this Johnny…" Taggart turned to him. "But shut your mouth. I don't know how it is, but it's truth. And I need it. So zip your lip."

Johnny and I were both shocked by that. Johnny and Taggart were good friends. For Taggart to say that to him over something that wasn't smartsy…it was definitely a new experience.

"Will you show us how to get saved, Chaplain?" Taggart turned back to Trevor.

Trevor nodded his head with a small smile. "Yes, Corporal Taggart."

CHAPTER TWELVE

You see what I mean about this guy? He was completely different than anyone else in that P.O.W. camp. And he was infecting my men! At least, that's what I thought at the time. I was so weirded out by it. I mean, his stories weren't even told that good. It was a miracle that we were even able to keep up with him.

Bratt, Taggart, and Tim changed. They were…happier. More like Trevor. It was really creepy. Other prisoners started to notice it. Even the German guards started to notice and they were asking them questions about it. With Taggart translating, Trevor began talking to **them** about his stinking Bible.
I wasn't sure if it did any good. I mean, the guards didn't do anything bad to Trevor. But they didn't fall under his spell, either. It was a bizarre time.
Weeks passed by. Trevor told us the rest of the life of Joseph. We read about how he fortune-told dreams or whatever, and how he became the second most-powerful man in Egypt. Taggart, Tim, and Bratt were just eating it up. Asking questions, giving answers, wanting to hear more.
But me and Johnny? We were growing worse. We were sick of the Bible. We were sick of Trevor. We wanted it to end.
So I tried something. I challenged Trevor to a rematch. If I won, we'd be done with the devotions. If Trevor won, he got to keep one of my heavier blankets.
…I had to get used to sleeping with one less blanket.
What was even worse is that he always kept putting me down. Nothing that I could really punish him for, though. It was teasing, but, boy, did it get under my skin! Whenever I would make fun of God, Trevor would make fun of me. He would disrespect me. Call me "Brad" like I was some snot-nosed kid from Iowa. And I couldn't do anything about it! He could beat me! I tried fighting him and hopelessly lost twice!

It was humiliating!

It made me so mad!

But I knew I couldn't stop him by force.

So, I broke one day and **asked him nicely** to stop.

It was such a sissy thing to do.

We were in the mess hall. I was sitting with Johnny, eating whatever the slop was. It sure wasn't good, but it filled our stomachs.

Well, sort of. We didn't get that much.

Then, **he** came around.

"Enjoying this God-given day, Brad?" Trevor asked me.

I stood up from the table, fists clenched.

"Will you stop it, Trevor?" I turned around to face him. Trevor raised an eyebrow at me. He turned to set down his plate on a nearby table and faced me again. His expression told me 'don't try and fight me again. You know what happened last time'.

And I was mad, yeah, but not stupid. I wasn't going to try and fight him. I knew I would lose.

So I tried something else.

"I get it." I swung my arms open. "I can't beat you. I can't outsmart you. I'm just a guy from New York that dropped outta' school after sixth grade. But will you please, **please** stop calling me 'Brad'? It's insultin'. I'm a captain. Don't I deserve just a smidge of respect just for my rank?"

Trevor's hard face suddenly broke out into a warm smile. "That's what I've been waiting for."

"What're ya' talkin' 'bout?" I asked, confused.

"Humility." Trevor said, still beaming.

"Yes, I have been humiliated." I folded my arms. "No need to push it, okay?"

"No, **humility**." Trevor emphasized.

"Okay, humility." I shrugged. "What about it?"

"Finish your food." Trevor instructed. "Then come meet me outside."

I was kinda curious, so I did eat a bit faster. Once I was done, I found Trevor right outside the mess hall doors.

"So, what did ya' want to tell me?" I asked him.

Trevor took a minute to piece his words together.

"Ever since you got here, you've been acting like you're some sort of hot-shot." Trevor explained. "Using your rank as some sort of 'I'm better than you' man-card, or something. But you know what I saw when you got here? The guy who got some of his men killed and the rest captured."

That hit me harder than a sock full of nickels slapping me across the face. I lowered my head, thinking on what Trevor was saying.

"Then, you start telling me that my faith is stupid, unreal, and you used your rank to try and make me stop from sharing it." Trevor kept going. "So, I prayed what God would have me do about it. And I came to this answer: if you will not respect God, I will show you just exactly how that feels. And how has it felt, *Brad*?"

I grumbled, cringing at that name. I didn't say anything, though. Then suddenly, a wave of intense anger spread across Trevor's face. It was anger under control, but that didn't make it less intimidating.

After all, I knew this guy could whoop me. It was a weird and unfamiliar feeling for me.

"And I don't care how you treat me." Trevor said with a low voice. "Slander me, fight me, do whatever you want to me. But my God? Don't you dare treat my Jesus like He's trash. You don't have to accept my beliefs, or even like them, but you *better* respect them."

I nodded, slightly afraid. I had never seen Trevor so angry. I didn't know what he might do next.

But all that happened was that his anger vanished.

"Good." He said calmly. "And you know what your problem is?"

I groaned. "You're gonna' tell me whether I want to know or not, huh?"

"Your problem is that you blame God for everything." Trevor said, not even caring about my question. "But, the thing is, God is not who you're really mad at. You've got a beef with Engel."

"Do we have to talk about this?" I asked frustrated.

"Yes, we do." Trevor said seriously. "You need to hear this. Because of what Engel did to you, you treat the whole of Christianity like dirt. As if Jesus Himself stabbed you in the back. He didn't. Engel did. And shame on him for what he did. Truly. He was wrong. But just because he did that does not mean that you have to unleash your hatred on God. God did nothing of the sort to you. God has only done good for you."

"God has only done good for me?" I repeated angrily. "Do you even see where we are?"

"That's not God's fault." Trevor replied. "You were the one who got yourself into the army. You knew the risks. Did that keep you from signing up? You made a choice and this is the result of that choice."

Technically, it wasn't my choice to get into the army. It was made for me by a judge. But it was my choice to stay in the army when the war began, so Trevor was right.

Trevor continued. "Anyone who tries hard enough can find something to accuse God of. But God is good, no matter what you or I say or think. It is His nature. It is His makeup. Just look at creation."

He spread his arms out towards beyond the gate. The snow-covered forest and the bright blue sky lied beyond the gate.

It was pretty. If you're into that sort of thing, I guess.

"Nature was made for two reasons: God's glory and our benefit." Trevor said as I looked at the forest and the sky. "That's just one reason out of potentially infinite reasons. I can give more, but time would fail me."

"And I'll be thankful to not have to listen to you more than I have to." I said back, more as a joke than an insult.

Trevor laughed at that. "I can be a bit of a chatterbox. But there is one more thing I would like to establish."

"And what is that?"

Trevor had a strange look on his face. It was a mix between dead serious and concerned. "As I said before, you don't have to

believe what I believe. I'm not even asking you to like it. But I do ask you to respect God and the Bible. Respect those two things and I'll show you some respect."
Then, Trevor held out his hand to me.
"What do you think about that, Captain Scoefield?" He asked me with a smile.
I slapped my hand into his, incredibly grateful he *finally* used the name I prefer.
"Deal, Chaplain." I gave a smile back.

CHAPTER THIRTEEN

I was finally let into the *kommandant's* office.
"Captain." Colonel Blume greeted without looking up from the paperwork on his desk. "I am told you wished to speak with me."
I wrung my hands nervously. I knew that if I did this wrong, it could end badly.
"Yes, sir." I spoke quietly. "I did."
"Well?" He began scribbling something on one of the sheets of paper. "Speak up. I haven't all day."
I cleared my throat. "Well, sir, it's gotten pretty cold out."
"This is Germany, Captain." Blume said irritably. "It's always cold out."
"…Yes." I said slowly. "But some of the men…they're sick, sir. Really sick."
Blume finally made eye contact with me. "Is that so?"
Then, he glanced at the door. "Johann!"
The guard that was standing outside the door came in. "*Ja, mein kommandant?*"
Blume barked some orders at him in German. I had no idea what he was saying, but I guessed it was something like "Make sure you don't catch what these filthy prisoners are carrying".
"*Jawohl.*" Johann nodded and closed the door.
"Thank you for telling me this, Captain." Blume told me as he returned to his paperwork. "I would be at quite a loss if one of my soldiers was taken ill."
I knew it.
"Well, sir, if ya' would be so kind…" I said gently. "I'd like to ask ya' if we could have some medicine."
Blume's pencil broke. The man's eyes bulged wide-eyed in anger. "Medicine?" He hissed.
I swallowed. "Yes, sir. Seein' it'll be Christmas soon, we figured it could be a sign of good will, or somethin'. The men may be dyin' and one of them is pretty close to me, if ya' don't mind me sayin'."

Blume turned his vicious eyes up at me. He had a snarl in his lips.
"What do you think this place is? A hospital? A charity?"
I wanted to say back "I was thinkin' more of a gumball factory,
myself", but I knew that wouldn't do me any good. So I didn't say
anything.
"Medicine!" Blume spat. "The idea! If you want medicine, I
suggest you appeal to the Red Cross, Captain! Not come in here
and try to connive me out of some money! Now, get out!"

I knew it was a long shot. It was mid-December. Me and my
men had been at Stalag III-D for almost three months.
It felt like it had been three years.
A sickness had moved through most of the barracks. German
guards wouldn't stay too long in the barracks because of that. That
was a nice thing to have, I guess.
But it was getting bad. Some men had already passed on. Others
were at death's door.
One of them…was Private Allan Pratt.
"How's he doin'?" I asked Trevor as I came into the barracks from
the biting-cold weather.
Trevor was sitting at Bratt's bed. He glanced up at me with a sad
face.
"To be real with you, I think heaven's calling him." Trevor
informed me.
On a normal day, I would've been so irritated with that answer.
Trevor had to put God into **everything**. It was so annoying.
But that day, I just became more worried.
I walked over to the bed as I rubbed my hands together to warm
them.
Bratt was pale. He would hack like he had been a smoker for
twenty years.
He turned his tired eyes to me. "Hey…Cappy. What did…the
colonel say?"
I lowered my head. "To be blunt, Bratt, he'd probably offer you a
$500 pistol to shoot yourself with rather than give ya' an ounce of
cough syrup."

At that, Bratt just laughed. That did my heart good. Even though he had been suffering for some time, Bratt still kept up a good spirit.

But the laughing turned to coughing, which made me only feel worse.

"It's okay." Bratt told me. "I know…where I'm going."

Bratt reached a hand out of his covers toward me. I knelt down and took his hand in my own.

"And you know…what?" He asked me. "I'm kinda…happy. I'll get to go…home to be with Jesus. That's much better…than this place."

I took an uncomfortable breath.

Bratt narrowed his eyes at me. "But you got to…promise me something…Cappy."

"Of course, Bratt." I choked up a bit. "Anythin'."

"You gotta…meet me there."

I was confused. "What'cha mean?"

"You gotta…get saved, Cappy." Bratt explained. He nodded towards Trevor. "He can…tell you how. You need to accept… Jesus as your…Saviour, or you won't be able…to see me in heaven. I don't want…that, Cappy. I don't want you to go…to hell."

More hacking. Bratt even threw up a bit. When he got control of himself again, he turned back to me.

"Promise me that." He said softly. "Please, Cappy?"

"I promise that…I'll think about it." I said hesitantly.

Bratt frowned. "Not good….enough."

"Fine." I grunted. "I promise that, before I die, I'll make everythin' good between me and God."

Bratt shrugged, which seemed incredibly tiring for him. "I guess…I'll take that."

He glanced back at Trevor. "Make sure he…keeps that promise."

"I won't let him die until he repents, Allan." Trevor vowed. "You can count on that."

Bratt died sometime in the night. By the time we were all up

the next morning, Bratt was as cold as the winter air. Blume wouldn't let us bury him. His reasons were "If I permitted that for him, I'd have to permit it for all and I can't bear the thought of wasting all that good, German land to enemy corpses".
In his defense, he did have a point, but that doesn't mean I wasn't angry at him for it.
But Blume did allow Trevor to give a funeral service for him, which was nice, I guess. It was very churchy, which was what Bratt wanted. We sang some churchy hymns that said something about the blood of Jesus, something about the Lord having His own way, and something about a dinner roll that was called 'up yonder'.
I found the last one very confusing.
After the singing, Trevor talked a bit about Bratt and how he knew him. Then, one by one, Taggart, Johnny, and I all spoke about his life. Once we were done, Trevor gave a small sermon about heaven and hell. I'm going to be honest, I didn't give the time of day to that sermon he preached. I was thinking of Bratt and, really, I just didn't want to hear any more preaching. But, from what I heard from the other prisoners, it was a good sermon. Powerful and convicting and all that good stuff. Some got saved. Not me, though, and not Johnny. We stuck to our guns.
But after everything was over and everyone was going back inside to get warm, I wanted to talk to Trevor. Sounds stupid, right? I didn't want to listen to his preaching, but I did want to talk to him. Yeah, I don't make sense sometimes.

"You still think God is good, Trevor?" I kicked some dirt as we stood alone outside.
"All the time, Captain." Trevor replied back instantly.
"I don't get you." I shook my head as I looked up at the pale sun that was hidden by some dense clouds. "You're goin' through hell, Trevor. This is hell. You can't say it ain't. And you say God is good all the time? You're bonkers."
"I've got a different perspective." Trevor said as he rubbed his hands together. "Did you know that my spiritual ancestors went

through much worse experiences than this?”
“You’re kiddin’ me.” I blurted.
“Not at all.” Trevor stated. “Stoned. Sawed in half. Burned at the stake. Fed to lions. I mean, come on, my own Saviour was crucified.”
“Fair.” I acknowledged. “But how does that show that God’s good?”
“Well…” Trevor thought a little before answering. “You say that this is hell. And you’re not wrong. At least, for the Christian. This life is my battlefield. My misery. My trials and persecution. But after life is over, I’m given my reward.”
“Heaven?” I guessed.
“Exactly.” Trevor nodded proudly. “And if you look at yourself in the right perspective, you will see that fact as exponentially amazing.”
“You’re losin’ me.” I admitted.
Trevor thought again. He suddenly pointed at a passing German guard. “You see Wilhelm there?”
“Yeah.”
“He steals prisoner’s food.” Trevor reported. “And sometimes Red Cross packages.”
“Yeah, I know.” I grumbled bitterly. “He’s stolen *my* food and Red Cross packages.”
“Yes.” Trevor continued. “Added to that, he works for Blume. Blume works for Hitler, who is probably the worst person ever. That, in turn, makes Wilhelm a pretty indecent fellow, right?”
“We all hate him, you’ve made your point.” I was getting impatient.
“Now, take that information and put it with this: God loves that man despite what he’s done.”
“And?”
“And God, who is *God*, came down from heaven to be among us, and ultimately die for that man personally.” Trevor explained.
“God gave His life for Wilhelm.”
“All that tells me is that God is stupid.” I huffed.
Instantly, Trevor gave me a death-stare.

"Sorry, sorry." I immediately apologized. "But ya' get what I mean, right?"
"What you see as foolishness is really love." Trevor calmed down. "You love your sister, don't you?"
Instant hurt.
"Of course."
"You would fight for her?"
"Yeah."
"Provide for her?"
"Yeah."
"Die for her?"
"A thousand times over."
"Even if she hated you in return?" Trevor asked.
I paused. "…Yes."
"Wouldn't that be stupid of you to do, Scoefield?" Trevor asked.
I saw the connection. "Oh."
"Mm-hmm." Trevor smiled. "That's what God did for us. For you."
"Yeah…" Was all I said in return.
Then, we stood out there in the cold for a brief moment of silence.

"You've really been hurt deeply by Engel, haven't you?" Trevor asked suddenly.
"Ugh, do we have to talk about that?" I groaned.
"I fear we do." Trevor said. "Because we both made promises to Allan, and if I'm going to be honest, I don't think I'll be able to uphold my promise until I get the ugly head of Engel out of your heart."
"Fine." I sighed. "Talk away."
"You've been hurt by him." Trevor said again. "That's not to be ignored. He betrayed your trust. He did something that was very wrong."
I found myself nodding to Trevor's words. Sure, Johnny, Taggart, and Bratt had always agreed with me, but it was nice to have even the preacher agree with me, too.
"But you're doing something wrong, too, Scoefield." Trevor told

me with a serious tone.

I gave him my "are you kiddin' me?" face.

"You're bitter." Trevor pointed out. "And you're letting that bitterness eat you from the inside out."

"Wouldn't you be bitter?" I shot back. "And what's so wrong with it anyway? My bitterness doesn't hurt nobody but Engel."

"To answer those questions chronologically: probably, much, and that's not true." Trevor said.

"What?"

Trevor sighed. "Yes, if I had a sister, I would probably be bitter towards someone who defiled her. Secondly, there is much that is wrong with bitterness. And thirdly, you say that your bitterness doesn't hurt anyone but Engel. That's not true."

"How do ya' figure?"

"Bitterness always brings self-destruction." Trevor replied. "If you want a biblical example, just take Jonah for instance. You know Jonah, don't you?"

"Everyone knows about the story of Jonah." I rolled my eyes.

"Good." Trevor continued. "He was bitter against the people of Nineveh. So much so that he didn't even want them to repent and place their faith in Jehovah. Because of that, he ran from God and took a ship to Tarshish. When God brought a terrible storm, Jonah told the mariners to throw him overboard."

"And he got eaten by a whale and the whale threw him up and everybody got 'saved' in Nineveh. I know, I know." I groaned. "What does that have to do with me being bitter?"

"Well, if you weren't so impatient, I would have told you by now." Trevor grinned goofily. "Has it occurred to you that Jonah didn't know God was going to send the great fish?"

It hadn't, I realized.

"No." I admitted. "So what?"

"So Jonah told the mariners to throw him overboard so he could die." Trevor explained. "He would have rather died then take God's message to Nineveh. That's what bitterness does to a man."

"He could've known that God was gonna' send the whale." I suggested. "He was a prophet, right?"

"It is possible." Trevor confessed. "But what about when he was in the belly of the fish? He didn't repent for three days and three nights. The fish didn't throw him up until Jonah repented. And Jonah referred to the belly of the fish as the 'belly of hell'. It wasn't like it was a nice place to be. He gritted his teeth and stayed there for *three full days* instead of taking God's message to Nineveh. That's what bitterness does to a man."

"Fine, ya' got me there." I shrugged angrily. "By the way, you're repeatin' yourself."

"Repetition is a good way to get things in people's memories." Trevor explained. "So, you think you'll turn out better than Jonah?"

"As a matter of fact, I do." I said firmly.

"Hm." Trevor muttered, scratching his chin. "Well, I've given you a biblical example. How about a real-life example?"

"Like what?"

"Like the fact that you murdered Norbert Schleim because you thought he was Engel." Trevor said quietly.

My eyes shot over to him. I hadn't told anyone about that. Absolutely no one. Not Johnny, Taggart, Bratt, or Tim. Not Colonel Blume. Irmgard didn't even know why I really killed Schleim.

And I was truly frightened about how Trevor knew that.

"How do you know that?" I gasped, keeping my voice down.

"You talk in your sleep sometimes, Scoefield." Trevor put his hands in his pockets. "I stay up pretty late, even in bed. And don't worry, no one heard but me. It was muffled behind the walls of your quarters."

"What did I say?"

"You say different things from time to time." Trevor told me. "But a couple of nights ago, you kept shouting 'I'll kill ya', Engel! I'll kill ya'!'. Then you stopped for a while. After some time, you started again by saying. 'I won't hurt you, Miss Irmgard. I just thought he was Engel. I won't hurt you. Just Engel'."

My face flushed as I held it low.

"I put two and two together." Trevor shrugged. "Figured that you had killed Schleim because you didn't see Schleim raping Irmgard Blume. You saw Engel raping your sister, didn't you?"

"…Yes."

"And *that* is what bitterness does to a man." Trevor stated sadly. "Still think it's harmless?"

CHAPTER FOURTEEN

It took a while to finally get through my heart and head that
Allan Pratt was actually gone.
Death isn't something that we understand or are familiar with,
even after you see it time and time again. You still expect to open
the door and see that person sitting where they always used to sit.
You expect to bump into them again.
But you don't. And it hurts.
It really hurts.
When someone dies, you need to have time to mourn over them.
Allow yourself to grieve for the loss and then accept what has
happened.
In a prison camp…well, it's not so easy. And I had good days and
bad days.
One day…I had a *very* bad day.

I sat outside in the biting, cold air. Looking down at the dirt, I
was just thinking.
It was Christmas day. The day when Jesus came to the world.
Peace on earth. Good will towards men. All that stuff.
And there was no peace on earth where I was.
There was no good will towards men.
There was no family. No Sarah.
There was no Christmas dinner.
There were no lights.
There were no carols.
There were no happy times.
And if you think on that stuff long enough…it begins to bring you
down.
And I was drowning.
To me, nothing was getting better. Everything was just getting
worse. And, thinking on that, I thought in myself that nothing
would ever get better. Everything would always just get worse and
worse and worse.

Calvin was dead.

Larkin was dead.

Sheldon was dead.

And now…little, innocent Allan Pratt was dead.

My fault, all of them.

Who knew who would be next?

Tim?

Johnny?

Taggart?

…Me?

Suddenly, I saw feet walk up to me. Two pairs. One's was a German guard's boots.

The other were a lady's boots.

I looked up. Irmgard Blume was standing before me, blocking the sun with her pretty face. She was carrying a bouquet of bright, red roses with her.

"Captain Scoefield." She smiled at me. "Merry Christmas."

She had a nice smile, too. It made me realize that it was the first time I actually saw her smile.

I stood to my feet. I almost stood at attention, but figured that might've been…too much? Or taken the wrong way, I guess?

"Ma'am." I nodded back to her. "Merry Christmas."

"Please, Captain." Irmgard kept smiling. "I would rather you call me 'Irmgard'. However, if you feel you must address me formally, I will also accept 'Miss Blume'."

"I'll take 'Miss Blume'." I told her, a hint of a smile on my face. Then, I glanced at the roses. "Oh, you shouldn't have."

Irmgard laughed genuinely. "Oh, no, they are from my father. Either for the holiday, or for an apology."

"Apology?" I asked.

"For bringing that pig, Schleim, into my life." She said with disgust.

Then a look of worry crossed her face. "Speaking of which, you look much thinner than when I last saw you. How is my father treating you?"

"Well, I'm treated…" I flicked my eyes at the German guard that was standing behind her. I knew I couldn't talk freely in front of him. "About as good as I deserve, Miss Blume."

Irmgard nodded sadly, understanding what I was trying to say. "I see."

Suddenly, she began messing with the bundle of roses that she had. She was looking through them until she found the brightest, most beautiful, most lively rose.

Irmgard took it out of the bundle as she snapped something in German at the guard behind her. The guard simply nodded as if he had just been given an order.

Then, turning back to me, Irmgard smiled again. And, before I could ask what she was doing, she gently tucked the rose into my right breast pocket of my shirt.

"Here." She said softly. "Maybe this will brighten up your Christmas day."

"I think you've already done more than the rose could, Miss Blume." I replied quietly.

Irmgard frowned slightly at that. She looked sad all of a sudden.

"You are very sweet, Captain Scoefield." She whispered, still looking sad.

"You don't have to call me 'Captain', Miss Blume." I told her. "You can call me…Bradley, if you like."

"That is your first name?" She asked, her sadness disappearing for a moment.

"Don't tell anyone." I gave a small grin. "But yes."

"Very well, Bradley." Irmgard tried it out. "I wish you well. Again, merry Christmas."

"Merry Christmas, Miss Blume." I again nodded my head to her.

Then, she turned and began walking away. The German guard followed her.

I felt my spirit sink a little as she walked away from me. Like a sad, slow burning in my chest.

The depression deepened the further she went. Soon, I was just as miserable as I had been before she came up.

"Wow." Trevor said as he approached me, his goofy smile

bigger than ever. "Getting close to the *kommandant's* daughter? Bold, Scoefield. Really bold. Way to go."

I didn't answer him. I didn't even look at him. I kept watching Irmgard. She was walking to a car that was parked outside the *kommandant's* office. The German guard opened the back door for her and she slipped in.

"Eh, let her go, Cappy." Trevor tried to shake me free. "She doesn't give a hoot or holler about any of us. Then again, she did give you a rose. Not sure what that means."

The car began to slowly pull towards the gate. The guards standing at the gate began to part.

I started walking away from Trevor, shoving my hands in my pockets. I walked towards the open area past the barracks. I was still watching the car. It was getting closer to the gate.

And the gate was opening. It opened all the way and the car passed on through.

And, even after the car had passed through, turned left onto the road, and started picking up speed, the gate was still wide open. On the other side of that gate was freedom. Hope. A chance for happiness again.

And it was wide open.

"Scoefield?" Trevor asked slowly. "You okay?"

I took off in a full sprint for the gate.

When I was in school, before my parents died, I was known as one of the fastest runners in the entire place. Coach Hamble was begging the principal to let me be on the seventh grade track team, even though I was in sixth grade.

I could run so fast sometimes that I could keep up with cars. I was never sure how fast those cars were going, but I figured it was decently speedy.

And when I charged for that gate, I hoped with everything in me that I was as fast as lightning.

"Scoefield! What are you doing?!" Trevor yelled after me.

I didn't pay him any mind. I ran for the gate.

I knew I wasn't as fit as I used to be.

I knew I hadn't been exercising like I used to, either.

But I was still going at a pretty good speed.

And the gate was still open. It was beginning to close, but I could make it.

I sprinted passed the *kommandant's* office. It was the building that was closest to the gate.

No turning back now.

Especially since the German guards all began to notice me bolting for the gate.

"Halt!" One of the guards at the gate shouted at me, putting his hand up in a "stop" motion. "Halt!"

I didn't halt.

I ran faster and faster.

The gate was halfway closed, but I could make it.

…If the guards didn't shoot me.

They were all raising their guns. Two at the gate. Two at the watch towers near the gate.

Four guns all trained on me.

"HALT!" The guard yelled one more time as he aimed his rifle.

"*I can make it.*" I lied to myself. "*They rarely use those things. Maybe they're bad shots. Maybe I'll get lucky and they'll miss. Maybe I could do a roll and dodge the bullets.*"

But I was fooling myself.

Firstly, there were four guns all aimed at me. Even if, by some miracle, three bullets missed…I couldn't bet that the fourth would.

Secondly, the two guards at the gate were standing in my way. I'd either have to run around them or through them. Either wouldn't really work.

Thirdly, even if I did get through them and the gates without getting shot, I would still have to run out into the woods with no food, no water, no shelter, no warm clothes, no way home, with guards all chasing after me with dogs.

Fourthly and finally…the gate closed.

I didn't make it.

But for some reason, I kept running straight at it.

It was too late for me. I was going to be riddled with bullets. I was going to die.

But I didn't really care anymore. It was better than rotting in that Stalag.

I would see Bratt again. I would see Sheldon and Larkin. I didn't really want to see Calvin.

I would see my Mama again.

I didn't really know what the afterlife would be like. I didn't believe in heaven. I just figured that everyone kinda just met up in some ghostly space, or something. Just wait there until the end of time.

But I didn't get shot. Instead, I heard something next to me.

I turned my head to my left to see someone catching up to me.

It was Trevor. Even with his itty-bitty legs, he had caught up to me like some speedster.

"GET DOWN!" He screamed at me before jumping in the air.

And, boy, could he jump.

He had hopped up so high that his head was an inch higher than mine. While in the air, he wrapped both of his arms around my shoulders. The pipsqueak latched onto my back like a monkey.

Then, using all of his weight, he dragged me down to the ground.

It was then that I heard rifle shots.

Trevor and I rolled through the dirt, skidding to a stop right before the German guards who were standing at the gate.

They were enraged. They immediately began kicking me, urging me back.

For a moment, I didn't do anything except pat myself down. I had heard four different rifle shots go off. I figured that I was filled with holes but just too high on adrenaline to realize it.

But, somehow, not one of the bullets had hit me.

I glanced up, completely dazed at how I was okay. But that was when I had seen Trevor…

Lying just a few feet away from me, face-down in the dirt, he had four bullet wounds in his back.

Trevor was already gone.

When he had tackled me to the ground, Trevor had covered me

with his own body, shielding me from the gunfire.
He had died because I ran for the gate. Because I had been stupid and made myself believe that I could escape when really…there was no chance.
Guilt swallowed me up like a whirlpool as the guards continued beating me.

I was placed in solitary confinement for two weeks. No privileges at all.
No blankets.
No bed.
No toilet.
Just four, cold, stone walls with me inside them. Bread and water once a day.
I shivered and hacked as I sat in my own filth. But as I sat there, sick as can be, I finally heard the keys unlock the steel door to my prison.
Kommandant Blume stepped in.
"That was some stunt you attempted." He scowled. "Had it not been for the chaplain, you would be in his place."
"Better than here." I coughed.
"Hm." Blume sneered. "Thinking about trying that again, Captain?"
"…No."
"Fantastic." Blume gave a fake smile. "Then the guards shall return you to your barracks."

CHAPTER FIFTEEN

For the next couple of days, I was nothing but a dead spirit in a live body. I didn't talk to anyone. I didn't laugh. I didn't play poker anymore. I wasn't anything.
I got up in the morning, did what I was told, ate what they gave me, and went back to bed.
I was just a dead man walking.
I felt nothing but grief. So many people in my life had been killed because of me.
I was worthless.
I was a monster.
I deserved to die.
And there were some nights where I wanted to die. The feeling would come and go, but I knew that if I didn't get out of that Stalag, I **would** die.
But I didn't die, so don't worry. After all, I am writing this, ain't I?

One day, guards came to our barracks early, shouting at everyone to get up and stand at attention. Blume was with them and something felt…different. The guards, and even Blume, looked antsy. Nervous. Something like that.
It made me feel good on the inside to see them like that.
The guards had all of us stand in a line. They commanded us to stand at attention, too.
Then I saw why.
A man in a black outfit stepped into our barracks. He wore an arm-band that had the Nazi symbol. A crisp, all black and red, officer's cap sat on his head. He wasn't too tall, but he was taller than Blume. His eyes were a deep brown that flicked here and there, as if he was looking for something.
He walked very deliberately. He took wide, slow steps with his polished, black boots.
All in all, he seemed completely business. Heartless, man-on-a-mission business.

"Gestapo…" I heard Taggart whisper to Johnny nervously.

The Gestapo man snapped his head directly at Taggart. Taggart flinched, his eyes wide.

"Who is this man?" The Gestapo agent pointed at Taggart. His accent was extremely German. But it was cold, too. Unfeeling. Cruel.

"Corporal Kenneth Taggart, *Herr* Major." Blume spoke quickly to the Gestapo agent.

The Gestapo nodded, narrowing his eyes at Taggart. "A chatterbox, hmm?"

"Not usually, *Herr* Major." Blume told him.

"Tsk tsk." The Gestapo agent clicked his tongue. "Of all the times to slip up, Corporal…I must divine a way to teach him respect. Prisoners must stay silent unless spoken to in the presence of the superior race."

Taggart let out a shivering breath.

"Of course, *Herr* Major." Blume agreed like a yes-man.

I knew him less than two minutes, and I already hated the Gestapo agent.

A new record.

The Gestapo agent began walking down the line of men that were in our barracks. Most looked down from him, so as to not join Taggart in offending him.

I had already gone through enough, so I did the same. As he began to walk past me, I lowered my gaze.

But…the Gestapo agent stopped right in front of me.

"*I don't need this.*" I groaned inwardly.

"Who is **this** man?" The Gestapo agent pointed to me.

"Captain Bradley Scoefield, *Herr* Major." Blume informed the Gestapo agent.

"Has he been trouble?"

"Some, *Herr* Major." Blume admitted. "He was involved in a recent and futile escape attempt. But he has assured me that he will comply from now on."

Then there was a pause.

"Look at me, Captain Scoefield." The Gestapo agent said in his thick, German accent.

I did so. Of course, I was still looking down to him because of his size, but I obeyed.

Up close, the man seemed different somehow. Vaguely familiar. It was like when I first saw Blume. I felt like I had seen his face before.

I examined the Gestapo agent closer to see if I could put my finger on who he looked like.

Under his cap, there was evidence of brown, curly hair. His eyes seemed a little soft to be a cold-hearted Gestapo agent.

But my examination was suddenly interrupted.

The Gestapo agent gave a quick smile. Very fast. Hardly noticeable, unless you were as close as I was. None of the other prisoners saw because they were all looking down. None of the guards saw because they were behind him.

It was only me.

When he smiled, his whole face changed. When he smiled, I recognized him immediately.

He was that kid I had met in New York.

"…Engel?" I whispered, not believing it.

Henry Engel was standing in front of me. It wasn't a Gestapo agent. It wasn't even a German soldier. It was Henry Engel. The piece of low-life garbage that had stolen my sister from me. Engel's face bulged into a frantic panic. He shook his head just enough that I could see it. His eyes were basically screaming "don't sell me out, moron!".

But what can I say? To say 'he caught me off guard' wouldn't even be scratching the surface.

At the same time that Engel was panicking, so was *Kommandant* Blume. Not one, but *two* prisoners had just spoken out of turn to a Gestapo agent. As far as he knew, his prisoners were going to get him in trouble if he didn't do something. Thankfully, he didn't actually hear what I said.

"Silence, Scoefield!" Blume ordered, his voice cracking. "You will show respect to Major Verkleidung!"

Suddenly, Blume ran up to Engel, saluted, and gave a worried smile. "Forgive me, *Herr* Major, they are not usually so disrespectful. I will teach **all** of them to know their place as soon as tomorrow."

I could barely contain my smile. On the other hand, I could barely keep my jaw from hitting the floor.

Henry Engel, the pathetic kid that had married my sister, had somehow made it from New York to Germany, stolen a Gestapo agent's uniform, and impersonated him good enough to fool not only me and other Allies soldiers, but even members of the **_stinking German army_**.

That kid had some grit. Even though I still hated him, I was glad to see him that day.

"No need, *Oberst*." Engel returned to his Nazi acting. "As a matter of fact, I wish to speak to this man."

"To Captain Scoefield?" Blume bumbled nervously. "O-of course. Yes, *Herr* Major. But, um, why would you need to-?"

"I shall require your quarters, *Oberst* Blume." Engel cut him off. "I wish to speak to him alone."

"…Yes, *Herr* Major."

"How in the Sam Hill are you even here right now, Engel?" I nearly yelled at him when we were alone in *Kommandant* Blume's quarters.

Engel immediately turned around and put a finger to his lips. He was telling me to "shush".

I admit that made me mad, but I shut my mouth. Engel took a small notebook and pen out of his Gestapo jacket. He scribbled some words on them and flipped the notebook around so I could see.

Are there any bugs in this office?

I had no idea what he was talking about.

"Bugs?" I scoffed. "What are you? Scared of spiders, now?"

Engel, once again, put his finger to his lips. His eyes were
maddeningly wide, trying to emphasize the "shush", I guess.
"Captain, I have some questions for you and you will not be
allowed to leave until they are answered." Engel said in his
German accent, glancing around suspiciously. He began checking
under lamp-shades and curtains.
"What'cha doin'?" I whispered to him.
Again, the shush gesture. Then, he scribbled on his notebook
again.

Bugs?! Microphones?! Listening devices?! Are there
any in this office?!

I rolled my eyes. "You've gotta' be kiddin' me. Engel, get your
head out of the spy novels you keep readin'!"
With that, Engel began to relax and spoke in his normal accent.
"So…there are no microphones?"
"Who's gonna' put listenin' devices in Blume's quarters?" I
snapped at him. "The guards? Of course there's no 'bugs' in here,
you idiot!"
"Sorry, Scoefield." Engel said, but also looked relieved.
"Ya' feelin' better now?" I asked him, walking up to him.
Engel thought for a second. "Well, in a way. I've been
uncomfortable this whole trip and-"
I didn't let him finish. I socked Engel across his jaw.
He toppled to the ground, clutching his face.
"Well, too bad." I growled at him. "Now tell me what you're doin'
here."
Engel slowly picked himself up, making sure he wasn't bleeding.
"That will bruise." Engel said quietly. "They'll know you hit me."
"Quit your cryin', ya baby." I snarled. "They'll never see it. Now,
why are you here? *How* did you get here? How did ya' know I
was even here?"
With that, Engel gave a tiny smile. "I can only give credit to the

Lord, Scoefield."

"I'll hit you again." I threatened.

"No, no, please don't do that!" Engel waved his hands frantically. "But…it is true."

"Just tell me what happened." I glared at him.

"Very well." Engel cleared his throat. "Thanks to the Red Cross, Sarah and I heard you were captured and sorted into a prison camp of some kind. Naturally, we were devastated. We've heard…some stories about what happens in places like this. None of them good. And so, we prayed for you. Every single day. Sometimes, multiple times a day. And, eventually, I began to feel like I could do something about it. I felt like God was wanting me to do something about it."

I hated hearing about God from him. I just reminded me of Trevor and my guilt. Trevor reminded me of Engel and my hate towards Engel. It was a vicious cycle that only made me sad, then mad, then even madder. But, as far as I could tell, Engel was there to help me out. So, I let him tell the whole story.

"I mentioned it to Sarah and she said she'd been having the same feeling. Even my Pastor, Bro. Benson, thought it was a good idea. Albeit dangerous, of course. But, because I'm German, I had some connections. I arrived here about three weeks ago."

"And you stole a Gestapo's outfit?" I marveled. "Did you mug 'im?"

"Oh, no, but there is a story behind it." Engel told me, looking at the suit he was wearing. "I didn't really have any money when I landed here, so I just decided to walk to Bonn. It's my hometown. Since I didn't know where you were, I thought it was a good idea. Once I was there, I ran into an old friend of mine. His name is Peter. We knew each other as kids, but he was now in the German *luftwaffe*. We decided to talk and catch up for a while and he kept insisted on buying drinks for us. It's…rather sad how much of a drunk he's become, concerning how he used to-"

"Engel." I snapped him out of his rabbit-trail. "Let's stay on track, huh?"

"Right. Sorry." Engel said. "He got drunk. Really drunk. So much so that I thought I could ask him some questions. I asked if he knew about some American prisoners and he told me that he hadn't seen many Americans, but had heard about a few that tried to rape a *kommandant's* daughter."

I flushed red. "That's a lie! That was **not** us! That was a stinkin' German! **He** was the sorry, low-down dog that put his filthy mitts on Miss Blume!"

Engel raised his eyebrows, but also seemed relieved. "Well, that's great! Well…sort of. I'm just glad it wasn't you. So you know the girl?"

"I was there." I confessed.

"You were there?"

"I heard her scream." I told him. "And I…killed the rapist."

Engel's eyes were wide with fear. "You **killed** him?"

"Smashed his face in…yeah." I added with a nod.

Engel gulped involuntarily. "Well…um, anyway, Peter told me that he heard you and your men were placed in a Stalag near Berlin. As it turns out, there are many Stalags near Berlin. Well, at least smaller ones. But, I started walking towards Berlin. And, halfway there, I found a car in the ditch."

Engel then glanced out a window and pointed. "**That** car."

I looked out the window. Right outside was a very official and a very German-looking car.

I couldn't help but grin. At that moment, a joke slipped from my lips.

"Stealin' cars again, boyo?" I chuckled. "Better not bring it back to New York. Nazi-mobiles aren't very popular there."

A second after I said that, I remembered who I was talking to. Engel wasn't my friend.

But…he was there to help. I felt very conflicted inside. I wanted to treat Engel like I used to…

But I couldn't. I couldn't forgive what he had done to Sarah.

"It's called a Horch Kfz." Engel told me. "And I have never stolen a car. That one was just…"

Then he stopped talking with a troubled look on his face. I guess he just was hit with the fact that he kinda did steal that car.

I grinned again. "Let me guess, 'borrowed'?"

"*Another joke?*" I frowned, thinking to myself. "*Stop it, Scoefield! This is the guy you **hate**!*"

"Well…" Engel cleared his throat. "I…I'm not sure who it belongs to now. I would give it back, once we're done with it, if I knew who it should go to."

I shrugged. "I was just kiddin'. If it was abandoned, it's not stealin'."

Engel shuffled his feet. "…It wasn't abandoned."

"Eh?"

"It **wasn't** abandoned." Engel repeated. "Where do you think I got this uniform? Anyway, don't worry. He won't miss it."

I blinked at him. "**You** actually killed someone?"

"Of course not." Engel shook his head. "They were already dead."

"Oh." I breathed. "What did you do with the body?"

"Bodies." Engel clarified. "There were two men with him. And, to answer your question, I buried them."

"Wow." I said sternly. "Bein' nice to the worst people on earth. You really are somthin', ya' know that?"

"That's not it." Engel defended himself. "I've no love for what these people have done to my home country. I just buried them because I didn't want anyone finding them if I was going to impersonate Major Verkleidung."

I thought on that. "You're not as much of a bookworm as I remember. That's somethin', I guess."

Engel accepted the praise. "Thanks. Anyway, I started making Gestapo 'surprise visits' at nearby Stalags until I found you here." Then, with a fiery look in his eye and wide smile on his face, he said: "And I'm going to bring you home."

I knew why Engel was at Stalag III-D. I knew he was there for me. Why else would my brother-in-law leave New York to a war-torn continent, dress up like a Gestapo agent, and search P.O.W. camps?

He was coming to save me and I had known that since I recognized him.

But when he said "And I'm going to bring you home", it really hit me. The full wave of realization hit me. Engel and I did not have a good relationship. If you have been paying attention at all in this whole book, you know that. I treated him like trash. I disowned him in every way I could. I even abandoned my sister for almost ten years because of him.

Yet…he came to save me when I needed it.

And, as I realized that, I kinda just stood there. Blank-faced and stupid looking. Like Engel had just asked me a math question.

"…Scoefield?" Engel asked me. "Are you okay?"

I drove my hands in my pockets, awkwardly. I bowed my head, not looking Engel in the eyes.

"You came all this way to bring me back?" I asked him quietly.

"I did."

I raised my head up to look him in the eyes. "Thank you."

Engel smiled big. Then, a look of guilt came over him.

"Hey, Scoefield…while we're here." He started. "I wanted to say that I'm so very sorry for all that I did back in New York. With Sarah. I betrayed your trust. I…I…"

I put up my hand for him to stop. I had already heard enough to get me fumin'.

"I don't want to hear it, Engel." I told him tensely. "I don't want to hear any of that right now."

"Right…" Engel lowered his head, a hint of tears in his eyes.

The tears made me angrier.

"Don't you dare cry on me." I hissed.

"Sorry…" Engel wiped his eyes.

I took a moment to think. I still didn't like this guy one bit. But he had sacrificed a lot.

For me.

"I tell 'ya this." I told him as I took a step closer to him. "You get us out of here, maybe we'll talk about it some other time."

"'Us'?" Engel blinked.

"I shall also need Sergeant John Smith, Corporal Kenneth Taggart, and…" Engel paused. "A Russian that is known as

'Tim'."
Blume seemed uncertain, but nodded anyway. The men of my barracks were still lined up. Taggart, Johnny, and Tim all were pale. Each of them looked horrified.
"What will you need these men for, *Herr* Major?" Blume asked gently.
"Questioning." Engel snapped with authority. "These men are believed to have information concerning Project Poltergeist."
I tried to not roll my eyes. Engel always came up with such weird stories.
"Project Poltergeist?" Blume asked, concerned.
"A secret American-Russian operation." Engel nodded. "I will need them for it. Well, that is, except for the Corporal."
Taggart sighed, relieved.
"He will not be joining you, *Herr* Major?" Blume questioned.
"I did not say that." Engel smiled evilly. "He is coming with. I was saying that he likely knows nothing of Project Poltergeist. Instead, I wish to teach him some respect back at Berlin. He shall be sent back to let the others know what awaits them if they cross the Gestapo."
Taggart nearly fainted.
"Have them all sent to my vehicle." Engel ordered loudly. "*Schnell!*"
"*Jawohl, Herr* Major!" Blume saluted Engel. "However…shall I send a guard to accompany you?"
"What are you saying, *Oberst*?" Engel pierced his eyes at Blume. "That I cannot handle myself?"
Blume hesitated. Engel was a tad bit bigger than him, but not by much. Blume's eyes flicked at Tim and I. I was the biggest, but Tim wasn't too much smaller. Both of us could handle Engel blindfolded and handcuffed.
And Blume knew it.
"Of course not, *Herr* Major." Blume responded. "It is just…
Captain Scoefield has shown himself to be quite a handful by himself. It would be a…"
Suddenly, Blume stopped, his brow furrowing. "*Herr* Major,

where is your driver?”

“Pardon?” Engel asked.

“Surely, a Gestapo Major like yourself would not drive yourself here.” Blume pointed out. “It’s beneath you. All Gestapo officers have drivers.”

All eyes moved to Engel. I swallowed nervously. In his eyes, I could tell that Engel was desperately trying to think of a reasonable answer to give Blume.

“My driver is ill, *Oberst*.” Engel said finally.

“Then why not have a replacement?”

“Replacement?” Engel shifted shakily in the snow. “Well, I…”

I was inwardly screaming. Engel was panicking and there was nothing I could do. Absolutely nothing.

“Do you know how long it takes to get a replacement driver?” Engel chuckled to Blume. “It is so hard to find good drivers these days.”

“Any soldier can drive, Major.” Blume was speaking with more suspicion, now. “It takes me less than five minutes to find a replacement driver.”

“I, uh, five minutes?” Engel asked. “Quite quick, if you ask me. For me it takes…”

“Tell me again why Berlin sent you here, Major?” Blume’s eyes narrowed at Engel.

“I am here to question prisoners on Project Poltergeist.” Engel began to get his stride back.

“I’ve never heard of it.” The *kommandant* replied quietly.

“Few have.” Engel nodded. “In fact, it may only be a wild goose chase. But the Gestapo likes to be certain.”

“Do they?” Blume said with a tint of anger in his voice. “That’s quite strange. The last Gestapo agent told me that they have no time for, as you call, ‘wild goose chases’.”

Engel tried to hold himself together, but fear was beginning to grow in his eyes.

“Erm, well, what one Gestapo agent says-” Engel tried to weasel his way out of it again.

But he was cut off.

"Who are you?" *Kommandant* Blume suddenly hissed. "You are not Major Verkleidung. You are not Gestapo. You are not even a member of the German army. Now tell me, who are you?!"

That was it. Engel was caught.

"*If there's anythin' good to find in all this…*" I thought to myself as I closed my eyes. "*It's that **I** won't die. I'll have to stay here, yeah. But I might live through it. Engel's toast, but I can keep goin'. Guess Engel'll finally get what I've been wishin' for him since I left New York.*"

But I was actually wrong.

Because instead of caving in to Blume's harsh tone and questions, Engel stood up straighter. He strode confidently up to Blume and stuck his nose in the *kommandant's* face.

"How dare you!" Engel shouted mightily. "Not a member of the German army?! You dare slander the *Fuhrer's* Gestapo this way?!" Then, in rapid fire, Engel began ranting in German. I had no idea what he was saying, but it was apparently very convincing to Blume. Blume's cold eyes began to show uncertainty in them. Finally, Engel returned to English. "Who am I?! Rather, I must ask, who are **you**?! You are a simple watch-dog, kept here to make sure the rodents don't get out of their cages! You are a bumbling buffoon that has done all he can to keep this post so that he may avoid conflict against the Americans and the Russians! If there is anyone here who is to be accused of not being a member of the German army, it is **you**, Blume! The rest of us put our lives on the line while you sit here, enjoying all the pleasantries life has to offer! Perhaps I can remedy that, *Oberst*! No! How about **Fahnenjunker**! I am certain we can find a post in the Russian front that would suit you nicely! Would you really like that, **Fahnenjunker**?!"

I, to this day, have no idea what a '*Fahnenjunker*' is, but it sounded insulting. Blume was completely convinced. He buckled down as he had before.

"No, *Herr* Major! Please! I-I-I meant no disrespect!"

"You will now add lies to the list of crimes?!" Engel's voice got even louder. "'Meant no disrespect'?! Every ounce of your accusations carried *nothing* but disrespect! You can hardly be considered worthy for this position any longer!"

Suddenly, Engel whipped his head around to a nearby guard. "Soldier!"

The guard snapped to attention. He even did the "heil Hitler" salute.

"Lend me your pistol so that I may shoot this man!" Engel ordered him.

"*Oh, yes. Please shoot him.*" I pleaded inwardly. "*Please shoot him, Engel.*"

"NO! Please, *Herr* Major! Have mercy!" Blume crumbled to the ground, hugging Engel's boots. "I have a daughter! I beg of you! Spare my life! I will never displease you again! I am loyal to the *Fuhrer*! I am a servant to the Gestapo! Please let me keep my life!"

With that, Blume bowed his head, still holding Engel's boots. Engel gave Blume a long, hard stare. He ended it with a dramatic sigh.

"Very well, Blume." Engel said, sounding bored. "I will allow you to keep your life."

"Oh, *danke Herr* Major!" Blume nearly cried tears of joy. "*Danke!*"

"Now…If you would be so kind as to stop wasting my time and get these men in my vehicle!" Engel shouted at the top of his lungs. "Handcuff their arms and legs, if you must! Just get them in my car so I may leave this embarrassment of a prison camp!"

All German soldiers, including Blume, saluted and cried out: "*Jawohl, Herr* Major!"

"That's better!" Engel roared as the soldiers began rushing Taggart, Johnny, Tim, and I towards Engel's car. Before they shoved us in, I watched Engel grit his teeth at Blume.

"I am a merciful man, Blume, but pray. *Pray* that I come back with your prisoners only." Engel hissed. "Should I report your accusations to the *Fuhrer* himself, he might just be in less of a gracious mood. Would you care to have him visit?"

Blume's face was whiter than the snow around us. "No, *Herr*

Major! Please forgive me. I was a fool to think of you anyone but who you are, Major Verkleidung.”

With that, the boys and I were stuffed into the car, handcuffed.

Moments later, Engel popped into the driver seat and slammed his door behind him.

He glanced back at the four of us and spoke in his normal accent. “Can you believe him? Calling me a phoney? Me, of all people?”

Taggart, Johnny, and Tim were all suddenly very confused.

I played along. “Tell me ‘bout it. We all know you’re the real deal, Engel.”

CHAPTER SIXTEEN

"So this is Engel?" Johnny raised both of his eyebrows. "The guy that stole your sister?"

"Well, 'stole' is a bit of a strong word." Engel mumbled from the front.

We had successfully made it out of Stalag III-D and were out on the road. Engel had told the boys who he was and how he had gotten here. He had also given us the keys to our handcuffs, so we were able to be more comfortable.

With Taggart and Johnny realizing who Engel was to me, they both began looking him up and down.

"He's a twerp!" Johnny laughed.

"Hey, now." Engel grumbled.

"How did this kiddo ever get your sister away from you?" Taggart eyed me.

I stayed quiet.

"Kiddo?" Engel glanced in the rear-view mirror. "We're around the same age. How old do you think I am, anyway?"

"I'm wondering if you're even legal to drive this thing, son." Johnny told him.

"I'm twenty-six." Engel frowned.

"You look like your sixteen." Taggart offered.

"Ah, he has the gift of youthfulness." Tim nodded with a smile. "I share that same blessing, my friend."

"How old are you, sir?" Engel asked him.

"Sir? Oh, no, brother." Tim waved a hand. "Do not call me 'sir'. We are equals, you and I. You must call me Tikhomir. Tikhomir Izmennik. But, if you have trouble with the pronunciation of that name, you may also refer to me as Timothy."

"Tikhomir." Engel tried out. "And how old are you, Tikhomir?"

"I am thirty-three years of age." Tim said triumphantly.

I was blown away by that. That made Tim older than me. I glanced at him. He sure didn't look thirty-three.

"Tim, you look ten years younger than you really are." I noted.

"Thank you." Tim stroked his mustache with a sly smile. "I have my mother to thank for that. My father's third wife. Though she is nearly fifty years of age, she does not look a day over thirty-five. Some have believed her to be my older sister."

"Wow." Taggart marveled. "Your father likes them young-looking, huh?"

"Indeed he does." Tim admitted. "Some of the older ones complain about that."

"His ex-wives still talk to him?" Engel asked.

"Ex-wives?" Tim asked in response. "No, they are still married to him. My father has five wives currently. The first one died before I was born."

"I guess your dad is trying to be like Jacob, eh?" Johnny nudged him.

"Ha!" Tim nudged him back. "My father already has more children than Jacob did. Not as much sons, however. There are fifteen daughters in our family."

"Fifteen daughters?" Taggart gaped. "That's more sisters than I'd like to think about."

"Too true." Tim shook his head sadly. "There are no words for the kind of torture I have endured."

"Why didn't you bring up the fact that you had fifteen siblings when we were asking if having twelve was possible?" Johnny questioned him.

"I wanted to let Taggart use his big brain." Tim grinned. "And I do not just have fifteen siblings. I said fifteen **sisters**. I have brothers, too."

"So, where are we headin'?" I leaned up towards the front to talk to Engel.

Engel made a "mmmmm" noise before speaking. "I'd really like to just find a secluded place where no one would see us."

"For what?"

"You guys changing." Engel pointed to a bag in the front passenger seat. "Unfortunately, I only have two other German uniforms."

"Two of us will still have to pose as prisoners." I thought out loud.
"That's right." Engel agreed.
"I can speak German fluently." Taggart spoke up.
"Good! Good!" Engel said happily. "Anyone else?"
Engel looked between Tim and Johnny.
"I hate to tell you this, bub." Johnny gave Engel an "are you kidding me?" type look. "But in case you haven't noticed, I'm not exactly the type to act as a German soldier."
He gestured to his light-brown skin color just to drive the point home.
"Oh. Right. Sorry." Engel said quickly. "What about you, Tikhomir?"
"I cannot speak anything but English and Russian." Tim confessed. "And even if I could, I cannot seem to imitate any accent but my own."
He did have a thick Russian accent. Even after all the time we had spent with him.
"Okay then, Scoefield, it looks like you'll be German guard #2." Engel looked to me. "You can do the German accent, right?"
"I'll do what I can." I said in my New York accent, which is really just my normal way of talking.
"Maybe you should just try not to speak, Cappy." Taggart offered after hearing my accent.
"Works for me." I shrugged.

We parked the car in a partly hidden area so Taggart and I could change into the stolen German uniforms. There were two uniform sizes. One was skinny and average height. The other was fat and tall. Taggart took the skinny one and I was left with the fat one since I was much taller than Taggart. They were a bit awkward, but they did fit…sort of.
"Any guns come with these?" Johnny asked as he rubbed his hands in the cold.
Engel nodded, opening the trunk. "The two other men each had a rifle."
He handed one to me and one to Taggart.

"You must understand." Engel said to Johnny and Tim. "With you being prisoners, we can't give you any guns that somebody could see. It'd give us away."

They both did understand.

"Would there have happened to have been another pistol?" Tim brought up. "One of us could conceal that in our clothes."

Engel thought about it before heading to the front passenger seat. He opened the glove compartment to show another pistol.

He took it out and offered it to Tim. Tim glanced at Johnny before taking it. "Would you rather have it, my friend?"

Johnny shook his head. "As long as you're a good shot, you have it."

Tim took it. "I do not wish to boast, but yes. I am an excellent shot."

"So, what now?" I asked Engel.

Engel looked back at me. "We drive to the border. Get to the Allies as fast as possible. Try not to draw any attention."

I considered his plan. "No."

"No?" Engel asked, confused.

The rest of the boys stopped what they were doing and looked at me, too.

"No." I repeated. "Not yet, at least. We got ourselves here a beautiful chance to take out some Krauts. You think we should just throw it away?"

"Scoefield, that's suicide." Engel tried to reason. "We start shooting people, they're going to shoot back. And five guys against a couple thousand aren't good odds."

"Wait." Taggart interrupted. "Cappy's right. In a way. Remember those two guards we eavesdropped on?"

I had no clue what he was talking about. "What?"

"At Stalag III-D, the day before Trevor…"

I tensed up. Guilt took hold of me.

"You know…" Taggart reluctantly finished, looking away from me. "I was listening to the guards outside our barracks. They were talking about a party, remember?"

"The big one." Johnny began nodding. "That even crazy ol'

Wonder-Mustache will be at."

It clicked in my mind. Taggart had told me about that after I was released from solitary confinement. "I remember that! That's perfect!"

"Who's Wonder-Mustache?" Engel was lost.

"His generals will be attending as well." Taggart added, ignoring Engel.

"Do you remember what day the big party was?" I asked him.

Taggart concentrated for a moment. "Yeah…It's this weekend. Three days from now."

"We can make that." I clapped my hands together.

"What do you have in mind?" Tim asked.

"Ken." I pointed to Taggart. He raised his eyebrows.

"You still remember how to blow a house up?"

"Oh yes. Yes, I do." Taggart smiled gleefully. Then he thought for a moment. "But we'll need to visit *several* farms."

"Would someone *please* explain to me what's happening." Engel asked forcefully as we were driving to the next farm.

"Hitler's throwing a party." Johnny told him. "In Berlin. Probably to raise up the spirits of his men. All the higher-ups will be there."

"Shouldn't we be avoiding that, then?" Engel looked in the rear-view mirror with a nervous look.

"We won't stay long." I spoke up. "Taggart's gonna' make a bomb."

"A bomb?" Engel gulped. "To…blow up Hitler?"

"He your best buddy or somethin'?" I shot back.

"Of course not." Engel defended. "I'm just…not the killing type."

"You ordered for a pistol at the Stalag so you might shoot Blume." Tim pointed out what I was thinking.

"That was just acting." Engel replied. "I knew he would beg for his life. I just acted like I would shoot him and then, 'forgive' him."

Engel pulled up to the farm. We had already visited one and gathered what we needed from it. Now, we just had to do it again.

"We shouldn't do this." Engel told all of us. "I'm not signing up for some desperate attempt at killing Hitler. I came to save my brother-in-law. I'm all for saving you three as well, but we should just get out of Germany while we have the chance."

"We're soldiers." I shot back at Engel. "And we're here to kill Germans so we can end this war."

Tim and Taggart grunted in agreement with me.

Engel swallowed. "'Germans'? I think you mean 'Nazis'."

I gave him a cold stare.

"Anyway…" Engel continued. "Seeing that I'm the guy who broke you out of the Stalag, I say that we should just-"

"Engel." I snapped.

Engel cringed and became quiet.

"We're not leaving." I told him firmly. "This is a chance we can't miss."

Engel turned around in his seat to look directly at me.

"Scoefield…I have a family. A family that wants me to come home. I've put a lot on the line already."

"Then go." I offered it to him. "Leave. We're big boys. We can take care of ourselves."

Engel let out a disappointed breath. He turned back in his seat and looked out the windshield.

A farmer had spotted the car and was slowly approaching, a look of terror on his face.

"Fine." Engel muttered quietly. "I'll help. But I need to know how we're going to do this. Step by step."

"We need ammonium nitrate." Taggart explained. "A good amount of ammonium nitrate. That can be found on farms for reasons I'll not get into because the explanation is a little lengthy. And for the sophisticated."

"Thank you." I told Taggart. I didn't need a smartsy speech. It wasn't until much later that I realized he had just called all of us dumb.

Well played, Taggart. Well played.

"We gather what we need and I'll fashion a bomb big enough to bring down the entire building that Hitler will be hosting his party at." Taggart continued. "We somehow sneak into the party with

the bomb, leave, and blow the place sky-high. Then, we get away
free and Germany is without its Nazi leaders. The war's over."
The car got quiet.
"That sounds far too easy." Engel muttered.
"I agree with him." Johnny added.
"The plan that we'll make for how we'll get the bomb in and
detonate it will be more complex and difficult, but it's doable."
Taggart offered. "And it's a good chance to end all the suffering
that this mad-man is inflicting on the world."
"I still say we leave now." Engel shook his head.
"If ya' want to chicken out, you can." I told him. "Us men will do
what needs to be done."
Engel sighed as the farmer was closing in on the car. "I'm with
you. Let's do it."

<u>CHAPTER SEVENTEEN</u>

We had to stop at fifteen different farms. Each time, Engel had to put on a show of how Hitler needed their ammoni-whatever for the German war-effort. Seeing Engel's good acting skills, they all fell for it and gave Engel whatever he wanted.
Once we had enough, we went back to the secluded place where we had changed earlier. It became our hiding spot. Our little base, I guess. Once we got everything that Taggart needed (which included some supplies from downtown Berlin. That was a risky trip that had a lot of close calls, but I'll not get into it now), he began working on his bomb. I watched him for a while, but was soon realizing that everything he was doing was going way over my head. So, I decided to give the guy an over-due compliment.
"I gotta hand it to ya', Taggart." I slapped him on the back. "You're a mad genius."
"Hardly." Taggart scoffed as he kept up his work. "It's just a simple explosive. Mostly ammonium nitrate, as I said before. Of course, simple doesn't mean easy. I had to dissolve the sodium bisulfate and nitrate salt individually in water, and mix the two solutions. Next, neutralizing the resulting acidic solution by-"
"Just take the compliment, Taggart." I told him. "I don't care what it's made of. I just want it to go 'boom' tomorrow."
"Right." Taggart sighed. "Thank you, Cappy."

From then on, the rest of us had nothing to do. It was Taggart's turn to do his stuff and none of us really had the brains to help him. Johnny, Tim, and I played poker. Engel, of course, read his Bible. I couldn't believe that even when coming all the way to Germany, Engel still had to bring his Bible.
Just seeing him with that book made my insides boil.
But I said nothing.
Hours went on and the sun began to set. Taggart couldn't work in the dark so we all started making camp for the night. We were in a dense enough area that we all agreed a fire wouldn't be too

noticeable. So, we made one. We kept watches one by one,
making sure no one stumbled in our camp.
First, it was me.
Then Johnny.
Then Tim.
I figured Taggart needed some shut-eye since he was the one who
was making an explosive. That kind of work sounds stressful.
As for Engel, I didn't trust him to stay up. Something inside just
told me he might have another knife to stick in my back.
Which was ridiculous, if I'll be true. Engel was the reason we
were out of Stalag III-D. But, as Trevor told me when he was
alive: "That's what bitterness does to a man".

"You're up." I shook Johnny as I moved close to the fire.
Engel had picked up some blankets when we went into Berlin for
Taggart's supplies. I immediately threw one over me and closed
my eyes. Johnny slowly got up, yawned, stretched, and walked
around a bit.
About twenty minutes passed. I should have been out after the
first thirty seconds of lying down, but sleep decided to stay away
from me that night. It was that horrible night when you're *so* tired
but your mind won't stop thinking.
Then, I heard Johnny talk.
"Why are you still up?" Johnny asked. It was a whisper, but I
could hear it well enough.
For just a second, I opened one eye. Johnny was facing Engel,
who still had his Bible in his hands.
Engel quickly glanced around to see if any of the rest of us were
awake.
I zipped my eyes shut.
"A little restless I suppose." Engel admitted, also whispering.
"You've been reading that for hours." Johnny said, probably
talking about Engel's Bible.
"Yes." Engel replied. "It got me through some very hard years. I
keep it close."
"*Yes, he really does.*" I thought to myself.

"You're just like Trevor." Johnny scoffed.

"Trevor?"

"A chaplain that was with us in Stalag III-D. He was terribly annoying." Johnny told Engel.

"Are you sure it was him?" Engel asked with a strange calmness in his voice. "Or was it the message he gave you?"

"Both." Johnny coughed. "I've been to church, but my parents showed me that you could be one way at church and another way at home. I always thought to myself 'if that's what Christians are, I don't want anything to do with them'. So, yeah, the message got my blood going, but the guy was a knucklehead, too. Forced his preaching on us like we were schoolkids. Hated every minute of it."

"What did he preach on?" Engel asked, still calm.

"Joseph." Johnny told him. "Had a real big problem against guys being with girls, if you catch what I'm saying."

Silence for a moment.

"…I do." Engel said hoarsely.

"Oh, sorry." Johnny apologized. "I forgot that…you and Cappy's sis…"

"Don't be sorry." Engel told him. "Sarah and I are guilty of that sin. It was our choice. But, let me tell you, this Trevor person was right to be so against it. What I did back then brought me nothing but pain."

Then, there was a pause.

"And it brought *him* nothing but pain."

I made sure I looked like I was in a dead sleep. I knew Engel was talking about me. Sure enough, they both were probably glancing my way.

"You two were close buds, weren't you?" Johnny asked.

"I would like to think so." Engel acknowledged. "But because of what I did, I think he turned part of his anger towards God. From what my wife has told me from his letters, Scoefield wants nothing to do with Jesus."

They stopped talking. The quiet went on for several moments. I figured they were done. It was nice to hear Engel was so sorry

about how he messed my life up. But, I was still mixed up inside.
Unsure of how I felt. Anger and pity were duking it out inside me.
I wasn't sure which one would win.
Then, Johnny started talking again.
"I have a kid."

My eyes nearly shot open at that. Johnny, when I first met him,
was a kid. He was seventeen when we were riding on that bus to
boot camp back in 1934. Now, ten years later, he was twenty-
seven. We had been friends for a decade. Out of all of the people
that I had known in the army, Doug had been my closest friend.
After he died, Johnny filled that spot.
And he never once told me what he told Engel that night. And to
Johnny, Engel was basically a complete stranger.
That hurt. Right then, it felt like Engel was even beginning to take
my friends from me, who had been through so much for so long
with me.
"I have three." I could hear Engel's smile. "Two sons and a
daughter."
"No, no, no." Johnny was saying in a serious tone. "I'm not
married, but…I have a kid. A little girl."
"Oh." Engel said, his voice sounding like he was frowning now.
"Yeah." Johnny said quietly. "So…I guess that's why I didn't like
the preaching. Trevor talked a lot about how we shouldn't lust. We
shouldn't have good times with the ladies. It's wrong outside of
marriage. Yadda, yadda, yadda."
"If you don't believe that then why are you confessing this to me
like it's wrong?" Engel asked.
"…I don't know."
"I think it's because you know it is wrong." Engel said plainly.
"When was the last time you saw your daughter?"
"…I haven't." Johnny sounded so sad. "I told her mother that I
didn't want a baby. I barely knew my daughter's mother. We were
just going to party together for one night. No strings attached. But
then she told me that she was pregnant. I told her to get rid of it.
Any way she could, you know? I wasn't going to be responsible

for some, little…thing."

Engel said nothing in response. He just kept waiting, it seemed.

"But she won't stop writing to me." Johnny continued. "The mom. She's been writing to me for ten years. She keeps saying how she found Jesus and how she loves me and how she prays that I'll find God and come back to her. I never loved her! I just wanted a good time! I don't need her or God! I'm good by myself!"

Engel still said nothing. The pause went on for a while.

Then, Engel spoke. "If you're so keen on justifying yourself, why do you look and sound so guilty, Sergeant Smith?"

Johnny got saved that night. The conversation went on for hours, but I'll let Johnny and Engel's talk be kept private. Engel did the usual and brought on the flood of Bible verses and Johnny eventually fell beneath the overwhelming conviction.

But that didn't matter to me at the time.

What mattered to me is that I felt so very alone. Engel was a Christian. Taggart was a Christian. Tim was a Christian. And now, Johnny was a Christian.

Not only that, but Engel had gotten closer to Johnny in a few days then I had in ten years.

But I didn't get angry at it. For once, I wasn't getting angry.

I was getting sad.

So sad.

Engel seemed to infect everyone he came in contact with. He had done the same with my sister all of those years ago. He did it with my friends.

Now, I was all alone.

All alone.

Even if we blew up Hitler without a single problem and went back home to New York, I would still be alone. Sarah wasn't Sarah anymore. I had no one. No one.

As a matter of fact, everyone I touched seemed to get worse.

Doug, Larkin, Calvin, Sheldon, Bratt, and Trevor all died.

But everyone Engel touched seemed to be happier. Happier…even without me.

He was doing good for everybody.
I was doing only bad for everybody.
Nobody needed me. In fact, people would be better off without me. That's what I thought that night.
And it was right then that I decided…
I would not go home with Engel.

CHAPTER EIGHTEEN

"So, here's the plan." I drew a line in the dirt. "Taggart and I have talked and we've hit a few bumps in the road."
It was the afternoon of the next day. Taggart had finished his homemade bomb and I was now going over our "blow up Hitler" operation with everyone else.
"What kind of bumps, Captain?" Tim asked, shifting uneasily from one leg to the other.
I motioned to Taggart.
"This is a primitive bomb." Taggart took over. "Because of our limitations, we have no detonation device and no fuse. Meaning, someone will not only have to get the bomb inside where no one spots it, but will also have to light it and run."
"I thought you said this bomb'll be big enough to blow up the whole place." Johnny said nervously. "How on earth is one of us going to get away from the explosion in time?"
"I'm lightin' it." I took the reigns again. "I'm the fastest one here. If there's anyone who can get away from it in time, it's me."
"But Scoefield, you're also the commanding officer." Engel piped up. "One of us should do it, not you."
"No offense to any of you boys, but none of ya' would be able to make it." I stood my ground. "Taggart's a wheezer when it comes to runnin'. We all know that."
Taggart nodded ashamedly.
"Johnny and Tim are both quick, but there's no way either of em' could get the bomb inside. Johnny'd never be mistaken for a German and Tim can't hide his Russian worth a darn."
Both admitted to that.
"And you, Engel, probably wouldn't even be able to carry the bomb." I eyed him.
Engel folded his arms. "I've muscled up a bit since we last saw each other, you know."
"Still, even if ya' could do it, you're not." I ordered him. "You're needed to get us out of Berlin and back to the Allies."

Engel paused. "Fine. But that brings up another thing: you can't speak German. You may look the part, but you'll get caught before you ever get inside."

"Taggart thought of that." I brought up. "So he's coming with me to get me in. Once I'm in, he'll be high-tailin' it out of there before I even light the bomb."

Engel shook his head at that. "Good idea, but not Ken. I'll go with you."

"It's okay, Henry." Taggart told him. "I'd be happy to do it. I am, after all, military. I know how these officers think."

"And I'm German." Engel shot back. "I know the culture. These officers won't be thinking military at a party. They'll want to unwind, meet some girls, have some well-earned delicacies. Get their mind *off* of the war, not on it. I'm the best chance for this mission to work."

I scratched my chin, irritated. The last person I wanted to go with was Engel. But I couldn't argue with him when he said that. Taggart was super smart, sure…but he was American. If he talked too much, even in German, he would sound out of place. People would get suspicious and we'd be more likely to get caught.

"Not only that, but I've a Gestapo uniform with genuine papers." Engel added to drive home the point. "If anyone suspects me, I can 'prove' I am who I say I am. Plus, with me being Gestapo, not many will question me. They'll avoid me, which is far better."

I hated it when he was right.

"Fine." I grumbled.

"The other problem is how to get the bomb in and where to put it." Taggart took over again. "This building that Hitler will be in is, obviously, well-guarded. No Allies have gotten anywhere near Berlin, but there have already been assassination attempts on Hitler's life by German natives. They will be careful. They will be on high alert. They will be everywhere and want to search everything that comes in there. We need to figure out a way to get it in without it being checked. If they check it, they'll know what it is and both of you will be shot on the spot."

"We pray, first and foremost." Engel chimed in.

I instinctively rolled my eyes, but I found that everybody around me was actually nodding and saying things like "you're right".

I hung my head slightly and coughed uncomfortably. "So, what? We pray and the bomb will magically get in on its own? I don't think so, boyo. We need a plan."

"Of course we need a plan." Engel replied. "But we need to pray in case the plan doesn't work."

"Ya' got a plan?"

"Well, as stated before, I am posing as Gestapo." Engel shrugged. "I've heard they've been able to slip things through checks with no questions asked. I show them the papers and we get through."

"What if that doesn't work?" I narrowed my eyes at him.

"I already told you." Engel smiled. "We pray."

"So, that's it?" I tried to resist rolling my eyes again. "That's your whole plan?"

Engel shrugged. "Unless you have a better one."

I didn't.

"We'll come back to that." I huffed. "Where to put it, then?"

"We may not have to get the bomb into the building at all." Tim cleared his throat. "I have taken the liberty of reviewing the plans of the building adjacent to the one that Hitler will be using to host his party." He rolled out the blueprints to the building out on the ground.

"Where in blazes did you get this?" I asked him.

"I picked them up while we were in town." Tim explained.

"You just magically found these plans in the building next to Hitler's and pocketed them without anyone seeing you or asking questions?" Johnny raised an eyebrow.

To answer that, Tim smiled and stroked his mustache proudly.

"One must be fast and stealthy when he has as many siblings as I. Little food is left on the table if someone like me does not have quick hands."

"I thought you said that you guys nearly got caught in town." Taggart blinked, looking at Engel and me.

"We *did*." Engel affirmed. "When did you steal these?"

"While that officer was questioning you and Captain Scoefield."
Tim cleared his throat again.
"Anyway, here." Tim pointed at the blueprints. "There is a wine
cellar in the basement of this building. From what I can tell, the
Nazis will still be using this cellar for the party, but it is not under
as much guard. You will have an easier time getting in and there
will not be as many eyes on you. I would recommend to place the
bomb in there. The alcohol could also be used as a short fuse,
giving you more time to escape, Captain."
"That's genius!" Engel applauded.
"Thank you, my friend." Tim smiled triumphantly.
"Looks like we got a better plan than just prayin'." I nodded at
Tim's idea. "Okay, we'll go with that. Taggart, Tim, and Johnny.
You all will be waitin' in the car outside the city. We don't want
anybody gettin' too close of a look at ya' and wonderin' why
you're all just sittin' in a car. Keep out of sight and Engel and I
will come runnin' to ya' not too long after you here a big 'boom'."
"I wasn't too sure about this plan at first." Johnny said with a grin.
"But you know what? We could actually do this."

The next day came. Party time for Hitler and his goons.
Crunch time for me and the boys.
Engel and I were making our way down the street, the sun already
past the horizon.
"Whatever happens, just stick to the plan." I said sternly at Engel.
"Ya' got me?"
Engel nodded, not saying anything.
I paused as we were getting closer to where we needed to be.
I took a shuddering breath.
"And…If I don't make it, tell Sarah-"
"You will make it, Scoefield." Engel interrupted. "I didn't come
all this way to go home without you."
"Just listen to me." I barked at him. "If, by some freak accident, I
don't make it…Tell Sarah I'm sorry."
"You'll tell her yourself." Engel spoke in a serious tone.
That was all the time we had, though. We were too close to be

speaking English anymore.

I was holding the bomb. It was pretty big, but I was able to carry it the whole time. Taggart told me it weighed like 30 kilograms, but I have no idea what a kilogram is, so…

It was heavy.

It was covered in a tarp so no one could see what it actually was, but it looked really suspicious.

I wasn't sure if this was going to work at all.

We approached the building next to the building where Hitler was having his party.

And…unlike Tim said, the building was just as heavily guarded as the one Hitler was in.

I gulped.

We were stopped before we got anywhere near the buildings. To make it easier, I'm going to call the building where Hitler was having his party "the party building". And I'll call the other one "the bomb building". Easier for you and easier for me.

Everybody wins.

Anyway, to me, the guard just looked like one of the many normal Nazi soldiers around. Not an officer. Not a Gestapo.

He snapped something in German. Engel without a word, handed him the papers for Major Verkleidung.

The guard looked them over. He flicked his eyes back to Engel, then to me, then back to the papers.

He handed the papers back to Engel, but had his eyes on the big, tarp-covered, stinky thing that I was holding.

He pointed to it and spoke something else in German towards Engel.

I knew what he was saying. You can probably guess too.

He, no doubt, asked something close to "What is that?". Engel and I had rehearsed this part, just in case it happened. Hitler, we knew, was a big superstitious guy. He had been searching for relics of power all throughout the war. Even before the war. So, if we were asked "What is that?", Engel would first simply say something like "That's classified. It's for the *Fuhrer's* eyes only".

We figured that would get most to zip their lips. But, if he pushed (which we figured some would because they were under orders) we had something ready to tell them for that, too. Engel was to say something like "If you must know, it is a powerful item the *Fuhrer* has been searching for. Fear not, we will store it in the basement of **this** building" (the bomb building) "until the *Fuhrer* is ready to see the item that will win this war for us."
Funny part was, that last bit wasn't a lie. If everything went according to plan, that bomb **would** win the war for us.
We figured that the guard would cave under the pressure that he could get in trouble if he asked any further questions. But, to our horror, this guard actually did more because of what Engel said.
He did look nervous, but he said something quick to Engel and ran off.
"Is that good?" I whispered to Engel.
"Keep calm." Engel whispered back. "But no. He said he's going to go get another Gestapo agent just to make sure everything is fine."
"Another Gestapo agent?!" I hissed quietly.
"Yes…" Engel gulped. "Probably one with more authority than me."
"We're dead." I sighed.
"Not yet." Engel said calmly. "Remember what I said before? We need to pray. Now more than ever."

The Gestapo agent that came out was clearly drunk. A drunk knows another drunk and when another drunk is drunk.
And that man was drunk.
"Some party." I muttered to Engel. "We might just make this."
The Gestapo agent came up, did a sluggish Nazi salute and asked Engel some questions.
Engel replied calmly and, before long, the Gestapo agent just looked back at the guard with a "I don't see what the problem is here" look. And with that, the Gestapo agent began stumbling back into the party building for more drinks.
The guard looked angry as the Gestapo agent went back inside.

Engel and I started making our way to the bomb building, when
the guard jumped back in front of us. He held up a hand to Engel
and started growling out some hateful German words. His eyes
were narrowed and he kept pointing a finger at Engel and at the
bomb I was holding.
As I glanced at Engel, I could tell something had gone wrong.
Engel was looking much like he had looked back in Stalag III-D
when Blume accused him of not being Major Verkleidung.
In other words, this guy was on to us and Engel didn't know what
to say.
So…I said something.
Yup. *I* said something.
I put the bomb down, marched up to the guard, got right in his
face, and said something.

I've been told I'm good at impersonating people. It was
something I liked to do as a kid. I did it because it was fun and it
usually made people laugh.
So, I figured I could impersonate Engel. I had somehow
remembered just a smidge of his German speech he had thrown at
Blume in Stalag III-D. True, I had no idea what Engel had said
then, but it was all I had.
And I shouted that at the guard. In a thick, German accent I had
somehow picked up from Engel or Taggart. They were just a few
phrases, but from what I could see in that guard's eyes, I was
convincing and I was terrifying. Whatever I was saying, it was
making his knees shake. And I barely got done before he started
apologizing, saluting, and getting out of our way. I picked up the
bomb and we headed inside the bomb building.
Engel shut the door behind us.
"You told me you couldn't speak German!" He gawked quietly.
"And you had a perfect German accent!"
"I *don't* know how to speak German." I whispered back to him. "I
was copying you from before."
Engel's mouth nearly hit the floor. "That was just an
impersonation of me?"

I nodded.

"Well, it was amazing!" Engel cheered. "It explains why it sounded familiar, but my, oh my, you did it perfectly! Wait, did you even know what you said?"

"No." I said bluntly. "What *did* I say?"

"You said something to the equivalent of 'I am more of a German than you'll ever be! This will come back down on you one hundred fold, I promise you! Every nightmare you have ever had will be nothing compared to the fire that I will bring down upon you! That is the wrath of the Gestapo!'."

I looked at him long and hard. "You said *that* to Blume?"

"Yes. And *you* just said that to that poor man outside." Engel pointed.

"Well, it worked, didn't it?" I shrugged.

Engel smiled big and bright. "Yes, it did. And I bet you it was all because we prayed."

It wasn't long or hard to find the wine cellar. It was, as you can figure, filled with wine. We set the bomb in place and it was about time for the fireworks to happen.

I just needed Engel to get out.

"Okay, boyo." I clapped my hands together. "I'll light the sucker once you're clear."

Engel looked back at me with a shake of his head. "No, I'll wait with you."

I blinked at him. "Uh, no ya' won't. Get goin'. Remember the plan."

"I am remembering the plan." Engel stated. "We were going to use the wine to make a bit of a fuse. Then, you don't have to stay behind alone. We can make a fuse, light it. Speed-walk out of here and, once it blows, run for our lives to the car."

I gritted my teeth. That had sorta become the plan. Tim had brought that up and everyone thought it was a great idea.

I sighed, trying to think of a way to get Engel to leave.

"Well, I can make the fuse myself." I excused. "You get goin'. We all know ya' can't run all that good."

Engel frowned. "What are you talking about? I've always been a good runner. I've not always been able to fight, but I've **always** been able to run just fine. No, I'm staying and helping."

"No, you're not." I started getting angry and it was showing.

"Yes, I am." Engel looked like he was getting angry too. And he wasn't backing down.

"Engel, ya' better get your tail out of here and back to the car!" I ordered him.

"Why don't you want me here?" Engel got straight to the point. "What are you hiding?"

"I'm not goin' back!" I told him.

Engel didn't quite understand. "You want to stay in Germany?"

"No." I began to deflate. I began to feel the depression take hold on me. The misery. The sadness. "I'm stayin' with this bomb. I'm gonna' blow up with it. I'm done with life. I'm a murderer and all I do is hurt people. Not like you. You make everyone's lives better. Happier. I'm…alone. And so I'm just endin' it."

"Scoefield." Engel walked closer to me. He grabbed my shoulders and shook me just a bit. "We can talk about this later, but you have to get a grip. You're not a murderer. You're a soldier who's gone through some horrible stuff. We'll light this thing and get back to the others. When I get you home to Sarah, we'll all have a good, long talk over some sodas, for old time's sake."

"Ya' don't know what I've done, Engel!" I shoved him back. "I am a murderer. I murdered long before ya' ever knew me. I just got away with it."

Engel started to look scared. "What…What are you talking about?

CHAPTER NINETEEN

It was summertime in 1924. I was eleven years old. Sarah was eight years old.

I was playing with some toys of mine. A couple of wooden trucks. I would always pretend to crash them together and have them both explode.

I was such a doofus.

"Hey! Bradley, ya' know what time it is?" My mama asked me as she came into the living room.

"Time for me to…keep playin'?" I smiled at her.

"Wrong, pally." She made a 'tsk' sound. "It's time for ya' to go to bed. Get washed up and get in your jammies."

"But Mama!"

"No 'but's, boyo." Mama snapped at me. "Get your patootey into that tub now."

"Just five more minutes, Mama?" I tried using my big, adorable eyes on her.

For a moment, Mama only gave me a hard stare back. But a smile soon broke across her face. She shook her head with her smile was only getting bigger.

"Can't do anythin' when you use them eyes on me like that." She laughed. "Fine. *Five* minutes more. Then tub, jammies, bed. Ya' got me?"

"Yes, Mama." I grinned at her and went back to crashing my trucks together.

I don't know if it would've been better to have gone to bed right then or not. If I had, things would've definitely have been different, but I'm not sure if they would've been better.

I was at four minutes and thirty-two seconds. Okay, that's a lie right there. I actually stayed up for probably something around eight minutes because I knew my mama was a softy and wouldn't get mad at me for it.

But then my pop came home. Amos Scoefield.

And he was drunk. And he was an angry drunk.

He trudged past me, not even looking at me. I was glad for that.
He stumbled into the kitchen and began glancing around. The
more he looked around, the more he began to growl like a mad
dog.

"Where's my dinner?" He asked no one. "That lazy wench! What
does she do all day?!"

Then, he spun around to find me.

"Boy!" He hissed at me. "Where's your Ma?"

I tensed, getting ready in case he wanted to hit me. "Upstairs."

"Ergh!" Amos bared his teeth and immediately began heading for
the stairs. I turned back to my toys.

Sometimes I stood up to him when he was like that. He would
go after Mama for no reason, or for a real stupid one. But that
night? I just didn't want to get hit then. I excused in my head that
he might not hurt Mama and I could just go get in my jammies
and go to sleep. I was packing up my toys as he was stomping
upstairs where my mama was.

"Woman!" He yelled. "Where's my dinner?!"

"Am-Amos, Honey, I'm sorry." I heard Mama say quietly. "I-I
didn't get to it yet. See, I just put Sarah to bed. Please don't wake
her, Amos. She'll cry."

"What've you been doing all day?!" Amos roared. "You couldn't
have put her to bed sooner?!"

"I'm sorry, Amos." Mama replied. "P-please don't yell. I've been
cleanin' all day. I had to do the laundry, the dishes…You also told
me that you wanted the basement picked up."

"Why'd it take you so long?!"

I heard him hit her. I gulped. A crashing sound came from upstairs.

"I can get that done in five minutes, you heifer!" Amos bellowed.
"Why did it take you all day?! What else have you been doing?!"

"Please don't call me that, Amos." Mama was crying now. "You
don't mean it. I know ya' don't."

"Oh, I do, you lousy, stinking, good-for-nothing free loader!"
Amos screamed. "I work hard all day, every day! I just expect a
couple of things done and you *can't do anything right*!"

I heard more crashing.

"Amos! Please! I'm sorry! I'm so sorry!" Mama was sobbing loudly.

That was it. I couldn't sit around anymore. If Amos was going to beat me for telling him to stop, then it would be better than just hearing Mama get walloped. I stood up and, with clenched fists, ran to the bottom of the stairs. I was so mad at myself for not stopping Pop before he went upstairs.

And then my life was changed forever.

Amos came into view with my mama. He had her by the hair, yanking her to the stairs. With each pull, she was crying out.

"Now go do something useful for once and make me some food, woman!" Amos shouted before throwing my mother down the stairs. Mama toppled down the stairs in a real bad way. It wasn't just falling or rolling down the stairs. She was flipping head over heels, smacking her head all the way down on those hard, wooden steps.

Then, she collapsed face-down at the bottom of the stairs, right at my feet.

Blood was running from her head. Not just a little bit, either.

I was frozen with shock. I didn't know what to do. I didn't know what to say. I didn't even know what to think.

Mama put her hands underneath her and tried to push herself up. She was shaking bad. Wobbling. I knew she was really hurt.

Then, she lifted her head to look at me.

Her big, green eyes.

"Bradley…" She choked, breathing real lightly. "It's okay. Don't be scared. I'm fine. I'm…"

Mama blinked her eyes a lot. Like there was some dust in her eyes or something.

But then, all at once, Mama fell back onto the floor. With blood pooling at my feet, I noticed that Mama wasn't breathing.

My mother, who had done nothing but love my father, had been murdered by him.

"Get up." Amos growled as he stumbled down a few of the

stairs. "I said get up, woman!"

Mama didn't respond. I started to cry.

"Mama?" I sobbed. "Mama? Are you okay?"

"Bah, she's fine!" Amos yelled at me as he trudged past her body. "She's just pretending to be hurt! Thinks it'll make me feel bad or something."

Amos didn't even realize that he had just killed his wife. He fumbled back over to the kitchen and I heard him open another beer bottle.

I fell to Mama's side, shaking her slightly.

"Mama?" I cried quietly. "Mama? Please wake up. Please. Please! Mama!"

"Shut up, boy!" Amos yelled from the kitchen. "She's just being the lazy piece of trash she's always been. She isn't worth anything I give her!"

Something dark came over me in that moment. Real dark. Something snapped inside of me. Winifred Scoefield, my mama… one of the best things in my life had just been forced out by the man who had always brought my family torment.

"You." I breathed angrily.

I stood up from my mama's body and hurried over into the kitchen.

There he was. Gulping down alcohol.

"You!" I pointed a finger at him.

Amos stopped and looked at me.

"You! You!" I started yelling. "You…pig-headed, sewer-suckin' numbskull! You piece of maggot's food! You rotten, stinkin' pile of goat slop! You dumb, ossified dewdropper!"

Amos' eyes were wide and furious. I had never, *ever* talked to him that way.

"You think you can talk to me that way?" He challenged. "I'm going to beat the snot out of you for saying that."

"Not if I beat it out of you first, ya' big, snobby ogre!"

I was really big for an eleven-year-old. I had always been big. I was a foot taller than all of my classmates at school. But Amos Scoefield was big, too. Too big for me to actually whoop.

Thankfully, he was drunk, so I actually got a punch in.
I smacked my knuckles right across his jaw. He fell back onto the kitchen table, shaking his head.
Then, his eyes were fixed on me. Up in less than a second, he bounded at me and fired his leg right into my gut. I was shot across the room and into the wall. I couldn't breathe for several seconds after that. Once I got the ability to start breathing again (though it was more like wheezing), I felt Amos' strong hand grab my shirt collar and lift me up to his eyes.
His evil, fiery, black eyes.
"That was a lucky shot, boy." He whispered at me. "I'm going to make you regret that."
But in the corner of my eye, I saw where my mama was still laying. Face down at the bottom of the stairs.
Gone. Because of him.
A burning explosion lit up in my heart and I kicked my legs. I nailed Amos hard in the stomach, just like he had done to me. The man coughed and dropped me. I plopped onto the ground.
I noticed then that Amos had dropped something else: his beer bottle. He had been holding it in his other hand.
I snatched the neck of the bottle. I turned it around in my hand to use it like a club. And, as Amos was still gripping his gut, I whacked that beer bottle right on top of his head.
Amos crashed to the floor, a nasty gash in his head. In my anger, I kept hitting him with the beer bottle. Over and over, I plowed that beer bottle into his head. All I was thinking about was that this man had killed my mother. My mother who was pure and innocent and kind and sweet and loving and everything good.
Amos killed her.
And by the time I had come to my senses…I realized that I had killed Amos.
Amos was lying dead on the kitchen floor. I dropped the now-broken beer bottle. I fell back, gasping at what I had just done.
I had killed my own father.
There were so many thoughts that went through my head in that moment. Thoughts like:

*"This isn't happenin'. This isn't happenin'. That **didn't** just happen. This is a dream. A nightmare. A trick."*
*"If **he** was a monster, what does that make **me** after I clubbed him to death?"*
"What do I do?! What do I do about this?!"
"I should call the hospital! I should call somebody! Maybe he's still alive! Maybe Mama is even still alive! Yeah! They're just… knocked out? Who am I kiddin'?! My parents are dead!"
"I'm a murderer! I'm gonna' go to jail!"
*"I gotta hide this. Sarah can't find out about this. **Nobody** can find out about this!"*
It went on like that for a while in my head. I panicked, as anyone would with something like that. But eventually, I calmed down and thought of a plan.

I opened Sarah's bedroom door.
"Sarah?" I whispered. "You awake?"
It was a really dumb thing to ask. There had been screaming, crashing, fighting, crying, and more screaming going on throughout the house since Amos got home. How could she **not** be awake?
But that's the funny thing. She **wasn't** awake. She was lying still, sleeping like a little angel.
I hopped over to her bed and shook her a little. "Sarah?"
She rolled a bit and moaned, but she opened her eyes after a little more shaking.
"Bradley?" She breathed. "What's wrong?"
"Hey, nothin's wrong." I tried to smile. "Um…Mama and I are just goin' to go out with Pop to…go to the candy shop. Mama… just told me to ask you what you wanted?"
"Candy?" Sarah sat up in bed. "But I thought Pop was mad at Mama."
"Ya' heard that, huh?" I gulped.
"Just a little." Sarah rubbed her eyes. "I heard them yelling about Pop's dinner. But I put the pillow over my head and sang Mama's favorite song. After a while, I didn't hear anything and I guess I

fell asleep."

I breathed a sigh of relief. "Well, that's good. See, um, Pop calmed down. He feels bad and he wants to get us ice-cream. Mama wants you to go back to bed, though. You got school tomorrow and all that. Ya' need your sleep."

"You have school, *too*." Sarah folded her arms.

I smiled at her. "Just go to sleep, Sissy."

My plan was to hide the bodies. Bury them out in the woods somewhere. The woods were pretty far from New York City, but I knew how to get there. Amos had a car where I could put him and Mama without too many people noticing. It was late, too, so no one would really be out.

After I cleaned up all the blood and mess, I checked outside before I brought a body out. I was so scared that someone would see me and call the coppers, but no one was out. And thank goodness for that because it took me forever to drag each body out and put them in the car. I sloppily threw Amos' body in the back of the car. I didn't care as much about his body as I did Mama's. With her, I tried to be as gentle as possible. I placed her in the passenger seat, sitting upright. I put a seat-belt over her so she wouldn't fall forward. I put myself in the driver's seat and put the keys into the ignition.

Then I stopped and took a minute to think.

"I'm an eleven-year-old kid." I thought. *"I've never even been in the driver seat of a car before. I don't know how to drive and if I try now, I'll drive like a drunk man."*

A drunk man. That gave me an idea.

I glanced at Amos' body in the back seat.

After a few minutes, I was backing the car out of our driveway. I was sitting on Amos' lap, trying the best to hide myself as I drove. Now, both of my parents' bodies were in the front seats. This way, if anyone saw the car, they would see that Amos was "driving". He was known for his drunken driving and people would probably get mad and maybe even call the police, but not report that there was an eleven-year-old kid driving with two dead people in his car. I ran over the Scoefield mailbox backing out of the driveway. I hit several trash cans, and other people's mailboxes, too, but I started to get the hang of it.

It would take me a good bit before I got anywhere near any woods. I lived in New York City. Nothing but pavement all around us. But I knew where I could find some woods. I knew the way because Mama would sometimes take us. Sarah and her both really liked to go and try to find little snakes.

I only went along because they wanted me to. I hated snakes.

After a while, I was coming along to a bridge. Nothing special about this bridge except what happened on it.

I braked before I got on the bridge. I saw something.

A police car was sitting on the side of the road right before the bridge.

I gulped, sitting even lower in my seat. This would be tricky to move past the copper without alerting him. I couldn't drive too fast. I couldn't drive too slow. Both would make him suspicious.

And I also didn't want him looking too closely.

I drove. Nice and easy. Not too fast. Not too slow.

I began to pass him, keeping my head down and not even looking at the police car.

Nothing happened.

I kept going. The bridge was coming closer and the police car was getting further away.

I was almost home free, glancing back at the police car to make sure his lights weren't flicking on.

I began to get excited, pushing my foot on the gas. I wanted to get away from the police car as fast as I could. I was speeding up, getting on to the bridge.

Just when I grinned to myself and put my eyes back on the road, I saw them.

Three dogs were walking on the bridge. A Golden Retriever, a Boxer, and an American Bulldog. Just strolling through the street around eleven O' clock at night.

Don't ask me how I noticed what kind of dogs they were in that split second. I was stressed, okay?

Anyway, they probably belonged to someone and just got out of their yard. I saw some collars on them in that instant that they came into my sights.

And I have to admit, I love dogs. I'm no girly guy that thinks dogs ought to be treated like a prince or anything, wearing shoes and sweaters, and licks inside people's mouths and everything.

That's weird. And gross. And unnatural. If you ever meet a guy like that, tell him that Scoefield says he's weird.

But I love me a good hunting dog. Or a guard dog. Those are what dogs were made for. They can be great pals and they can love people more than people love themselves.

So, yeah, I like dogs.

And I swerved that car so I wouldn't hit them. And I didn't hit them. But I swerved too far to swerve back. Instead of hitting the dogs, I hit the railing on the bridge. And before I could start panicking, I busted my head against the glass.

And I was out.

I woke up coughing. Smoke was pluming in the car. I had no idea what was happening or how long I had been out, but the car was on fire. The engine was already blazing, black smoke pluming from the flames. And the wind was blowing just right that the smoke was pushing right through the shattered windshield and into the car. I was hacking and wheezing like…well, a smoker. Starting to see why it's bad for you?

I started to move back, trying to catch my breath. That's when I felt something. The entire car swayed back. I froze as the car was gently rocking back and forth until it came to a stop again. I slowly gazed out the driver's window. The car was balancing on the edge of the bridge. It had crashed through the railing altogether. The front wheels were hanging off into the air. The back of the car was balancing on the bridge, but just barely.

I was sitting on a sea-saw that was just itching to tip.

I gulped as I counted my problems.

1. I was in a car with two dead bodies. If I was found by that copper (who was still just down the road, mind you), questions would definitely be asked. Worse case scenario, I would be going to juvenile hall and Sarah would be put in some orphanage. I didn't know if I would get to see her again if that happened. And what would the coppers tell her? "Your brother killed your parents"? I couldn't have that.

2. I was trapped in a car that was ***on fire***. Fire. Not like a little sizzle or just a cute, little candle-sized flame. No, hot, growing, deadly fire. I had to get out, no question. The flames were bigger than me and they weren't hunky-dory with just staying in one place. No, they were spreading closer and closer to me. But, at the same time, I couldn't move because…

3. The car was ***hanging off the side of a bridge***. With each of my coughs, I felt the car sway. Just opening the driver door could have tipped the car right into the river below and I would be as dead as my parents. Not that opening the driver door would do me any good. Outside of the driver door was just empty air. The bridge was too far to reach from the driver door. The only way I could make it out onto the bridge was if I climbed into the back seats and got out of one of those doors. But any movement could make the car slip and plummet down like a shot-up airplane.

The smoke was really getting to me. I was constantly coughing, not being able to breathe very well. I needed to try something, so I tried turning around in my seat.
Then, the car leaned forward.
Too far forward.
The back side of the car lifted and the car fell off of the bridge.
"No no no no no no no, DON'T FALL!!!" I screamed.
The car fell.

*"My arm **really** hurts."*
That was the first thing I thought.

It wasn't "*I'm alive!*"
Nope, that was the second thought.
I had fallen, in a car, twenty feet from the bridge into a cold, dark river. I don't know how I lived through it, but I had hurt my right arm pretty bad. I wasn't sure how I had hurt it. I guess I had slammed it against something or whatever. To be honest, my eyes closed at the last minute. The fire was out because of the water, but the water turned from being a helper to a new danger.
The car was sinking faster than shoes filled with rocks. Water was pouring into the car where the windshield used to be.
I had to go.
I grabbed the handle to the driver door and pushed, but the more the car sunk, the harder it was to open the door. And water was already rising above my shoulders.
I thrusted my entire left side against the door, but it was too heavy to open.
The car was nearly beneath the water.
Of all the deaths I had thought of, drowning was always the scariest to me. And I was very close to dying that way.
In a desperate panic, I balled up my left fist and flung it against the driver door window.
Somehow, that worked. The window shattered and my fist plowed through. Don't ask me how. Maybe I've got some crazy-stupid strength. Maybe God was really just looking out for me.
But that window broke and the pressure against the door wasn't as heavy. So, I took a deep breath and I opened the door. As I swam out, I took one last look at my parents. Amos had fallen over to the right since the crash. Mama had done the same thing, but to the left. They were leaning against each other. They looked like they had fallen asleep while resting their heads on each other. It was an "aww" moment if I ever saw one.
But that "aww" quickly zipped out of there when I remembered that Amos had killed Mama. And I had killed Amos.
Not exactly an "aww" moment when you add murder to the mix.
Then, my lungs began to remind me that I needed to breathe in order to keep living. I was near the bottom of the river and needed

to get my tail to the surface as fast as I could. Thankfully, Mama had taken Sarah and I to swim classes so I knew how to swim pretty good. I began frog-stroking my way up to the surface. With each stroke, my right arm burned like fire. I had definitely done something bad to it when the car fell.

I burst through the water. The river had carried me down some ways. The bridge we were on was about a football field's distance away now. I gently paddled to the river bank and climbed on up to dry ground. I sat down and let myself breathe a little. Then, I checked my arm. Bleeding. Didn't look too good.
But I was alive. And, though I didn't mean for the car to end up in the river, no one would find out what really happened to my parents. If they were ever found, everyone would just blame Amos' drunk driving. No one would ever think his eleven-year-old son put them there.
I was safe.
For some reason, that thought made me think about the police car that had been next to the bridge. I glanced back over just at the perfect time. The police car was puttering along, without its lights on, near the bridge. The car went right by the busted railing and, for a moment, I figured it would just keep on going.
But then, the car stopped. It backed up to the broken railing and parked.
The lights flicked on.
The policeman stepped out and stared at the railing for a good, long while. He scratched his head.
From that, I could tell the guy was thinking "What happened here?"
That meant that he didn't see anything. He didn't see me crash. He didn't see the car fall. And that also meant that he didn't see the car that was at the bottom of the river.
I let out a sigh.
And I headed home.
I headed home to lie to Sarah to her face. I headed home to pack up what we could and go live somewhere else before someone

came around asking questions. I headed home to start a new life
and forget everything that had ever happened that night.
But I never did forget.

<u>CHAPTER TWENTY</u>

I had finished telling Engel the truth. He stared at me, his eyes as big as dinner plates.

"You killed your father…" He said quietly.

"Yeah, I did!" I admitted. "And he deserved it, too! He killed my Mama! A sweet woman that never did nothin' bad to nobody!"

"Scoefield…" Engel said sadly. "I'm…I'm so sorry."

"Sorry doesn't help, Engel." I snorted back to him. "So, ya' understand why I gotta do this? I'm a terrible person. A terrible, terrible person. You…you're much better than me. And if I can just do a good thing by bitin' the dust with these crazies, I'll do it."

"You expect me to understand why you're going to kill yourself?" Engel questioned. "Scoefield, we're all terrible people. Remember what Sarah and I did to you?"

"*Don't* remind me." I growled.

"We're all sinners." Engel continued. "None of us are better than another. That's why we need a Saviour. Come home with me and Sarah and we'll tell you about Jesus."

"I think I've heard enough about 'im." I glared as I reached into my breast pocket for a match. Engel had given it to me before the mission started. I struck it against the wall and put it near the bomb.

Engel froze, his eyes terrified.

"Now go, Engel." I commanded. "Get out of here. I'm goin' with this bomb and if you don't start hittin' the pavement, you'll go with me."

"Scoefield, please." Engel started slowly walking towards me. "Don't do this. Just stop for a moment. What would Sarah say if she saw you right now?"

"She'd probably say 'good riddance'!" I shouted in despair. "Everythin' I touch just gets worse! And I'm done with it!"

I put the match to the bomb.

"Scoefield, NO!" Engel cried out.

I closed my eyes tight. I waited for the pain. The heat. The booming sound.

…None of that came.

I peeked through one eye at the bomb. The match had burned out. There was no fire. So, the bomb didn't explode.

Engel sighed in relief. But behind him, a creaking sound was heard.

Both me and Engel zipped our heads over to the stairs, where the sound had come from.

A German soldier was standing there, eyes gaping at us. Mouth open.

He saw the bomb.

He saw me with the match.

He probably heard Engel scream in English.

"Uh, *guten abend*?" Engel said nervously.

"ALARM!" The German soldier screamed as he ran back up the steps.

"We're caught!" My anger replaced my recent misery. I held my hand out to Engel. "Give me another match! We gotta light this now!"

"I don't have any!" Engel said in a panicked screech.

I blinked twice at him. "You brought only **one** match?!"

"I didn't think we'd need any more!" Engel threw his arms out.

I could've strangled him. I really could've strangled him.

But instead, I just shouted.

"RUN!"

We thankfully made it out of the bomb building without any Nazis getting in our way. But as soon as we made it to the streets, guards were popping up everywhere. Most of them with automatic weapons.

Gunfire was everywhere, shattering car windows and busting up sidewalk. Engel and I were screaming for our lives as we were running for the same thing. We ducked in and out of alleyways, behind cars, any shelter we could get to as we booked it out of town.

By some miracle, we were outrunning the Nazis and getting out of range. I guess they were cautious to run after us, thinking that there was no way a bomb had been brought in by only two enemy soldiers. There had to be more, right? Also, they were probably making sure that the generals and Hitler were kept safe.

As we were sprinting through Berlin, I saw that Engel was actually keeping up with me just fine. In fact, he was a little bit ahead of me. I took that moment to look back and I also saw that there were some guards chasing after us. Not too many, but more than us.

We made it to the outskirts of town. Before long, we were hitting the tree line.

"We're almost there!" Engel cheered as we trudged through the snow as fast as we could. "We just need to get back to the car and then we're racing to the Allies!"

I remained silent. My depression episode had passed in the sheer terror of being caught by the Nazis. I knew that Engel was going to talk to me about what I said before. Sarah would probably talk with me, too. I wasn't looking forward to that.

But, as I said, the episode had passed for the moment. If I really didn't care about living or dying, I would have just stayed put when the Nazis caught Engel and I. My thoughts were interrupted when I heard more gunfire. The guards behind us were closing in. They were in better shape than a P.O.W. escapee and a...well, Engel.

And then, I felt something slam into me from behind.

For a second, I just found myself falling. Face-first into the snow.

And then it came.

The pain.

I had been shot. Shot in the back.

And I couldn't hold back my scream as the agony exploded all around in me. The scream just kept growing and growing.

Engel, who had heard me, was climbing up a hill. He instantly spun around and saw me lying in the snow.

"Scoefield!" He cried as he slid back down the hill. He grabbed my shoulders trying to pull me to my feet.

"Get up! Get up, Scoefield!" Engel urged me. "They're right behind us!"

And I tried. I tried pushing my legs to get under me and start bolting away again.

But I realized something…

My legs weren't moving.

My head was telling them to jump up and speed away.

But they weren't doing anything. They weren't even twitching.

My muscular, powerful, tall legs were as good as dead.

"I…can't!" I grunted out in between deep, sharp breaths. "They won't…move! They won't move!"

Engel quickly checked my back where I had been shot. "You've been shot in the lower back." He muttered more to himself instead of me. "You're legs…may be paralyzed…"

"What?!" I gasped.

Engel whipped his head in the direction we were running from. German shouts were close. Very close.

"Stay here." Engel told me. "I'll take care of them."

"Take care of them?!" I shouted at him as he hopped through the snow. "You'll end up worse than me, you moron!"

Engel ignored me as he hid behind a tree, messing with the snow.

Germans were coming into view, all running at me.

In total, there were six. More were definitely on the way, but these six were the first to reach us.

They came into the clearing where I was lying. I held up my hands, showing I had no weapon.

Three had their guns trained on me while the other three were talking quietly to each other. Probably discussing what should happen now.

Then Engel jumped out from behind the tree.

The first reaction from the Germans was that of uncertain panic. Engel was dressed as a Gestapo agent. They had no idea if he was the real deal or not.

He wasn't.

He showed them this by firing snowballs at them.

I'm not kidding. ***Snowballs***.

But, they worked. They were thrown by a quick and strong arm. Each snowball plowed right into each of the six German's eyes. For a moment, they were all blind. Each of them tried to wipe the icy snow from their eyes.

That gave Engel some few precious moments. He put up his dukes, boxer style, and charged at them.

The first thing he did was disarm them of their weapons. He would take and throw a gun, or punch and kick it out of the Nazis' hands. Then, he went to town on them. Like a professional boxer, Engel began slamming his small fists right into the noses, throats, ribs, jaws, and backs of those six men.

At this point, the Germans had the snow mostly wiped away from their eyes. They began to get their wits back. But they were angry. They were panicking. Both don't do well in a fight. Though they outnumbered Engel, they were swinging wildly, missing him entirely. In fact, they were actually hitting each other, knocking each other in the dirt. All the while, Engel would bounce around, dodging, and jumping back in to give several quick jabs to sensitive areas.

I was so impressed.

Before long, Engel had taken six, military-trained, Germans and had them lying in the snow. None dead, like I would have done, but all taken care of.

"I'll be a monkey's uncle." I groaned quietly. "The twerp is actually a man now."

"More of them will be here soon." Engel ran back up to me, panting a bit. "You can't move at all?"

It was so painful to try, but I tried again anyway. I kicked, ran, jumped, even tried to just twitch…

Nothing. Absolutely nothing.

I put my head in the snow, realizing what would probably happen to me.

"No." I said softly. "My legs are gone. I'm useless. Dead-weight. They'll find me and they'll shoot me."

At that, Engel began to turn into that little kid I remembered from New York. His mouth drooped into a frown and tears started to build up in his eyes.

For once, it was nice. It was nice to be cried over. It was nice that someone cared enough to be sad for me. So, for that moment, I let him cry a bit before saying:

"Leave me, Henry."

"What?" He croaked.

"Leave me." I repeated. "I'm…done. I can't run. Can't get up. This is it for me. And I deserve it."

I looked Henry right in the eyes. "I've hurt people all my life. I killed my own Pop. Got other friends of mine killed. This is what I get for it. But not you. Ever since I met you, you've tried helpin' people. Why, you helped Sarah the first night ya' met her. You did hurt me. You really did hurt me for what you two did. But…I forgive ya'. I really do. It took me a while, but I'm lettin' it go."

I could feel tears start pushing at my own eyes. "Just…Just tell Sarah that I'm sorry, will ya'? I should'a come seen her one last time. I was just so stupid and now…it's too late. Go, Henry. Go."

I guess I expected Henry to bawl. Break out in crocodile tears like he always used to do.

I was surprised at what he really did.

The boy drew in a sharp breath, his tears gone. A terrible look came on his face that made me think he was having bad gas or something. I guess it was his "determined face". Henry waltzed right up to me in the snow, jabbed a finger in my face and said:

"Now you listen to me, Bradley Leonard Scoefield." He said with a strong voice. "I did not come all of this way to just leave you behind in the snow. Like it or not, you are my brother-in-law, and I intend to bring my family home."

And before I could say anything in reply, Henry took both hands and clasped them under my arms. And with a mighty, straining pull, Henry began lifting me off of the ground.

Which is crazy. I weighed one hundred and ninety pounds. Mostly muscle, of course. Henry weighs, like, five pounds, and that's when he's soaking wet.

But he was lifting me off of the ground. I'm pretty sure his eyes were popping out of his head while he was doing it. His breathing sounded like an ice-cream maker. I even think I heard him strain out a fart or two. It was a disgusting experience.

But he got me up in the air. And with some unseen strength, that boy lifted me onto his shoulder.

Henry Engel was carrying me.

"I'm especially not letting you go now." Henry wheezed, trying to breathe. "I've been waiting to hear 'I forgive you' for ten years!"

I was too shocked to say anything. That, and, in pain. When you've got a bullet in your back, being lifted off the ground is agonizing. So I just marveled as Henry began marching uphill with me over his shoulder. Henry really did expect to carry me back to the stolen car where we could get away to freedom.

And that would have been so wonderful if it had happened that way.

But it didn't.

See, because, when we reached the top of the hill, we saw someone there.

A German soldier, aiming his rifle right at us.

As soon as I spotted him, I flung my hand to Henry's pistol that was attached to his belt. I whipped it out, aimed, and fired.

But the Nazi fired first.

CHAPTER TWENTY-ONE

Henry and I rolled back down the hill. It wasn't a large hill, but it felt like we were toppling down a mountain. Plus, there was a bullet in my back, so I was screaming all the way down it. The world rolled around several times before I plowed into the snow, gasping in agony. But as soon as I recovered, I snapped my head up and whirled my pistol to aim at the top of the hill.
As it turned out, my shot was good. The German was face-down in the snow, his rifle lying out of reach.
For a moment, I cheered.
Then, I saw him.
Henry was lying next to me. He was on his back, staring up.
He had a blood stain on his shirt that kept getting bigger. Henry had been shot. Right in the stomach.
I used my arms to push myself closer to him.
"Henry!" I cried, putting my hands on his gunshot. I needed to keep pressure on the wound. "Henry, ya' with me?! C'mon, kid, snap out of it!"
"I'm still here, Scoefield." Henry said. He was creepily calm. His eyes slowly moved to me.
"Don't ya' worry 'bout a thing, Henry." I told him, feeling my throat close up. "We'll get ya' to Taggart. Taggart'll know what to do."
Henry simply shook his head at that. "No, Scoefield. I can feel it…I'm dying."
"You're not dying." I started choking on my words. "It just hurts. You'll be all-right."
Henry gave me a small smile. "It's okay, Scoefield. Really, it is. I'm not afraid of dying. I'm not even upset. I was able to live for Christ while I was on this Earth. I was able to serve Him and do His work. Write godly songs. I was able to be married to a beautiful, wonderful woman for ten years. Have such dear, sweet children."
Henry then reached out with a shaking hand and placed it on my

shoulder. "And I was able to get my best friend back. I am content with going to the Lord's paradise now."

Then, a frown sprouted on Henry's face. "The part that I am sad about is that all of you will be left behind here. You'll mourn over me. I don't want you to, but I know it will happen."

I couldn't answer him. I was full-fledged crying now. Just like he used to do all the time.

"Scoefield…" Henry said sadly. "Don't cry. It's okay. I'll be okay. But you…I don't know about you, to be honest."

Then, an idea flashed in his eyes. He slowly fiddled around with his pockets and brought out his small Bible. He handed it to me.

"If you make it back home, you read this." Henry ordered. "I mean it, Scoefield. Read it. Start with the Gospel of John and the book of Romans. If you don't make it back home, remember these verses: 'For God so loved the world, that He gave His only begotten Son, that whosoever believeth in Him should not perish, but have everlasting life. For God sent not His Son into the world to condemn the world; but that the world through Him might be saved. He that believeth on Him is not condemned: but he that believeth not is condemned already, because he hath not believed in the name of the only begotten Son of God. And this is the condemnation, that light is come into the world, and men loved darkness rather than light, because their deeds were evil'. That was John 3:16 – 20. Listen to those words. Meditate on those words. And, when you're ready, accept those words and call out to Christ. 'For whosoever shall call upon the name of the Lord shall be saved'."

I still couldn't answer him. I just kept blubbering and bawling. Then, Henry began messing with his hands. He was pulling at something on his left hand.

His wedding ring.

"One…one more thing." He started taking bigger breaths. "Sarah…Give this to Sarah."

He put the ring in my hand. Then, he dug something out of his pocket. A folded-up piece of paper that had "Now I'm Here" written on it.

"And this." Henry put the piece of paper in my hand. "Tell her that I love her and that I will…will see her again someday. Tell the children that I love them, too. They'll all need you, Scoefield." Then, with his final breaths, Henry smiled at me. "And I know… you'll think it's sappy. But I love you too, Scoefield. You're my friend and my big brother. I hope…I really hope that I'll be able to welcome you into heaven one day. Do that for me…please?"
I didn't get the chance to answer.
Henry died in my arms.

…How do you undo something horrible that can't be undone? You can't. It's that simple.
But don't you wish that you could? With all of your heart, don't you **wish** you could undo it? Doesn't it make you stay up all night in frustration and in tears and you wish you could just sleep? But you can't. Because what's done is done. And even though it is so horrible, it can't be undone.
My name is Bradley Scoefield.
And I am a murderer.
And now you know why I say that.
I murdered my Pop. There's no question there.
Indirectly, Calvin, Sheldon, Larkin, Pratt, and Trevor all died because of me, too. That blood is on my hands.
And now, Henry's.
So many people tell me that I shouldn't blame myself for Henry's death. He was shot by a German soldier. But he wouldn't have even been there if I hadn't smashed up Ronny's bar.
He wouldn't have been there if it wasn't for me. He was a better man than I will ever be.
And, Henry, I know you can't hear me…
But I'm sorry. I'm so sorry.

<u>CHAPTER TWENTY-TWO</u>

I didn't get captured by the Nazis that day. More came and trained their guns on me, but I was rescued by Taggart, Tim, and Johnny.
Those three had heard the shooting. They snuck closer to check it out. They found me just in time.
As it turns out, Tim really is an excellent shot. Nailed nearly all of them Nazis before any of them knew what was happening.
I was rescued.
We abandoned the mission, seeing we had failed miserably and knew we wouldn't get another chance to try it. Especially with my legs not working. We drove to the front where the Allies were pushing through. Thanks to Taggart, we got through the German lines without much trouble. Once we were on the other side, Johnny took charge and we were taken in to safety. I was taken to a hospital where my bullet wound was checked.
The damage was bad. My legs really were lost and they weren't coming back. The bullet had been lodged in my spine and everything below my waste had been zapped.
So…I was sent home.

Johnny, Taggart, and Tim all stayed behind to fight. I was flying home alone. I was awarded the purple heart medal for the injury I had suffered. It was a great honor to have. Many higher-ups thanked me for my sacrifice and my service. I had been treated pretty well.
But when I wheeled onto American soil and saw my baby sister…
None of those honors meant anything.
There she was, tall and more beautiful than ever. Seriously, Sarah had grown so much. She had to be easily taller than Henry was.
Her hair was long and looking like it belonged to a movie-star.
Worry-lines were all over her face, but her eyes still sparkled.
Or maybe…that was the tears. But I'll get to that later.
In each of her hands, she held another hand. The hands of her

babies.
Three of them. Lucas, Gary, and Michaela.

Lucas was tall. Just like Sarah. His face was strikingly similar to Henry's, but his nose was pointed, like Sarah's. His hair was dark, like Sarah's, but not curly. It was wavy. His eyes, were the same green as Sarah's, but held all the emotion of Henry's. Lucas looked older and stronger than he should have. From what I recalled, he was only nine years old. He was standing in front of Sarah and the other kids. He was doing a little dance with his legs. It really looked weird. Like he had to go to the bathroom, or something. But, after looking at him for a second, I realized that he was nervous. Eager to see his father. Scared that he wouldn't. Gary and Michaela were the ones who were holding Sarah's hands. Gary, even though he was Lucas' twin, looked almost opposite of him. He was short and chunky. He had the curly hair that both Henry and Sarah shared. His face looked closer to Sarah's than Henry's, but he had the dark brown eyes that Henry had.
Michaela was a spitting image of her mother. She looked exactly like Sarah when she was seven. She was thin, pale, and very fragile-looking. Her nose was pointed and she had curly brown hair.
It creeped me out. It was like seeing 1923 Sarah come zooming up to the future.

I said nothing as I wheeled down the ramp to them. Sarah was already gasping, seeing me in a wheelchair. She was looking around anxiously for Henry. But she didn't ask. I guess she was scared to, knowing what the answer might be.
Lucas' dancing got more violent as I came closer. He looked down-right terrified. Gary and Michaela just kept looking up at their mother.
Then, the words came:
"Where's my Papa?"
It was Lucas. He came walking up to me and asked it very

directly.

For that, I gave the tiniest hint of a smile. He was already acting like a man, asking me questions like that.

But the smile blew away in the next second and I wheeled past Lucas, ignoring him.

I went straight up to Sarah. I held out my hand.

I gave her Henry's wedding ring.

And Sarah fell to her knees, sobbing.

I tried to get back into living life in New York City. Only, except of being able to walk. I was stuck in a chair. So, I couldn't work. Sarah was forced to do that since Henry was gone. She had to work two jobs. A waitress and a house-cleaner, just to make ends meet. My wages as a retired army captain helped, but Sarah still had to work so hard.

Lucas and Gary were old enough to look after themselves and Michaela at home, so I wasn't stuck babysitting them when they were home from school. I had loads of time to myself. So I did what I felt like doing. I didn't talk to anyone. I didn't laugh. I didn't play poker anymore. I just went to the bars.

I got up in the morning, ate, drank, drank, drank, drank, and went back to bed.

That was my life.

I felt nothing but grief and guilt. So many people in my life had been killed because of me.

And because of that, I drowned my pain in whiskey. Until whiskey had a hold on me so deep that it was like oxygen. Let me tell all of you: nothing good comes from drinking. Alcohol is good when doctors use it on you, but drinking does nothing but poison you. You know why? Because it actually is **poison**.

Guess what doctors use alcohol for? To **kill** bad viruses. That's what alcohol does.

And I was poisoning myself and everyone around me for that time.

For almost two months, I treated Sarah and her kids like garbage. I would come home drunk sometimes and call them all filthy things.

Lucas, who had once looked up to me, hated my guts and never wanted to be around me. Gary and Michaela would always cry when I yelled at them. They would cry and cry and cry.
Sarah was just miserable, but she was always too tired to do anything about me.
Oh, if Henry had saw me…He would have kicked me out of that house faster than you can say "tell it to Sweeney!".
Forgive me, Henry.
Which reminds me, I never did read the Gospel of John or the book of Romans during that time. I didn't want to think about anything that was associated with Henry's death.
At the mention of Henry's name, I would either blow up like a volcano or my eyes would become waterfalls. There was no in between.
I forced Henry's kids to never speak of their father around me. I bullied Sarah into not talking about her husband.
There was just too much guilt hanging over my head for that.

To give you an idea of what I was like, I'll tell you of a particular day when I decided to go out and drown myself in drinking, but didn't.
But only one day. I don't want to talk about how I used to be. It's shameful, it's sad, and it only gets people down.
And that is not the point of this book.
I wheeled out of the house on a Tuesday. A Tuesday in February. Sarah had already been at work for three hours and the kids had been at school for one. I wheeled my way into the city. It was a long and tiring way to get into the city, but my arms were still very strong. It was a good workout to keep me from getting too out of shape.
Once I was in the city, I started heading for Ronny's bar. Even after all this time, Ronny was still in business. I had promised him that I would never smash up his bar again (and how could I?), and Ronny forgave me and let me start coming. At first, he put a shortage on my drinking just to make sure. Now, he was fine with letting me have as much as I could pay for, which wasn't all *that*

much.

I was about to turn the corner to Ronny's bar when I saw a familiar face.

Nancy Barber. An old friend of mine that I worked with at the old diner, back before the war.

She was standing across the street at a grocery store. She was waiting outside with two bags full of groceries. And she had gotten big. As in fat. Her belly looked swollen and ready to pop. Still, I had changed a lot, too.

I glanced at Ronny's bar and figured it could wait a little bit. I wheeled across the street and through the parking lot. Her eyes spotted mine and she gave a small smile. I smiled back at her.

"Well, I thought I heard you were back in town." She said happily. "How are you, *Captain* Scoefield?"

I waved dismissively at her. "Eh, stop it with all that. I'm still just 'Scoefield' to ya', Nancy. And I'm…fine."

Nancy's smile looped down into a frown. "Mm-hmmm. Just fine, huh?"

"Well, ya' can see I'm not exactly all in one piece." I grumbled. "But enough about me. How've you been?"

Nancy smiled again. "Oh, blessed beyond my imagination. The Lord's been good and I'm not ashamed to tell people that."

I was blown back by that. The Nancy that I remembered…well, she wasn't the churchy type. Hated church, in fact. She went to a few, but unless they were Negro churches, they treated her terribly.

White people were pretty cruel to Negro people back then, and Nancy was no exception.

"When did you get religion?" I shot at her.

"I didn't." Nancy said back. "I got a *relationship*. A relationship with Jesus Christ."

"Same thing." I muttered. "But when did that happen?"

"You should ask your sister." Nancy told me. "She's the one who got me going to Bible Baptist Church. There, I got gloriously saved."

"You go to Sarah's church?" I gaped.

"You would know that if you ever went." Nancy pooched her lips a bit. "I miss seeing you. And you need to have a talk with my husband."

"*Husband*?" It just kept getting bigger and bigger. "When did *that* happen?"

"When Henry, God rest his blessed soul, invited a wonderful man to church." Nancy explained. "And he got saved as well. Let me tell you, Scoefield, he has a heart of gold and-oh! There he is now!"

Nancy pointed slightly. It was hard for her to do since both of her hands were holding sacks of groceries. But after squinting down the parking lot, I spotted a car heading towards us. The car stopped within a few feet of us and the man was slowly getting out of the car.

"So I guess you're not Nancy Barber anymore, huh?" I glanced at her.

Nancy showed off a sparkling wedding ring. "No, sir. Nancy Butters, now."

"*Butters*?" My eyes probably popped out of my head at her.

Then I glanced back at the car. Fat, bald Wesley Butters stepped out of the car.

He still wore the same, old hat.

And somehow, he had gotten even fatter than last time I saw him.

"*Last time I saw him...*" I groaned in my head. Last time I saw him, I was plowing my fist in his face.

Then I looked closely at his nose. It was crooked. Stuck that way. Bent to the side like…

Well, like someone had nailed him in the face over and over. I swallowed guiltily.

"Hey, darlin'!" Nancy waved excitedly.

"Hi, honey!" Butters called back. "Who's your friend?"

Then, Butters got a good look at me. His eyes popped and a terrible look came over his face. He turned pale like a bed sheet. Then, his foot began tapping.

He remembered me.

"M-Mr. Scoefield!" Butters stuttered in a panic. "I-I mean, no! Not 'Mr. Scoefield'! Just Scoefield! Right! I remember, sir! I'm s-so sorry to have, um…"

Butters' foot was tapping a mile a minute. He was sweating like he was in summer, but it was winter out.

I just lowered my head, not looking at him.

"Hey, honey, why don't I just get those for you and wait in the car?!" Butters squeaked, talking to Nancy.

Without another word, Butters sped toward us, snatched the groceries out of Nancy's hands, zipped back to the car, stuffed the groceries in the back seat, and flew into the driver seat.

A moment of quiet passed as Nancy and I sat there. I didn't say anything. I was afraid that Nancy knew what I had done. And sure enough, she did.

"He's terrified of you." She spoke finally. "He has nightmares of you, sometimes."

I still didn't say anything. I didn't know I had been so scary to him on that night.

"When I first heard what happened, I thought 'Nah. Not Scoefield'." Nancy sighed. "But I remembered how you treated them Tanner boys. They deserved it, all-right. But…it was still pretty rough. You hurt them bad. And you hurt Wesley worse that night."

I still said nothing. How could I say anything?

"His nose is stuck that way, in case you were wondering." Nancy kept going. "It's hard for him to breathe out of it."

"I'm sorry." I finally spoke.

"Don't tell me." Nancy looked at me. "Tell him. And tell your sister and your nephews and niece."

I looked up at her, a little confused. "What're ya' talkin' about?"

"You think I don't hear what kind of trouble you bring to those poor babies?" Nancy shot an angry scowl at me. "What kind of trouble you bring Sarah? When you first came back, I wouldn't stop asking about you. And you know what I heard? 'He's just like Pop was: an angry drunk'. Shame on you for that. Sarah and her

babies are precious. She's done you nothing but good and you treat her with anger and drunkenness? Shame on you. You better put a lid on both of those things. Because if you don't, I'll start praying to the Lord Almighty that He sends *so **much*** trouble your way that you have no choice but to turn to Him for help."
Nancy pointed a finger in my face. "And believe me, Bradley Leonard Scoefield, you do not want me to pray that. God answers my prayers."
I could feel myself getting angry at her. Instinctively. It just happened whenever someone spoke against me like. I felt excuses bubbling up. Bitter words boiling up.
Of course, I never got a chance to use them.
"Don't you start." Nancy waved a finger at me. "Another thing you do not want is to start yelling at a pregnant lady. I've got hormones going through me that will turn me into a raging mama-bear in seconds. Do not start yelling at me, Scoefield."
That actually stopped my anger in its steps. I glanced back down at her gut. Then back at her.
"Oh." I grunted, not thinking. "I just thought you had gotten fat."
…That's something you should never say to a pregnant woman.

    I decided to skip the bar that day. I had gotten enough guilt driven into me (and a hard slap by Nancy after I had called her fat) that I wasn't feeling like drinking.
Which is weird. Drinking usually made me feel better.
But I just wandered around for a while, trying to think. Trying to make myself feel better.
Of all the great ideas to make me feel better, I went to the cemetery.
Great place to put a smile on you, isn't it?
I visited a couple of graves that I knew.

LEPPY WILKINSON

1843 – 1923

My grandfather. Grandpa Leppy. He was always a cheerful guy. Liked church but didn't like my pop. Then again, who *did* like my pop besides my mama?

Speaking of which, the next grave I visited was…

WINIFRED SCOEFIELD

1896 – 1924

My mama. There was one made for her, but not Amos. He didn't get one because no one cared enough about him to buy a tombstone for him. And you know what? I was okay with that. I didn't want to go to the cemetery to see my mama's grave and have to see his, too.

Lastly, I went to…

HENRY ENGEL

1916 – 1944

That was the hardest one to see. Henry's body had been left in Germany, but we did have a funeral service for him there in New York City. The church had raised up money to buy Henry a tombstone right next to his parents' grave.

I stopped there the longest.

I didn't say anything. I just sat in my wheelchair and looked at his grave.

Thinking.

Remembering.

Stuff like that.

I figured, after half an hour or so, it was best to go home. Nothing in the cemetery was making me feel better. Big shock there, right?

I began to wheel back the way I came. I was going to take one last look at my mama's grave when…

I noticed someone standing in front of it.

It was a policeman. A policeman that looked familiar.

I stopped for a moment, wondering if I was wrong and he was looking at some other grave.

I squinted at the tombstone and, sure enough, it was my mama's. Just as I was wondering why this copper was looking at my mama's grave, he spotted me.

"Sorry. Can I help you?" He asked as he munched on a carrot that was in his hand.

I immediately recognized him. Call it a great memory or just bitterness, but I remembered him instantly. He was the policeman that had told me I was just like my father, back when I smashed up Ronny's bar ten years ago.

I glared at him. "Don't need anythin' from you, Buttons."

The policeman's look changed. I could tell by his look that he remembered me, too.

"Oh yes, the Scoefield punk." He curled his lips. "Not busy busting up any bars, I hope."

I simply spat in his direction. I didn't want to talk to this guy. But I did have one question for him.

"Why ya' lookin' at my mama's grave?" I questioned him.

The policeman turned his face back to the tombstone. His face sunk again in sadness.

"I come here often to pay my respects." He said quietly. "It's probably guilt, to be honest."

"Guilt?" I laughed. "Makes sense. Where were you when Amos would beat her? Treat her like trash? Where were you when we were all cryin' through the night because of Amos, Buttons? Probably just gettin' fat on doughnuts, right?"

The policeman swelled up with anger. He puffed up like a balloon. It was kinda funny to see, but I could tell he was serious.

He jabbed a finger at me. "You hold your tongue, boy! I've never heard such disrespectful words! I do my job and I like to think I

do it well, but…I just didn't know about what Amos did to
Winnie."
"Ya' didn't see that he was drinkin' all the time?" I mocked. "That
he was angry all the time? That he was gettin' himself in jail all
the time?"
"Well, maybe I should keep a close eye on you, then." The
policeman shot back. "Because you are fitting pretty good into
your father's shoes."
"Hey! Ya' better watch what you say, Buttons!" I shouted in rage
at him. "I ain't nothin' like Amos Scoefield!"
"I have a name." The policeman kept his cool. "And it's not
'Buttons'. It's Matthias. And, yes you are, son. Like you just said,
you're drinking all the time. You're angry all the time. You've
been in jail, too. You are **exactly** like your father. How long will it
be until that dear sister of yours turns out like your mother?"
"That'll never happen!" I just kept getting angrier. "I'm a good
man!"
"You've got quite the temper there." Matthias replied. "You've no
respect for anybody. Does that sound like a 'good man' to you?"
"Leave me alone!" I shouted at Matthias. "You've got no idea
what I've been through! You've been sittin' on your keister here in
New York while I was gettin' shot at by Germans! I lost these legs
because of them! So, I reckon that I've got some pretty good
excuses why I am the way I am! Ya' got me?!"
Matthias was still unfazed by my shouting. He just took another
bite out of his carrot and shook his head. "You won't believe me
when I say this…" He spoke quietly as he chewed his carrot. "But
that's almost exactly what your father said to me years ago."
I wasn't sure what he was talking about.
*"Why in blazes would my pop say anythin' about Germans and
gettin' shot at?"* I wondered. *"It's not like he was ever in war…
right?"*
"I knew your father very well." Matthias interrupted my thoughts.
"Amos was…a friend of mine once. We went to school together.
We graduated together. He was the best man at my wedding. And
then…we were drafted together."

I was shaking my head the more he talked. "Nah, nah. My pop never talked about you. My pop was never in war."
"Oh, yes he was." Matthias continued. "We fought in France during World War I. It wasn't called that at the time, though. We went into that war as best friends, but we both came home changed."
Matthias knocked on his right leg with his knuckles. The sound wasn't normal. It sounded like…metal.
"My change was physical." Matthias continued. "Couldn't run anymore. Couldn't do a lot of things I used to. Amos, though? He lost himself. Turned to drinking. Turned angry. Bitter. Beat his wife. Smashed up bars. And you know what he always said to me when I threw him in that jail cell?"
Matthias looked me dead in the eye.
"'You know that I've got pretty good reasons for being the way I am'." He said slowly. "Not too far off from what you just said. But you know what they say about the apple falling from the tree."
Matthias started to walk away from me. It was then that I saw how he limped on his right leg.
"I just hoped…" He said over his shoulder. "That the way you always talked about how awful he was…well, that it would keep you from turning into him. Guess I was wrong."

CHAPTER TWENTY-THREE

I came home that night very sour. It had begun to rain and I was caught out in it. Completely soaked, I wheeled up to the front door and banged on it with my fist. Nobody answered it. I banged again. Still no one.

I swore to myself and fumbled around in my pockets for the house key. I finally got it out and jammed it into the key hole. I pushed the door in and wheeled up the ramp. As I shook the rain from my hair, I wheeled into the living room. I knew that Gary and Michaela were probably already hitting the hay, but Lucas was still up. He was sitting on the floor, reading a book.

"Geek." I scoffed at him.

Lucas' eyes flicked up from the pages with an angry scowl.

"*Schurke*." He spoke back.

"What did ya' say, pipsqueak?!" I raised a fist at him.

Lucas didn't even budge. He just continued glaring at me. "I was just saying 'hello' in German, Uncle Scoefield." He said politely, but I could tell that anger was boiling in him.

I narrowed my eyes at him. I knew that wasn't what he said, but I couldn't prove it.

So, I left him alone. I wheeled into the kitchen to find my dinner.

I glanced on the table. Nothing.

I peeked over at the stove. Nothing.

I looked all over the kitchen counters. Nothing.

I checked in the ice-box. Nothing.

No dinner for me anywhere.

My sour mood turned even worse.

"Boy!" I yelled at Lucas. "Where's your mother?"

Lucas tensed at my yelling, but kept his eyes on his book.

"Upstairs." He muttered quietly.

"Gargh!" I fumed. Going upstairs was hard for me. True, Sarah had the stairs replaced with a ramp so I could make it up and down the 'stairs', but it wasn't a picnic doing it.

Still, dinner was more important than having a hard time getting up the stairs.

So, I pushed myself up the ramp and got to the second floor. I wheeled past Lucas and Gary's room and Michaela's room. I came to Sarah's and pushed the door opened.

She was sitting in a chair, still in her waitress outfit, fast asleep.

"I think **now** would be a good time to make dinner, don't **you**, Sarah?!" I shouted at her.

Sarah jolted from her sleep and fell off of the chair.

"What in blue blazes, Bradley?!" Sarah yelled back. "You could've given me a heart attack!"

Then, she softened as she stood up, looking at me.

"You're soaking wet." She noted.

"Ya' don't say!" I snarled at her. "Someone kept me stuck outside in the rain!"

Sarah tensed. "You have a key, don't you?"

"It's not easy for me to get a key out of my pockets!" I raised my voice at her. "Don't you see the wheelchair?!"

"Oh, I'm sorry." Sarah spat sarcastically. "I didn't realize that a wheelchair means you can't move your arms either, you lazy tub of booze."

"You watch your mouth!" I hissed at her. "Ya' better show me some respect, woman!"

"'**Woman**'?" Sarah furrowed her eyebrows. "What am I to you? Your personal butler?"

"Well, ya' do make my dinner." I growled. "Speaking of which, chop chop! I'm starvin' here!"

"Oh, of course, your majesty." Sarah taunted, bowing to me. "I'll just get back to serving you after I've put in **fifteen** hours at work today!"

Sarah suddenly rubbed her chin, like she was thinking. "Oh, and what have you done? Have you washed the laundry? Cleaned the dishes? Watched the kids? Helped Lucas with his homework? Have you done anything useful today?"

Then, her eyes fired up in anger. "Not. A. Single. Thing. And you expect me to do everything when I am dead-tired. But, in order to show you patience and love, because I'm a Christian and your sister, fine. I'll go make you some dinner."

She bumped past me, still steaming.

But I was steaming, too. No, scratch that, I was already on fire. "Hey! Don't you talk to me like that! Get back here!" I shouted at her as I chased after her with my wheelchair. Sarah stopped at the stairs, looked back at me, and folded her arms.

"You have no idea what I went through over in Germany!" I pointed a finger at her. "I went through things that are one hundred times worse than what you could ever go through over here! Not to mention I lost my legs! So maybe I'm allowed a little bit something extra! So watch your tongue, Sarah!"

"I'll ignore the fact that you think losing my husband is something small." Sarah sneered back at me. "But I'll say what I want to say until you stop drinking. And until you start helping out around here. And until you stop acting like Pop!"

That did it. It pushed me too far.

I had already been compared to Amos too much that day.

In a fiery fury, I struck her. I back-handed her across the jaw. In an instant, Sarah flew off of her feet and began crashing down the ramp. She was smacking her head all over the wall and hard, wooden ramp.

Finally, she collapsed hard on the first floor.

…At the feet of Lucas.

Lucas was at the base of the ramp. He stared at his mother in horror, fearing the worst.

And in that moment, my eyes were opened.

I had experienced this very same thing, over twenty years ago.

But this time, I was in my father's place.

"SARAH!" I screamed after her. I pushed myself off of my wheelchair and fell down the ramp to get to her as fast as I could. I banged myself up a little, tumbling down that ramp, but there was something much worse on my mind. After I came down the ramp, I crawled to my baby sister.

"Sarah! Sarah! Are ya' okay?! Answer me!"

Sarah was bleeding from her head, just like my mama had been twenty years ago.

I began crying. "Please, Sarah! Don't do this! Please! I'm sorry!"

Then, Sarah began to lift herself up.

"It's okay." She muttered quietly. "It's okay. I'm fine. I'm not too hurt."

Her voice was etched with pain. I could easily hear it. She was hurt.

"Lucas!" I turned to the boy. "Call an ambulance! Quick! Call 911 now!"

Lucas only nodded and then ran towards the kitchen.

"Bradley, stop." Sarah sat up and looked at me. "That really hurt, I'm going to be honest, but I don't need an ambulance. I'll be okay."

I took her in my arms and hugged her tightly. "I'm so sorry! I didn't mean to do that! Please forgive me! Don't die on me! I'm so sorry! I'm so sorry!"

"Bradley…" Was all Sarah said back.

The ambulance got there in not too long of a time. They checked Sarah and told us all that she was fine. She had a nasty gash on her head, but nothing serious. Not even a concussion. They bandaged her up and left.

Sarah was told, just for good measure, not to go to bed for a while. And since it was a school-night, Lucas couldn't stay up with her. So I did when the boy went to bed.

Sarah and I stayed in the kitchen. I sat near the table, ringing my hands in guilt while Sarah was making me dinner.

"I'm glad you're okay." I said quietly, not looking at her.

"I told you I was." Sarah spoke back just as quietly. "I was born a Scoefield, you know. We're tough."

A flash of a smile came across my face. Then it was gone.

"Yeah."

"Are…you okay?" Sarah asked me, turning from the stove to look at me.

"Yeah."

"That didn't sound convincing." Sarah said plainly. "Talk to me,

Bradley."

"It's nothin'." I said back.

Sarah walked over to the table and put my supper on it.

"It's not nothing." Sarah put her arm on my shoulder. "I know that you're not okay. Talk to me."

"What do ya' want me to say?" I finally looked at her. "You were right. I am actin' like Pop. No, worse. I'm just like him."

Sarah looked guilty. "I shouldn't have said that. I'm sorry, Bradley. I was just angry."

"But you were right." I said again. "Another guy told me the same thing today. An ol' buddy of his. I'm just like Pop. I'm just like Amos Scoefield."

It was the first time I had ever admitted that. I was exactly like my terrible father.

And it was something I could not bear. I began sobbing again. Uncontrollably. Hopelessly.

Sarah did her best to soothe me by holding me and telling me it would be okay. But I knew better.

Ever since Bratt's death, there would be this dark, deep, bottomless despair that would creep up on me. Over and over I would fight against the terrible dread that was eating at me. Sometimes I'd win. Sometimes I'd let it come over me.

But right then…I felt like I had completely fallen into that pit. And I didn't think I was coming out of it.

I came to a solution much like the one I had in Germany. My time was done. It was time I just give up and die. But I couldn't do it while anyone was home. Sarah left for work before sunrise. That was easy. Then, the kids left on the bus to school around eight o' clock.

I was left alone in the house.

I went to my safe and put in the combination. Once it was opened, I found one of my favorite guns that I had used in the war. An M1 Garand.

I snatched it, wheeled back near my bed, and began cleaning it. I took it a part, cleaning each individual piece. Once I was finished with that, I put it back together.

I loaded it.

I put the barrel of the gun against my chest. I closed my eyes and took a deep breath.

I put my finger on the trigger…

"Don't. You. Dare." Sarah's voice suddenly broke through to me. I snapped my head back over to the door to my bedroom. Sarah was standing there in her house-cleaner outfit. Her eyes were filled with out-right terror. She was shaking slightly.

As it turns out, her boss had sent her home about as soon as she got to work. Sarah was still wobbly from hitting her head and her boss told her she needed some rest.

If her boss hadn't have done that day, I wouldn't be here.

"Put that gun down now." Sarah said so softly I could barely hear it.

I didn't say anything back to her. I just dropped the gun. It clattered on the ground.

As soon as it did, Sarah ran in and embraced me.

"What did you think you were you doing?" She asked me in a broken voice, still very quiet. "You think shooting yourself would make my life better?"

I didn't answer her.

"Bradley, I can't do this." She was full crying now. "I can't keep carrying myself, the kids, and now you. I'm at the end of my rope. I can't have you doing this. I love you too much."

"I'm sorry." I finally said something.

"No you're not." Sarah saw right through my lie. "No you're not." Sarah then pulled away from me and looked at me through red, puffy eyes. "What do I have to do, Bradley? What do I have to do to help you?"

"Nothing can help me." I told her, matter-of-factly. "Not even Jesus can help me."

Sarah took a sharp breath in. Then, she slightly calmed as a thought came over her.

"You want to bet on that?" She asked me.

"What do you mean?"

"Come to church with me tomorrow." Sarah told me. "Come to church just one time tomorrow. That's all I'm asking, Bradley. Just come to church with me tomorrow."
"But Sarah-"
"You are either coming with me tomorrow…" Sarah told me sternly. "Or I'm telling Pastor Benson that you are suicidal. He'll come and talk to you about it. Either way, you'll be listening to that man. Would you rather it to be in a crowd where he's not staring at you constantly, or one-on-one with just you two in this room?"
I took a deep breath.
"Fine."

CHAPTER TWENTY-FOUR

I went to church for the first time on February 14th, 1945. It was Valentine's Day, so the preacher was going to talk about love stuff.
I grumbled, thinking about that. The one thing I had no need to hear about was love.
But I promised Sarah I would go and listen. That's what I was going to do.
I didn't dress up. Didn't feel like it and I didn't want to go through the extra trouble. I wheeled into the big church behind Sarah and the kids.
I had asked them if it was okay to sit on the back row. Knowing Henry, they had probably sat on the front row every service. But I didn't want to be seen there. I was too embarrassed about my legs and feeling guilty just by being in Henry's church. Nancy saw us and decided to come sit right next to Sarah. Next to her was Butters. He looked nervous being so close to me, but I made sure not to look at him.
We had a time of welcoming. So many people came to greet me and shake my hand during that time. It already made me grumpy. I didn't want to meet these people. I didn't want them asking me questions or anything.
But they did.
They were too friendly to not.
After a couple "meh"s and "get outta' my face"s, they finally let me be.
After that, we did some singing. One of them sounded familiar. It was one of the same ones that Trevor sang at Bratt's funeral.
Then, finally, we got to the preaching.

"Take your Bibles, turn to Genesis 42." Pastor Benson began. "Genesis 42…And we're going to start with just two verses. Once you've found your place, Genesis 42, go ahead and stand with me."

Everybody stood with their Bibles but me. If you're betting I wasn't standing because I didn't like church, I don't think you've been reading good enough.

"We're going to read verses 7 and 8 this morning. Genesis 42:7 – 8. 'And Joseph saw his brethren, and he knew them, but made himself strange unto them, and spake roughly unto them; and he said unto them, Whence come ye? And they said, From the land of Canaan to buy food. And Joseph knew his brethren, but they knew not him'."

My ears twitched at the name "Joseph".

I immediately thought of Trevor…

And the guilt and sadness came with it.

"Why did I come to this place?" I groaned. *"It's supposed to make me happy, not sad, right?"*

"You may be seated." Benson finished.

Everybody sat.

Benson looked up from his Bible. "Today, we're going to look at the life of Joseph, as we consider the subject topic (again, it's not going to be exhaustive, by any means) 'I Love my Family'."

For some time after that, after a fluffy prayer, Benson was asking people if they were wanting to share examples of love. If you ask me, it was just a bunch of ooey gooey baloney.

"Real quick, Lord willing I want to recap Joseph's life." He finally got on track with the preaching. "In order to understand – I think most of us get the point of Joseph's life – but I want to remind you of these things that happened in Joseph's life that led to the place in chapter 42. We're not going to read through all of these verses. I'll sum up most of Joseph's life, if you'll bear with me. I may have to paraphrase a bit, but I want you to have the background right now so you can understand how loving Joseph was. So, if you go all the way back to Genesis 37. Genesis 37…"

"Why does he always say the Bible verse twice?" I grumbled to Sarah.

"Because men need to be told things twice." Sarah whispered back.

I gave her a glare, but she simply pointed back up to Benson. "Jacob and his sons have already been introduced, but it talks about Jacob being in Canaan, and verse 2 says 'These are the generations of Jacob. Joseph, being seventeen years old was feeding the flock with his brethren;'. Again, we're not going to read through all of these." Benson reminded us.
"Thank goodness." I muttered to myself.

"Joseph is seventeen years old." Benson said. "He's a young man, for sure. He's not a grown-up. He's not on his own. He is the next to the youngest. But we find out in verse 3 that Jacob loved Joseph more than all of the other brothers. We know from that passage of Scripture that Jacob gave him that coat of many colors. That was an important thing in their day. It was being declared in no uncertain terms that Joseph is the favorite. Joseph is the one that is preeminent above everybody else. And his brothers hated him yet the more for it. In verse 2, he already told his dad of his brothers' evil report, and now with this coat, they just hate him. They cannot stand him. Then he has two dreams. The first one is him and his brothers are out with their sheaves, gathering together sheaves of grain of some kind. And Joseph's sheaf stands upright and the brothers' sheaves bow down to it. And they did not like that. In his second dream, the sun, and the moon, and eleven stars bow down to him. And he tells his brothers, and he tells his father. And even his father was a little bit astonished, but he heard it and said 'Well, we'll consider that'."
Benson gave a small chuckle. I narrowed my eyes at him. What was so funny?
"The brothers, as well as the parents, understood that this is God showing forth that they would bow down to Joseph. They had a hard time believing it. But this is what God revealed. And I think these dreams carried Joseph through a lot of hard times that were coming in the near future. Verses 18 – 30 of this chapter, the brothers are out and their taking care of some sheep. Joseph is sent to find them. They see him coming a far way off and they say 'Here's our opportunity: We're going to kill our brother. We know

he's Dad's favorite. We hate him for it. And so, we are going to
kill him'. Thankfully, and by the grace of God for sure, it's
Reuben that stands up and says 'Hey, let's not kill him. Let's just
throw him in this pit'. His plan was to come back later and rescue
Joseph, but that didn't end up coming to pass. Because Judah had
a 'better' idea as he saw the slave traders traveling by. He saw
those slave traders and thought 'We can kill two birds with one
stone. We can get rid of Joseph, and we can make a little money
on the side. Let's sell him to the slave traders, and we will be done
with him'."

Benson paused for a bit, gathering his thoughts. "Now, we
understand enough about those type of slave traders, that when
you were going to be made a slave…that was pretty much the end
of your life. They were fairly certain that, while they would not
have to kill Joseph, Joseph was a dead man. Whatever work he
was put to…it was more than likely that he was going to have a
short and a troublous life. He wouldn't be too old at his final
birthday."
I lowered my eyes. Many guys I knew weren't too old at their last
birthday.
Benson continued. "Chapter 39 starts off with Joseph being taken
down to Egypt. There, he is bought by the captain of the of
Pharaoh's guard, Potiphar. The captain of the people that watched
over Pharaoh and the palace."
My attention was turned away from the preaching for a moment
when Michaela started asking Sarah if she could get a glass of
water. Sarah quickly hushed her.
"Well, Joseph is under these difficult circumstances." Benson said
as I looked back at him. "We're not making this the focus of the
day, but we need to understand that Joseph, even in the midst of
difficult circumstances, continued to trust God. He had done
nothing wrong. He wasn't paying for sin in any way, but this was
a trial upon his life. Yet, he continued to follow God. I'm certain at
the back of his mind was the thought that God had showed him
those dreams for a reason. So, he continued to put God first. And

because Joseph did that, then we have verse 2 of chapter 39: 'And the LORD was with Joseph, and he was a prosperous man'. That, as he was working in Potiphar's house, he came up to the position of 'top slave', if you will. He's promoted to being in charge of everything in the household. There is nothing in this house that is not under Joseph's control, with the exception of Potiphar himself and his wife. Everything else is under the supervision of Joseph. He knows everything that's going on. Potiphar trusts Joseph enough because Joseph has been trustworthy, and God has blessed him. And Potiphar has prospered because Joseph is the one in charge and leading things."

Benson took a minute to take off his glasses and rub his eyes. "But you see, whenever somebody continues to do the work of God, Satan is going to throw opposition. Satan is going to throw some kind of monkey wrench in the works. And what opposition Joseph faced was Potiphar's wife. She wants to have him. But Joseph refused time and time again. Until one time, Potiphar's wife caught him by the coat and the only recourse Joseph had was to 'get him out'. To drop his coat and run. And he ran and got him out. I love that statement, because that's exactly what the Bible says in verse 12: 'And he left his garment in her hand, and fled, and ***got him out***'. He was not going to be in that place. It did not matter how many people would never know about it. He said 'I refuse to do this sin against God'. It would be sin against Potiphar, his wife, but it would be first and foremost sin against God. The most intelligent thing he ever did was that move right there. He got him out. But you see, the opposition of Satan isn't going to stop there. It didn't work out the way Satan wanted, but another opportunity is set up. Potiphar's wife has already revealed herself to be unfaithful and untrustworthy. She obviously cares little for her husband and she cares little for anybody else. So, in putting herself first, she thinks 'If I can't have him, I'll ruin him'. And she does everything in her power to make Joseph look bad and succeeds."

Benson paused as he looked back at his Bible.

"I've always found it interesting by the time you get to the end of this, that while Potiphar is angry, it never says he's angry with Joseph. He's just angry. I'm convinced he knew enough about his wife to know she's lying. There's nothing about Joseph that would ever indicate he would have any part of what she is accusing him of. But because Joseph's a slave, and she would have been a part of Pharaoh's court, calling her a liar would have been tantamount to treason. So Potiphar has to imprison Joseph. Still, Joseph says 'I'm going to be faithful to God'. He's imprisoned at the end of chapter 39."

I knew a little about prisons. This sermon sounded a lot like the things Trevor preached to us.

I felt a pain in my gut. I didn't want to keep thinking about Trevor.

Benson continued. "In the prison, the Lord is with him. He is promoted, again, to being in charge of all the other prisoners under the prison-keeper…being a prisoner himself."

Benson laughed, along with many in the audience.

"How does that work?" Benson shrugged his shoulders with a smile. "It wasn't the most desirable situation, that's for sure, but Joseph still is determined to follow God. He was going to do what was right. He wasn't a whiney-baby about it. He lived right and put God first. He retained his integrity, dignity, and love for God. Regardless of what his brothers did, of being in slavery. Regardless of being imprisoned in a prison nothing like what we have in America. He continued to put God first. And while he's there, he has the over-sight of the other prisoners. And one day, two prisoners come in. Pharaoh's butler and baker. The butler was the one who served him, who taste-tested all the food, who poured wine for him. It was a very trusted position. He was the one who, if someone was trying to poison Pharaoh, died first."

Benson snickered again.

This guy just laughed at everything.

"The baker, of course, made all the food." Benson explained. "Pharaoh thought one or both of them had betrayed him. So, they

were put in prison. Some short time later, they both had dreams. We find those dreams in chapter 40. Both of those dreams were told to Joseph and Joseph interpreted them. Both interpretations came to pass. The baker was killed and the butler was restored to his position. And Joseph asked the butler 'Remember me before Pharaoh. I'm here unjustly. I ask that you remember me before Pharaoh'. And the butler forgot him." Benson nodded, his expression saying 'Bummer, right?'.
"Two years." Benson emphasized. "Two years. Based upon-let's see, what verse is it?"
Benson started searching through his notes.
"Hold on just a second. I've got it written down."
More scrambling through his notes.
"Verse 46 of chapter 41: 'And Joseph was thirty years old when he stood before Pharaoh'. So, if he's thirty when he stood before Pharaoh, you go back two years, he's twenty-eight. He's twenty-eight when the butler and the baker were in prison. He was seventeen, maybe eighteen, when he was sold into slavery. It's been eleven years, approximately, since being sold into slavery to when the butler and the baker were there. Thirteen years before he's standing before Pharaoh."
Benson looked up from his notes, seemingly appreciating his successful math. Much of the audience, including me, didn't seem to care.

"Whatever that means to you." Benson shrugged. "He's still a young man. He has spent the majority of his early adult life in slavery and imprisonment. But still, he did what was right, regardless of the circumstances, and God prospered him. Then, in chapter 41, Pharaoh has two dreams. For all the people that were brought forth, none of them could explain those dreams. Nobody could tell him what they meant. And then the butler…"
Benson slapped his forehead in an "Oh, I forgot!" gesture.
"Finally, right?" Benson said. "He remembers 'You know, there was this guy, two years ago, down in the prison. I and the baker had a dream, he told us the interpretation, and they came to pass. I

wonder if he's still down there. He could help you out, Pharaoh'. And Pharaoh said 'Get him up'. Once he 'got him out', now he's 'getting him up'. So, Joseph comes before Pharaoh and the dreams are told. And the dreams were put forth to Joseph and Joseph says- ah, let's look at the verse."
Benson, along with everyone (except me) in the auditorium looked down at their Bibles.
"Verse 25: 'And Joseph said unto Pharaoh, The dream of Pharaoh is one: God hath shewed Pharaoh what he is about to do'. Verse 16 says basically the same thing: 'And Joseph answered Pharaoh, saying, It is not in me: God shall give Pharaoh an answer of peace'."

Benson looked up from his Bible. "Thirteen years. Slavery. Imprisonment. And *still* he gives God the glory. Let's get to the interpretation. So, seven good years are coming, they'll have more than they can stand. And after that, there'll come seven bad years where they'll have nothing."
Benson made a "zero" with his hand as he said "nothing".
"I love how Joseph not only gives them the interpretation, but he says 'Here's what you need to do: you need to find somebody who will collect during the seven good years so you will have food during the seven lean years'. And I see it in my mind every time I read through this account."
Benson closed his eyes. Probably for dramatic effect.
"Joseph presents the interpretation. He tells Pharaoh what to do and, as soon as he's done, he starts turning around to walk away to go back to the prison. Prepared not to be elevated. He has done what God asked him to do and he is prepared to go back to his cell. Back to the dungeon, where it is dark, and dank, and moldy. But it's Pharaoh who says 'Hey, wait up a second, son. Who else is there that is better prepared? If you can interpret this, and you can give me exactly the plan that we need, then we want you to enact it'. The best of everything was represented in Pharaoh's court. Yet, he says 'This man, who has come from the lowest life that could possibly be and wants nothing more, *he's* the man that

we're going to choose'."

Benson took a moment to collect his thoughts.
"I know we haven't even really looked a whole lot at 'I Love My
Family'. But know this: if you want to love your family, you got
to love God first."
That was really the first moment where the sermon struck
something more than my ears.
My family.
Sarah. Henry.
Lucas, Gary, Michaela.
That was my family.
"You got to love God first." Benson repeated.
Was he saying I didn't love my family? I *did* love them. I didn't
love God, but I *did* love my family. How could he say I didn't?
But my mind went back…
I struck Sarah.
I treated Lucas, Gary, and Michaela like dirt. Made them all cry or
hate me.
….I killed Henry.
"If you don't love God right, you cannot love your family right."
Benson kept going with his sermon.
I had not loved my family right. My heart started beating faster.
My breath shuddered.
"You can't expect to have any kind of godly love for your family
if you do not love God first." Benson kept firing his words. "You
cannot hope to lead your family properly if you do not put God
first. It can't happen. You might be able to muddle through. You
can get the best of education, put the best food on the table, have
all kinds of great things…but if you're not putting God first,
you've failed your family. You've failed your family."
Failed?
I couldn't deny it, whether by my mind or my heart.
Benson was completely right.
"All the money, all the stuff, all the things that can be amassed in a
life-time won't matter a hill of beans if those of your family die

and go to hell."
Hell. That word struck me like the bullet in my back. It scared me. For the first time in my life, the word 'hell' scared me.
Why? What was happening to me?
"We've got to lead them." Benson continued with a sad nod. "And, please, I understand that we're not giving the whole picture. A child can be given everything to follow God. They do have their own will and they can choose 'No thanks' when it comes to God. But what I'm trying to say is that there's **no** hope if you're not putting God first. There's no hope if you don't love God. If He's not first in your family, how dare you be so presumptuous to think that your kids will serve God. Could it happen despite your parenting? Despite your lack of love and service for God? It could. Does it usually? No, not often."
Benson silently counted to himself.
"I can think of…a handful of people that have done that, but not many. I can think of a whole lot more that had the opportunity to serve God, but said 'No'."

Benson took a deep sigh and shook his head sadly.
"We've got to put God first. Joseph has been doing that now for much longer than thirteen years. But certainly, these thirteen years, he has continued to faithfully serve God. And God elevates him. Verses 37-45 shows Joseph ruling in Egypt. He's under Pharaoh only by the throne. Pharaoh tells him 'You have control of everything. Only in the throne am I higher than you'. Joseph is *truly* second-in-command at thirty years old. So what does Joseph do? He puts his plan into action. Verses 47-49, during the seven plenteous years, Joseph starts rationing everything. He starts bringing together all the extra. Then, as the seven years of famine come, Joseph then sells the food back to the people. He was a smart guy. He didn't use it all up. He didn't waste it. He saved and managed. Then, he sells it back, and even that was to the benefit to Pharaoh. Verse 57 tells us that all the other countries came to buy food from Joseph. Chapter 42 starts in with that passage of Scripture where Jacob sends his tens sons to go get food. He's

heard there's food in Egypt."

Benson briefly looked back at his notes. "I don't know why, but I like the math parts of these things."

I hated math. I wish he would just get back to the sermon and leave all the math alone.

Something really was wrong with me. I actually *wanted* to hear the rest of the sermon.

"Joseph was seventeen when he was sold into slavery." Benson pointed out all the math. "He's twenty-eight when the butler and the baker were put into prison. He's thirty when he stands before Pharaoh. Seven years of plenty have passed, so that's thirty-seven. I assume Jacob and his sons would have had provision for some period of time. I don't know how long. Maybe up to a year. So, Joseph is around thirty-seven or thirty-eight years old. They have not seen him for twenty to twenty-one years. A seventeen year old kid changes a lot in twenty to twenty-one years."

Okay, I admit it, that was an interesting thing to think about. I changed a lot since I was seventeen. And I wasn't yet thirty-seven.

"We can go beyond that." Benson added. "It's not just twenty years. Here in America, twenty years go by and fashions change, but we don't generally go through dramatic life changes. Joseph went through some *very dramatic* life changes in twenty years. He was sold into slavery. Who knows how he was treated at first? What happened to him while he was in the prison? Who knows what the other prisoners thought of him? Who knows what the guards did to him? We have no clue what happened during those thirteen years. No idea. By the time he was before Pharaoh, he could have looked dramatically different from when he was seventeen. Being a slave, maybe he was working outside all the time. Turned his skin to shoe-leather. Being down in the dungeon, maybe he was out of the sunlight. Turned all pasty. Who knows how he could have changed? Now, he's been seven years in Pharaoh's court. He's had the best luxury that Egypt could provide. He's had some *dramatic* life changes. So, when his brothers show up, it is no surprise that they do not recognize him."

"*Good point.*" I thought to myself.

"Can I add another point to this?" Benson asked. "Joseph's brothers sold him into slavery. What did we already establish was their thoughts concerning that?"

"He's a dead man." I whispered to Sarah.

"He's a dead man." Benson answered his own question.

I chuckled to myself, glancing at Sarah with a feeling of victory. Sarah coughed out a chuckle too. She looked breathless, though. Worried, maybe. No. Nervously happy.

It was bugging me. Making me uneasy.

I turned my attention back to Benson.

"They were not thinking of Joseph in any way, shape, or form. Even when he comes into their mind later, all they're saying is 'We sold him to die and now we're paying for it'. There is not the foggiest idea in their mind that they could possibly be standing before Joseph. They're just there to buy food. Verses 2 through 8. The ten brothers come to buy food. Joseph recognizes them but they knew not him. They've basically been doing the same thing for the last twenty years. Joseph was the youngest, so some of them have to be five to ten years older than him. One of the things that I have realized is that people's looks change the *least* from about thirty to fifty, maybe fifty-five. People generally look the same for that time. They change really fast from infancy to sixteen. There's a lot of major changes, but from the twenties up to near fifty-five, people look generally the same. Again, it's no surprise to me that Joseph looked at them and thought 'These are my brothers'. Knows them immediately. So, he develops this plan. And lest you think that Joseph is trying to get his revenge, that is not anything near Joseph's mind. What he is thinking is 'I want to see if they are the same. Are they the same ten who threw me in a pit and sold me into slavery? Are they of the same character or has God done something in their lives?'. Let's see what happens."

Benson once again put his face into his Bible. "Verse 6, Joseph's brothers bow to him. I think that's important to point out. That was the first of Joseph's dream. Joseph's first dream was about sheaves bowing down to his sheave. What are his brothers there to do? Buy grain. Bowing to get food. I don't think that's on accident. God put the dream in that way because He knew what was coming. It centers around food. Verse 9 through 17, Joseph tells them 'You're spies! You're an espionage group! You're here to see if you can take us over!'."

Benson pointed his finger violently while he spoke for Joseph.

"If Egypt was the only nation that had food, don't you think that there were enemies that say 'We want that'?" Benson kept nodding his head.

Then, he took another glance back at his Bible.

"They are imprisoned until their story can be corroborated. Here's what Joseph ends up offering them: 'One of you will stay in prison, the other nine will go back home. *But* if you want food again, you'll need to bring your youngest brother'. After all, they told him 'There's twelve of us total. Ten of us are here. One is at home. One is not. We're the sons of an old man back home'. And Joseph tells them 'One stays here. You bring that twelfth brother here or you're liars'. And they'd probably die if they were found to be liars. That's the deal."

Benson took a moment to appreciate the story he was going through.

Seemed weird to me, but whatever.

"Another thing I love about this story is that, the whole time Joseph has been speaking to them, he's been speaking through an interpreter. As far as they know, he does *not* speak Hebrew. Joseph can hear everything they are saying and understand it perfectly. Yet, they have no idea that he's clued in to what's being said. Verses 21 to 22 is where they reveal their guilty conscience concerning Joseph. 'We are verily guilty concerning our brother, in that we saw the anguish of his soul, when he besought us, and we would not hear; therefore is this distress come upon us'. When Joseph was down in that pit, I doubt he was just sitting and twiddling his thumbs. I'm sure he was crying 'HEY! LET ME OUT OF HERE!'."

The yell made Sarah jump. I ignored her. I was concentrating on the message. I couldn't stop hearing.

"It was probably a lot more pitiful than that." Benson commented. "And they refused to listen. They would not hear. Reuben basically says 'I told you so! I tried to keep you from this and you refused to listen. Now we're in this mess'. Simeon is taken and bound before the rest of the brothers' eyes. He's bound until the youngest brother is brought."

This story…it was filled with imprisonment. Out of the entire church, I'd say that the one who knew best about being in a prison…was me. Every time Benson mentioned 'imprison' or something like it, a cold shudder ran through me.

Still, I listened.

"The brothers go home. Some time passes. I'd say pretty near a year. Finally, in verses 36 to 38, Reuben goes to Jacob. 'Hey, look, we can't go back for food unless Benjamin comes with us'. Jacob won't have it for however long. I wish we knew how long the brothers had spent back in Canaan before finally going back to Egypt. Because in all that time, where's Simeon?"

"Prison." I whispered to myself.

"In prison." Benson answered. "Jacob wouldn't send Benjamin. He says 'You're going to kill me if he doesn't come back. I'll die of a broken heart'."

Another arrow hit my heart. I wasn't sure why…

But something was speaking to me. Something was making my heart ache. I felt tuckered. I felt weighed down.

Benson flipped through his notes. "Back on track. Time passes. Judah comes to Jacob. He promises to be surety for Benjamin. He's the insurance policy. If Benjamin doesn't come back, Judah won't come back. Jacob says 'Fine'. He sends them and some gifts to buy favor with Joseph. Verses 18 through 30, the brothers are at Joseph's house for a feast. Simeon is brought forth and they are going to have a meal. The brothers are seated in birth order. They're amazed by this."

Benson's chuckle revived. "That is a very interesting

coincidence."

Much of the church snickered with him. One person raised his
hands and made quotations marks with his fingers. Benson
laughed at that. "'*Coincidence*', that's right. Joseph knew it. It's
his house. He set them up that way. You'd think that would start
cluing them in, but they don't seem to recognize it. As food is
served, more is given to Benjamin more than anyone else. He's
given a worthy portion. Benjamin is, after all, his only whole
brother. After the feast, the brothers are sent towards home with
food in their sacks. But Joseph has instructed that his special silver
cup to be put in Benjamin's bag."

Benson tapped his Bible with his pointer finger. "*This* is the
test. They go out a ways until they're chased down by Joseph's
servants. They tell the brothers 'We're going to search these bags
because one of you has stolen our master's cup. And the one who
has it will be put into slavery'. The brothers say 'If you find it, you
can have the whole lot of us, but you won't find it'. And the
servants say 'No, we just want the one who took it and then we'll
be out of your hair'. And they find it in Benjamin's bag. Now if
they were the same, if they were the *same* brothers that heartlessly
threw Joseph down in a pit, listened to his cries, and ignored him,
they would have said 'Take Benjamin. We'll go'. But that is not
what they do. They *have* changed. They are in mourning now.
They're in mourning. They're like 'What in the world is going to
happen? We are going to kill our dad if Benjamin does not come
back home with us. He's going to die of a broken heart'. They go
back to Joseph. *All* of them. The whole lot of them go back to
Joseph. And they are pleading for their brother. Let's get down to
it. Verse 14 of chapter 44: 'And Judah and his brethren came to
Joseph's house; for he was yet there: and they fell before him on
the ground.' There they are again, bowing down to him. 'And
Joseph said unto them, What deed is this that ye have done? Wot
ye not that such a man as I can certainly divine? And Judah said
What shall we say unto my lord? What shall we speak? Or how
shall we clear ourselves? God hath found out the iniquity of thy

servants: behold, we are my lord's servants, both we, and he also
with whom the cup is found. And he said, God forbid that I should
do so: but the man in whose hand the cup is found, he shall be my
servant; and as for you, get you up in peace unto your father.'
Joseph gives them another out. 'I don't want all of you. I should,
but I'm not going to. I just want the one that stole from me. The
rest of you can leave'. But Judah comes forward to Joseph, saying
'Oh my lord, let thy servant, I pray thee, speak a word in my lord's
ears, and let not thine anger burn against thy servant: for thou art
even as Pharaoh. My lord asked his servants, saying, Have ye a
father, or a brother? And we said unto my lord, We have a father,
an old man, and a child of his old age, a little one; and his brother
is dead, and he alone is left of his mother, and his father loveth
him'."

Benson began to tear up as he read the passage. A choke was
heard in his voice. His emotional state was contagious. I felt a
throb in my throat and a burning in my eyes. Why was I getting so
pathetic because of one lousy sermon?
Benson composed himself before speaking. "Judah knew that
Benjamin was now the son his father loved. *He* was the beloved
son! If Benjamin were to not come back, Jacob would die,
certainly of a broken heart. Remember what Jacob said? 'Ye know
that my wife bare me two sons: And the one went out from me,
and I said, Surely he is torn in pieces; and I saw him not since:
And if ye take this also from me, and mischief befall him, ye shall
bring down my gray hairs with sorrow to the *grave*'."
Benson began to choke up again. He kept reading from his Bible.
"'Now therefore when I come to thy servant my father, and the lad
be not with us; seeing that his life is bound up in the lad's life; It
shall come to pass, when he seeth that the lad is not with us, that
he will die: and thy servants shall bring down the gray hairs of thy
servant our father with sorrow to the grave. For thy servant
became surety for the lad unto my father, saying, If I bring him not
unto thee, then I shall bear the blame to my father for ever. Now
therefore, I pray thee, let thy servant abide instead of the lad a

bondman to my lord; and let the lad go up with his brethren. For how shall I go up to my father, and the lad be not with me? Lest peradventure I see the evil that shall come on my father'."

Tears came to my eyes. I had been struck to the heart. The Bible pierced right through to my calloused, dead heart.
I saw it. I felt it. I knew it.
I was Judah.
Henry was Joseph.
Sarah was Jacob.
Her children were Benjamin.
I'm not into symbols. Things are things. They're not other things. But if I can bear it, so can you. Keep up with me.
I was the one who had taken Sarah's beloved away from her. Henry had come to Germany to save me. He never returned because of me. Sarah's heart had been broken the moment I came home without her husband. She was shattered without Henry. And me…I was only making life hard for her. Weighing her down. Hurting her with my words and my attitude. And the last bit of light in her life…her children…I was poisoning them.
I was taking the last piece of her heart and crushing it.
And it was that moment, inside Bible Baptist Church of New York City, that I realized it. That sermon hit me like a train and I was instantly in tears. I began to cry like…well…
Like Henry used to.
Like a baby. Bawling like a sap.
But still I listened. Benson wasn't done.

"Sounds like twenty years changed Judah." He wiped his eyes again, sniffling. "Twenty years had made him a different man. A little more tender. A little more loving. He still understood the fact that Benjamin was the beloved son…and he was okay with that. Because he loved his father. He could not bear to come before his father without Benjamin. I am absolutely certain that part of the reason Judah feels this way is because of the guilt of already depriving his father of one son."

Judah had deprived Jacob of Joseph.
I deprived Sarah of Henry.
I did.
"To do a second…he could not bear it." Benson shook his head.
"Can I add this? Sin will always takes us farther than we want to
go. It costs us more than we want to pay. It has a way of causing
pain that lasts far longer than the pain of doing right in the first
place. The brothers didn't like Joseph. They hated him. 'He's got
these dreams and he thinks he's going to rule over us. We'll show
him!'. Little did they know how much those actions would haunt
them the rest of their lives. Twenty years they dealt with that guilt.
It's still fresh on their minds. They've come to the place where
they will not do that again. Can't you see Judah with his heart-felt
plea? We don't see this in Scripture, but I have a feeling that they
might have said 'You can take all ten of us if you let Benjamin go
back. Don't deprive our father of his beloved. Whatever it's going
to take, we'll do it. Just let the lad go'."
That was it. I broke. I could not take any more. I sobbed out so
loud that the entire church could hear me. Eyes were turning to
look at me.
Sarah's especially.
"Bradley?" She asked quietly.
I couldn't be in there. I spun my wheelchair around and pushed it
out of the auditorium as quick as I could. I wheeled out of the
church and began rolling down the sidewalk as fast as my arms
could push.
All the way, I was crying. Just crying.

    I had taken myself to the cemetery where Henry was "buried".
I zoomed past Grandpa Leppy's grave and my mama's grave.
I came right to Henry's and collapsed at it.
I thrusted myself out of the wheelchair to fall on the ground next
to Henry's tombstone.
"Okay!" I cried out pathetically, hugging the tombstone. "Ya' got
me! I get it! I understand! I'm a sinner! I've done evil all my life!
And I need your God, Henry! I need your God! I don't want to be

like I am anymore! I don't want to be like Judah! I want to be like Joseph! I want to be like you and Sarah! Help me to get saved, Henry! Help me!"

Now, I know that Henry wasn't there. Even if Henry's body was actually in that grave, that's all it would be: a dead body. Henry's spirit was in heaven with God. But I didn't exactly know how all that stuff worked out. So, I went to the "person" that knew that stuff the best: Henry. Thankfully, though, God heard me that Wednesday night. And He sent somebody who would actually have been able to lead me to His saving grace.

Sarah.

Sarah, after I had left the church, quickly asked Nancy to watch over the kids. Then, like a shot, she took off after me. And she had caught up to me right as I was screaming at Henry's grave. She heard everything. And, after I sobbed a bit, she thanked the Lord quietly and knelt beside me.

Then she led me to Jesus Christ.

In a place of death, I found life.

CHAPTER TWENTY-FIVE

I won't go into how I got saved. That was personal and I'm kinda embarrassed to keep talking about how much I cried.
But I got saved that day.
Saved once and for all of forever.
Bratt, Henry…I kept my promise.
Sarah walked me through the Romans Road, as she called it, and I prayed to Jesus Christ to save me from my sin and from the eternal destination of hell.
And Jesus Christ did just that.
Now, if you're reading this, and you need to be saved, I ask you to pray right now that God would send you someone who can lead you to Him. And trust me, He will. If you really mean it, God will send you someone. Just try it. But don't you try to fake it, because God will know and it doesn't work that way.

Anyway, so that's what this book is about. It's about me, one of God's biggest unbelievers, becoming a Christian.
I was a murderer.
I was a drunk.
I was a lot of bad things, but God saved me. And if God can save a guy like me, He can save a guy or gal like you.
And trust me, you need Him. Desperately. You gotta trust Him.
This book is also partially to honor Henry Engel. He wrote a book to me before he died and I thought it would be right (even though writing is still girly. This is the only book I'll ever write) to write one back to him. It wasn't a competition, because if it was, I totally won. Henry wrote like a 202 page book. Mine is like eighteen times that! Seriously, look at the size of this thing! Who'd have though Bradley Scoefield would ever write something so big. It wasn't easy. I started out with: "Henry Engel saved my life. He was a good man and a good Christian. Now I'm a Christian because of him" and that was it! That was my whole book at first. Sarah took one look and said "I don't think so".

It took me three stinking years to write all this! Everybody who's reading this better appreciate that! Writing's hard!
But, anyway, it's not about that. It's about what God did through Henry. And I want everyone to know that.
Henry…I'm sorry.
And thank you, little brother.

I even did something I thought I would never do.
In front of the whole church.
It happened in March.
I wheeled up my wheelchair on to the platform. I came up to the microphone.
I looked out at all the people who were just staring back at me.
Dang, I hated being in front of people.
Especially since many of my pop's buddies were in the congregation. I had invited all of them. Ronny and Matthias, too.
They were about to hear little Scoefield's horrible voice.
I glanced over at Sarah at the piano. She nodded back.
She was ready.
I swallowed. My throat was so dry.
I cleared my throat. "Hey."
The audience remained silent. I should have known better than to say that. Audiences aren't supposed to say "hey" back to someone on the stage.
Except a little girl in the second row. She said "hi" back.
That made me chuckle.
It made speaking a little easier.
"For those who have no clue who I am, I'm Captain Bradley Scoefield." I introduced. "My mother's name was Winifred Scoefield. My father was Amos Scoefield. I fought in World War II and lost my legs in it. I was rescued from a prisoner of war camp by a very courageous man."
I took a deep breath. By thunder, I was **not** going to cry in front of all those people again.
I kept it under control.
"His name was Henry Engel." I continued. "He was my brother-

in-law, and he was my friend."
I saw sympathy in many people's eyes in the congregation. Many knew Henry. Many knew what happened.
But I wasn't really talking to them. I was talking to my pop's friends. I was talking to the other people who were invited to this. Other soldiers who were sent home early. Police officers, including my pop's old war buddy with the metal leg. A lot of people who thought like I used to.

"Henry was a singer." I mentioned. "Loved doin' it. Seems odd to me, but it was his callin'. And he touched a lot'a lives by doin' it."
I took another deep breath. No crying. *No* crying.
"Henry died savin' Corporal Kenneth Taggart, Sergeant John Smith, a Russian guy named Tim, and me from the Nazis." I said quietly, staring at the floor. "And while he was alive, he wanted me to know who God was. Tried to get me to see that God was there for me, even though I didn't want God."
I looked up at the audience again. "Henry was writing one last song before he died. He wasn't able to finish it, so Sarah and I worked to write the last bit. And today, even though I'm no singer, I want to share it with you. It's called 'Now I'm Here'."
That was Sarah's cue and she began playing the piano.
My face began to get burning red. I hated singing.
But I sung for the Lord.
I sung for Henry.
I sung for those in the pews who used to be like I was.

"I'm here today
Because a man
Told me of
The spotless Lamb

How He died
That was the price
To save my soul

To give me life

But I refused
I tried to hide
From this Lamb
Who offered life

But I was bound
Trapped in my sin
And saw that Jesus
Could cleanse me within

Now I'm here
To tell you that He died
He rose and He's alive
He wants to set us free

Now I'm here
To tell you that He's real
Regardless of what we feel
And He didn't give up on me

I'm here today
Because a man
Spilled His blood
In a distant land

He's done more than
Heal my scars
He changed my fate
He changed my stars

Now I lay down
My stubbornness
Lay down my will
I'll trust and rest

That this man
Who for me did fall
Deserves my praise
Deserves my all

Now I'm here
To tell you that He died
He rose and He's alive
He wants to set us free

Now I'm here
To tell you that He's real
Regardless of what we feel
He didn't give up on me

What can wash away my sin?
Nothin' but the blood
Nothin' but the blood
What can make me whole again?
Nothin' but the blood
Nothin' but the blood

I'm here today
Because a man
Honored and served
The great I AM

He's in heaven
His journey done
His work is over
His race is run

Now it's my turn
My work begins
To tell others of
He who cleanses sins

So brother, sister
Listen to me
Run to Jesus
Just bow the knee

Now I'm here
To tell you that He died
He rose and He's alive
All this He did do

Now I'm here
To tell you that He's real
Regardless of what we feel
And he wants to rescue you

He wants to rescue you"

Everybody says I did good when I sang that. They probably lied, but hey, they were nice.
As it turns out…a couple of people got saved from that church service. Not from my singing, oh no. We still had a sermon after that. A good, fiery sermon from Pastor Benson. Ronny got saved. Some of my pop's buddies got saved. Vincent Doeler, Mr. Butters' boss, got saved. Matthias the policeman didn't, but he got saved a couple years later after he saw how much I changed.
That's not bragging, that's glory to God.
Something happened to me, too, during that church service in March of 1945.
See, Pastor Benson preached not only on salvation, but on missions.
And God spoke to me through that.
I talked with Sarah about it when she was driving me and the kids back home from church.

"I gotta tell ya' somethin', Sarah." I said softly so the kids in the back wouldn't hear.

"What's that?"
"God spoke to me during that message."
"Good." She smiled at me. "What about?"
"The mission field."
"You thinking about giving more money to missions?" Sarah asked.
"Eh, no." I scratched my neck. "I'm thinkin' God wants me to give me."
"Pardon?" Sarah glanced away from the road for a minute to look at me.
"Watch the road, please." I told her.
"Sorry." She looked back on the road. "But what do you mean?"
"God's called me to the mission field." I told Sarah.
"The mission field?" Sarah asked, surprised. "But, Bradley…your legs."
"Yeah, I know." I nodded. "But God can work past that."
"Well, and you'll have to learn more about the Bible." Sarah added.
"Yup."
"And learn how to preach."
"Yup."
"And get enough money to go and start a life wherever you'd be going."
"Yup."
"And just where do you think God wants you to go?" Sarah asked.
I laughed a little nervously. "Uh…Germany."
Sarah looked away from the road again with wide eyes.
"Germany?"
"Yeah." I pointed back at the road. "Sarah, look at the road."
"Sorry. But…Germany? As in Nazi Germany?" Sarah was very concerned. "The place where you were a prisoner of war?"
"Uh, yeah."
"The place where you got shot?"
"Yeah."
"The place where Henry died?"
"…Yeah." I said hesitantly.

"And the place where a world war is *still* going on?"

"That's the one." I said.

"Bradley, I think you need to pray more on this." Sarah suggested. "You've only been saved a month, you can't walk, I still need you here, and there are a lot of other reasons why you can't go to Germany."

"That's the thing." I clicked my tongue. "About you needing me?"

"Yes?"

"Well, I don't think that will be a problem." I told her gently.

"Why won't it?"

"Because I think the Lord wants you to come with me."

TO BE CONTINUED…

Dear Reader,

As you've read through this book, you've probably noticed how much of the story centers around Christianity. Now, I don't know what you particularly feel about Christianity, but I would like to say something, if that's all right. What I am about to tell you does not come from a heart that is holier-than-thou or just wanting you to join my church. I tell you this because I am concerned for your soul. It's similar to a man at a beach that sees a shark in the water. Some of those who are swimming in the ocean don't notice the danger. So what should he do? Make them aware of the danger by yelling "SHARK!" And that's what I'm endeavoring to do. I want to warn you of the danger that's coming at the end of your life.

Recently, there have been a decent amount of people I have known that suddenly passed away. Most were unexpected and very shocking. It reminded me of a rather depressing truth: death is coming for all of us. We don't know when and we don't know how, but death will eventually come. And, for some, I kept thinking to myself "Where are they now?" I didn't know some of their faiths or beliefs. But I believe in a God that made the heavens and the earth. I believe that, in the beginning, the world was perfect. I believe that mankind sinned against God, thus shattering the perfection of creation. I believe that all have sinned and are worthy of judgment. I believe that Jesus Christ, God in human flesh, lived a sinless life and died on the cross so He might pay the price of our sin for us. I believe that anyone who calls upon Him will be saved from a literal, eternal hell. And I, as one of His believers, am to go out and tell others of His salvation so that they can be saved as well.

In today's age, there are thousands of faiths that someone can believe in. And people flock to religions because we, as humanity, have an inner knowledge that there is something bigger than all of us that first brought everything into being. Even atheists know that a higher being exists out there. They just choose to reject it. When my friends died, it forced me to think of their eternal destination. Their opportunity to choose is past and they are either in heaven with the Lord, or burning in the penetrating darkness of hell. This is not the most cheery stuff, I admit. But, as I said earlier, I'm concerned for your eternal destination. And I don't want anyone to go to hell. I wouldn't wish that on my worst enemy. So, if you'll permit me, I'd like to tell you about how you can get away from the shark, so to speak. Now, before I get into it, I will let you know that I'm not trying to make you my disciple or anything. I'm not trying to get accolades for converting someone to Christianity, and I'm most certainly not trying to force you become a Christian against your will. No, I'm telling you about it so you can make the choice for yourself. From my perspective, people are in grave danger. And, again, we don't know when our life will end. So what kind of person would I be if I believed in a real place called hell, but never told anyone how to be rescued from it?

So, without further ado, I'd like to lay out the steps of salvation, if that's all right with you.

1. <u>God is holy and cannot be in the presence of sin.</u>
"For I am the LORD that bringeth you up out of the land of Egypt, to be your God: ye shall therefore be holy, for I am holy."
Leviticus 11:45

"There is none holy as the LORD: for there is none beside Thee: neither is there any rock like our God."
1 Samuel 2:2

"Holy, holy, holy, Lord God Almighty, which was, and is, and is to come."
Revelation 4:8b

Holy is a word that means "set apart", "morally blameless", or "sacred". Essentially, it means to be without sin. Since God is holy, associating with sin would nullify His holiness. It's like mixing oil with water or trying to put light and darkness together. It can't happen. If God and humanity are going to be in each other's presence, one of them needs to change. And it's not going to be God.

2. <u>Every human is a sinner. Even the tiniest sin makes you incapable of being in God's presence and worthy of His wrath.</u>

"For all have sinned, and come short of the glory of God;"

Romans 3:23

This is where some believe that they are "good enough" with God because they haven't committed the big sins like murder, rape, etc., but if you think that, just look at the Ten Commandments and ask yourself "Have I broken any of these?":

1. Thou shalt have no other gods before Me.

2. Thou shalt not make unto thee any graven image.

3. Thou shalt not take the name of the LORD thy God in vain.

4. Remember the sabbath to keep it holy.

5. Honor thy father and mother.

6. Thou shalt not kill.

7. Thou shalt not commit adultery.

8. Thou shalt not steal.

9. Thou shalt not bear false witness.

10. Thou shalt not covet.

People usually acknowledge that they've broken at least one of the Ten Commandments (usually the one that deals with lying, at least). But, in the New Testament, Jesus added a higher standard with a few of these commandments. He said that if you held anger in your heart towards someone, you've committed murder in your heart. He also said if you look upon someone with lust who is not your spouse, you're committing mental adultery (adultery here is actually referring to sexual sin in general, not necessarily the specific act of cheating on a spouse, though that is included). Now, most people have done those things as well, which makes them lying, murdering adulterers. And that's just three of the Ten Commandments. But even if someone had only broken one little aspect of God's law, the New Testament also says this:

"For whosoever shall keep the whole law, and yet offend in one point, he is guilty of all."

James 2:10

It's like having a string tied to a ball. The string has ten knots in it, representing the Ten Commandments. If someone were to cut the knots with scissors, how many would they have to cut before the ball hits the ground? Just one. The same is true with God's law. If you just broke only one part of it, you're guilty. You're a sinner. And you cannot be in His presence. Thankfully, that's not where it ends.

3. <u>Sin leads to spiritual death, but Christ leads to spiritual life. The spiritual death will separate sinners from God to eternal hell. But Jesus paid the penalty so we can go to heaven.</u>
"But God commendeth His love toward us, in that, while we were yet sinners, Christ died for us."
Romans 5:8

"For the wages of sin is death; but the gift of God is eternal life through Jesus Christ our Lord."
Romans 6:23

A price needed to be paid because of humanity's sin. It can be likened to someone committing a crime of property damage. Someone has to pay for to repair the damage. But let's say it wasn't just any property that was damaged. Say it was something incredibly valuable, like the Eiffel Tower. If someone destroyed the Eiffel Tower, that would probably cost millions of dollars to replace. A price that most people cannot pay. When it comes to sin, the cost was even higher. Humanity in of itself could not pay for the cost of redemption. We needed someone to pay the debt for us. That someone is Jesus Christ. He paid the price by being a sacrifice for humanity. He is God, which means He is perfect and able to pay the cost for sin. But He is also man, because only a man could redeem mankind. His innocent blood was shed in order to give everyone an opportunity to be forgiven of their debt.

4. <u>Repent and place faith in Jesus. Believe that Jesus is the Son of God and claim the gift of eternal salvation that He offers you freely.</u>

"For God so loved the world, that He gave His only begotten Son, that whosoever believeth in Him should not perish, but have everlasting life."

John 3:16

"Repent ye therefore, and be converted, that your sins may be blotted out, when the times of refreshing shall come from the presence of the Lord;"

Acts 3:19.

"That if thou shalt confess with thy mouth the Lord Jesus, and shalt believe in thine heart that God hath raised Him from the dead, thou shalt be saved."

Romans 10:9

This sounds too simple to a lot of people. But Jesus already did all of the work for us. All we need to do is accept the gift. Imagine that we are all on death row, but a pardon has been offered to everyone. All we need to do is accept the pardon and we're set free. But we have the choice to also refuse the pardon. In history, there have been people placed on death row that were given a pardon from the president, yet they refused and were put to death anyway. The same is true for spiritual salvation. You can refuse it. But the consequence is eternal hell.

Again, I want to make it crystal clear that I'm not trying to force any of this upon you. I'm simply telling you this because I believe it to be true and I don't want you to suffer a terrible fate of going to hell when you die. Now, I realize that this is not always what people want to hear, but you must understand my motives and that they are not malicious or deceptive in any sense. And I hope this hasn't come across as judgmental or unfeeling. I promise that is not my heart behind this. As a Christian, it is at the core of my belief that all people are bound for hell without Jesus Christ's gift of salvation. And I don't want you to suffer in hell for all eternity. I would like to see you in heaven someday.

Sincerely,

Nicholas M. Krohn.

ABOUT THE AUTHOR

Nicholas M. Krohn has always had a love for both writing and the Lord. Nicholas received Jesus Christ as his Lord and Saviour at the age of nine, thanks to his faith-filled mother and a godly church. After his salvation, Nicholas spent most of his childhood free-time jotting down fantastical stories that had a deep sense of Christianity within them. When he was a teenager, Nicholas discovered that writing was his calling from God. When attending Heartland Baptist Bible College, Nicholas began seriously writing and self-publishing novels with the desire that they would both wholesomely entertain readers, yet bring glory to God's name. It was here that he met his wife, Marissa, whom he married in 2017. Halfway through college, Nicholas also realized that he could do more than just write Christian Fiction. After deep study in the Bible and graduating from Heartland Baptist Bible College in 2020, Nicholas made it his mission to not only point to the Lord with his fiction novels, but to expound on the Word of God itself through commentaries, in-depth studies, and other such works of literature. Nicholas continues to pursue this work while living in Iowa with his wife and children.

OTHER KROHN'STORIES BOOKS

(All of which are available on Amazon)

MARISSA KROHN

The Silent Princess (*Children's book*)

NICHOLAS M. KROHN

BIBLE COMMENTARY SERIES

Krohn's Commentary of the First Book of Samuel

Krohn's Commentary of the Second Book of Samuel

THE SCOEFIELD SERIES (*HISTORICAL FICTION*)

Scoefield

Engel

Blume

THE ZALIAN CHRONICLES (*CHRISTIAN FANTASY*)

Heroes & Thieves I: The Noble Bandit

Heroes & Thieves II: A Bundle of Fools

Heroes & Thieves III: Clapia's Rebirth

Heroes & Thieves IV: Two Wastelands

KROHN'STORIES POETRY

Trains, Bridges, Cups, & Cheese

The Rambling of a Cart Pusher

<u>CONTACT US</u>

Website: <u>krohnstories.storiad.com</u>

Facebook Group: <u>Krohn'Stories Books</u>

Instagram: <u>krohnstoriesbooks</u>

Email: <u>krohnstories@gmail.com</u>

Fan mail, inquiries, suggestions, and critiques are all welcome. We will do our best to reply to all messages/emails, but cannot promise due to a busy schedule. Please be appropriate. Any swearing, vulgarity, threatening, or otherwise inappropriate messages/emails will be deleted without any response.